EVERNIGHT PUBLISHING ®

www.evernightpublishing.com

ISBN: 978-0-3695-0676-4

Cover Artist: Jay Aheer

Editor: Audrey Bobak

MAFIA MONSTER'S FORCED BRIDE

MAFIA MONSTER'S FORCED BRIDE

Mafia Brides, 1

Sam Crescent

Chapter One

Alex Smith—no, that wasn't right—Alex Greco glanced around the luxurious sitting room at the many different faces of the world she had married into. Not willingly. No, her father had come home one day, sat her down, and told her that he had big plans for her. Whenever he had big plans for her, she knew they were lies. The truth was, he had big plans for himself. Not that she hated her father. Liam Smith was a scary man. Abandoned as a child, he grew up on the streets and fought his way out, earning himself a reputation and wealth that rivaled the mafia family she was currently sipping drinks with.

No champagne, not for her. A bad experience on her eighteenth birthday put an end to her alcohol-drinking days. Now, she kept to water or juice. Nothing alcoholic.

Not that she had a drink of her own. That would require the waiter to come close to her, and no one ever did that.

Her husband, Roman Greco, stood near a bunch of men, talking, probably business, or perhaps they were discussing who they were going to kill. He paid no attention to her, not that she minded.

They were like chalk and cheese.

Keeping her arms folded, she tried not to feel so self-conscious. In a room full of strangers, it was impossible.

This marriage was supposed to unite the Greco mafia with her father, who was the biggest crime boss in the country. His businesses had expanded and crossed the boundaries of illegal into legal.

Her father had never kept his life secret from her. She wasn't a fool and knew he wasn't a good man. He'd tried to do right by her, but her husband couldn't stand her. Their wedding night had been a huge sham. According to tradition, he had to marry a virgin. She had refused to take the doctor examination.

Her father had kept her shielded, but he'd also been sure to allow her to have her own mind. So her virginity had been questioned. It had nearly caused a war on the streets because Liam refused to subject his daughter to the test. Lucas Greco had insisted. Her father had told him if he wanted to make this about blood, and not trust, then so be it.

The test hadn't gone ahead, but the wedding had.

On their wedding night, Roman had refused to touch her. She didn't know if it was because she didn't look like any of his other women or because he didn't think she was a virgin.

Anyway, she got a shitty night's sleep. He cut himself and gave the whole bloodied sheets a real feel to them so he could present them the following morning. To the world, they were married, but she knew she could get it annulled.

She was a virgin. Alex refused to put herself through such an archaic examination. How dare they ask that of her? Her wedding night was three months ago. Since then, she had rarely seen her husband, and when she had, he had nothing kind to say about her. Always critical. Then, of course, she was dragged to these kinds of functions where she stood out because she didn't quite fit in. Unlike all the women present, she didn't possess terrified gazes, nor did she fear being around men.

"You are all alone once again," her father said, surprising her.

She turned to see him, hands in his pockets, looking as stern as ever. "Dad." She went to him, wrapping her arms around him and breathing him in.

Her mother died many years ago when Alex was just a toddler. She had no memories of her. It was a drive-by shooting, and Alex, well, she hadn't gotten away unscathed either. A bullet had done a through-and-through on her leg. One rival war gang had taken his wife and injured his child. Liam had gone to war within hours, and Alex didn't want to think of the damage he'd done.

"What are you doing here?" Alex asked, smiling.

He was the first friendly face she'd seen all evening, and she'd been standing here for two hours, in the same spot. She could barely walk in the heels Roman made her wear. The dress she wore was also uncomfortable, as it went around her neck and fell to the floor. It was completely unflattering, and Alex hated it. Years ago, Liam once told her to choose her battles wisely, and she used that advice in her marriage.

If she didn't fight Roman on the simple things

like her clothing, then there was a chance for her to fight for something she did want, like freedom, or … something. She didn't know exactly what she wanted, but being stuck in his country home or his apartment all day sucked. He'd given her a credit card to go shopping with, but she wasn't one to shop.

"Business," Liam said.

"Of course. It's always business." She had nothing to say.

"You're upset."

"I'm not." The lie was easy to say, but he didn't believe it.

Liam took a deep breath. "Excuse me."

"Dad, don't," she said.

They had already started to gain some attention. Public displays of affection were frowned upon. After she'd hugged her father, a lot of people frowned, clearly talking about her.

She was the stupid wife of Roman Greco. The outsider. The weirdo with the strange name. She happened to love her name. Admittedly, it was because her dad wanted a boy, but Alex was a nice name. She liked it.

"I am going to deal with him."

"And what, force him to come and stand with me? Why? We have nothing to talk about. I … I don't fit in here." She hated how pitiful she sounded.

"Sweetheart, you fit anywhere you want to be."

"No, I don't. You didn't raise me to be…" She looked toward the women who were in their own private circle. She'd never been part of the in crowd, never cared to be. This was no different. "This."

"Alex," he said, and she held her hand up, stopping him.

"Please, don't. I don't need my dad trying to deal

with my husband." Even saying the word *husband* was difficult. She had never intended to get married. Never wanted to be married. Her parents had never married. According to her father, her mother hadn't wanted to tie the knot, didn't feel it was necessary.

"I didn't want you to be put in this kind of situation."

"You arranged this for us, Dad. How could you not have wanted it?" Alex and Roman were two people who'd never met before their wedding.

Liam had always kept her far away from his other business dealings. She was aware of it, and he never lied to her about what he was, but that didn't mean he exposed her unnecessarily.

The first time she actually met Roman was when she walked down the aisle to him. There had been other opportunities for them to meet, but they had never happened. Mainly because he was busy, like, all the time. Even when she refused to have the virgin test, he hadn't been present for any of it. His father had.

"Bringing our families together was necessary," Liam said. "But that doesn't mean I wanted you to be miserable. I can fix this."

"Dad there's nothing to fix. I think we're just strangers, you know. Trying to get used to each other and all of that." She forced a smile to her lips, which was again difficult.

She'd never been a good liar. Liam had told her many times that she was terrible at it. The worst person, and he'd even advised her not to attempt it when she was older either. He probably had the nicest, easiest kid to hang out with. She had never rebelled against him. They had an amazing relationship, father and daughter.

Liam's nostrils flared as he looked toward Roman.

Her husband was looking back at her, and she couldn't exactly read the look on his face, but she could imagine he was … pissed. Maybe something more, she wasn't sure. Either way, he wasn't happy.

What more could she do?

Did he not like her talking to her father?

"You promise not to make waves?" she asked.

"I promise not to meddle, but if he does anything, or if in any way you're scared, you come to me."

"Promise."

Roman didn't scare her, not really. Okay, there were a few times he might have made her a little afraid, but at those times, he was angry with someone else, and he just told her to fuck off or to get out of his face.

They didn't have the best communication, and what also didn't help was that she hated confrontation. Rather than call him out on the crap he said, she left it.

Liam pulled her in for another hug, and she saw everyone's disapproval. What kind of family was this?

"Mr. Smith, I heard you'd joined us," Lucas Greco, Roman's father, said.

She pulled away from her father in an attempt to create a little space. The two men shook hands, and Roman made that his cue to join them.

Alex stayed perfectly still, not saying anything.

Lucas glanced at her, and she saw the disapproval on his face. He hadn't liked that she refused to be part of the virgin test. The man didn't believe in trust. It was completely clear to see with the way he treated her.

As far as he was concerned, she was a hussy, or whatever word he used to describe her.

"It's a nice gathering," Liam said. "How could I turn down a personal invite from you. Roman?" He nodded at her husband.

She stared at her father, who looked at the

distance between them. Alex wasn't going to step closer to the man she couldn't stand.

Silence descended upon the group. It was because of her.

"I think I would like some fresh air," she said. "Lovely party."

Without waiting for a word, she turned her back on them and stepped away, finding any excuse to be as far away from them as possible. She didn't even care to step outside.

Instead, she found the stairwell in the main corridor and lowered herself, taking a deep breath.

She hated parties and functions like these. They sucked.

"Not one for the crowds?"

Alex looked up to see Antonio Testa, one of Roman's best friends. She met him on their wedding day when he was Roman's best man.

"No, I'm not." She shrugged. "You?"

He chuckled. "I just needed a breather from all those women." He winked and then nodded at where she sat. "Do you want some company?"

"Sure." She didn't see a reason why not.

Antonio was a large man, and she had no choice but to move a little closer to the banister for him to be able to fit on.

"You look nice tonight."

"Thanks."

This was Roman's best friend, not hers. She didn't trust him, even though Antonio had never given her any reason not to trust him.

"I know that Roman can be a little difficult, but you've just got to give the guy a chance. He's under a lot of pressure."

She turned to him and then smiled.

Unless it was her father, she had no intention of talking to strangers about her marriage to Roman. Especially not a best friend.

"I don't know if you're needed in there…"

"Trying to get rid of me?" He nudged her shoulder.

Alex frowned, but rather than try to make a big deal out of what was happening, she forced a smile. "I don't want to be held responsible for, you know, keeping you away from business. I know how important it is for you all." Antonio had never been overly friendly with her, and she didn't quite like that he was being so now.

****

Roman Greco hated these small little party get-togethers. His father arranged it as a way of inviting him and his new wife, as well as Liam. He'd seen the older man give her a hug, and he just knew it was a dig at him, or in some way telling him he wasn't good enough.

Liam had told him plenty of times that he was merely the best of the worst. He didn't understand what the big deal was. He married his daughter, and business was going great between them. All the boxes for this union to work had been ticked, and still, Liam looked at him like he wanted to slit his throat.

It just so happened the feeling was mutual. He didn't like Liam Smith.

The man wasn't mafia, he wasn't family, and in no way was he blood. There was no denying Liam had worked himself from the ground up, building a reputation for himself and becoming the feared crime boss that he was. His name rivaled the Greco name for fear. Men were loyal to him, and they never, even under threat of torture or being tortured, turned on him.

Lucas Greco, Roman's father, had been impressed and wanted to finally meet the man that no one would break from. Not even to save their own skin.

Who instilled that kind of loyalty?

The man in front of him was deadly. Roman saw it in the man's eyes. There was nothing living there, and he heard the rumors that the only person who was ever safe from this man was his daughter, Alex.

So much rumor and gossip followed this man. Roman didn't believe it all.

He sipped at his whiskey and stared at the man over the rim of the glass. He didn't fear Liam.

Roman was the only man in the history of the mafia to have killed a man at the ripe old age of ten. Serving his father and the Greco name was in his blood, as was becoming the boss, when his father would hand the reins over to him. Until that time, he still had to do what his father instructed.

"How is married life treating you?" Liam asked.

"Fine." He clenched his teeth, wanting to beat the crap out of the man in front of him. There wasn't much difference between them in age, just twenty years. Liam was fifty-five years old while he was thirty-five years old.

Unlike the women in their world, he didn't have to marry at a young age. Most of their daughters were often betrothed by the age of twelve and married at either eighteen or twenty-one.

Alex was twenty-one, and she was nothing like the women of his world. She didn't bow her head or try to be hidden. She held herself tall and proud. There was also defiance within her gaze. His father had told him of her denial to take the virginity test and how Liam refused to enforce it.

Liam stated that his daughter was a virgin and he believed her.

Roman didn't. He also hadn't fucked her either,

hadn't consummated their marriage. He expected Alex to tell her father they hadn't had sex, but she still kept quiet.

He didn't know what her game was, but he intended to find out.

No one took him for a fool. When it came to Alex, he already had people in place to find out her weaknesses. So far, she showed none. She had also not proven to be a liar either, which … baffled him.

Liam chuckled. "Just fine."

"I think we should talk business," Lucas said, interrupting. "I've gotten word—"

"Business is for the morning where booze hasn't been so freely offered," Liam said. "Do you think I got to where I am by taking the words of drunken men?" His gaze turned back to Roman. "I have it on good authority that you've been with Denise."

Roman tensed up. He didn't know how Liam knew of his ex-lover, or her name, and to be honest, he wasn't happy with it either.

He kept his personal life very private, and his lovers were always protected.

Since his marriage, he hadn't enjoyed another woman, not even his wife. He'd been so focused on dealing with the fallout from taking an outsider as a wife. Alex was … so different.

She didn't know their customs and often just stood by herself, ignoring everyone, or being ignored, he wasn't quite sure.

What was with her? He couldn't read her.

Women like Denise, his ex-lover, were interested in power and money. They only wanted what was best for themselves. When it came to Alex, he wasn't sure what it was. He also couldn't find out the relevant information he needed to know more about her. Her father kept it all under wraps.

No one knew anything, and that pissed him off.

Whenever he had a computer guy onto something, there was always some glitch or problem that stopped him from finding out everything there was about his wife.

"My son wouldn't ruin his marriage vows," Lucas said.

That wasn't entirely correct. His father had pulled him to one side and said that if he ever needed to, there were always mistresses who would help deal with his needs. Lucas, besides having a wife, had three mistresses.

Roman hadn't been interested in going to another woman. Being married wasn't what he expected. First of all, he had to make sure Liam didn't find out he hadn't actually consummated the marriage.

The only piece of information he could truly get was that Liam Smith loved his daughter. Adored her. She was treasured by him, and that made her an interesting pawn in this game.

Liam Smith was an ally, and his father had told him to treat Alex with respect. He had no interest in hurting a woman.

"I had dinner with Denise at her request, two weeks ago. She had a problem and needed me to fix it."

Her boss was getting handsy, and with his and Alex's marriage announced in the press, people assumed the women in his life were now easy targets.

He hadn't seen Denise for a long time, and they had ended things rather amicably.

Roman finished off his whiskey as Liam glared at him. "My daughter has not returned. Go and find her."

In his father's home, he didn't expect to take orders from anyone but Lucas. He had a quick glance at his father and saw the nod. It annoyed him to even be seen doing as that bastard asked.

Still, he turned on his heel and made his way out of the main party, going along the corridor and coming to a pause when he caught sight of Antonio, one of his best friends, with his wife.

Antonio attempted to put his arm around Alex, but she immediately stood up. She hadn't seen Roman yet. "You know what, I think it's time I headed back to the party. It was nice meeting you, Antonio." She stepped away, and the moment she caught sight of him, she stopped. "Roman."

"Alex."

He stared at her from the tip of her head. She had luscious brown hair. It was thick and fell around her in waves. From the short time he had spent with her, he knew she often wore it up, most of the time in a clip, rarely falling down around her shoulders.

Staring down the length of her body, he saw her black dress that was more fitting for a funeral than a party, and it wasn't a flattering fit either. The dress fell to her tits and then seemed to hang off her body. None of her gorgeous curves were on display. He knew she hadn't picked this outfit herself.

The maid who came to clean his home three times a week had picked it out for her. He made a note never to ask her to help his wife again. No wonder the women were making snarky comments behind their hands about her. She looked like … death.

Neither of them spoke, and Alex's gaze moved from his, to the wall, and then to the floor before returning to his.

"I better go and join them," she said.

"I'll be there in a moment."

She didn't stop, just nodded as she kept on walking.

"I think you're wrong about her," Antonio said, getting to his feet.

He stared at his friend and tilted his head to the side. "How?"

"She does not like me being anywhere near her. Did you see?" Antonio asked.

"I saw her move the moment you put your hands around her."

"Yeah, and she kindly removed my hand from her thigh as well," Antonio said.

"What?"

"You told me to get close, to push her. You said there were no limits, that if needed, to take it all the way. I merely put my hand on her knee." Antonio's gaze swept over him. "But tell me, Roman, if you don't care about your wife, and you want everyone to know that she is a manipulative, cheating bitch, why are your hands clenched, and you look like you want to kill me?"

"I do not want to kill you. Good job." Roman didn't like the fact that he felt this way. Alex meant nothing to him. She was a job. A woman who had been forced on him.

She played her part of innocent daughter well, but he knew the truth. She was a slut and Liam's greatest weakness. He would find the truth one way or another.

It wasn't lost on him that Liam had given them the key to making his life miserable. They could kill her and start a war. It would be so easy. His father had told him that he respected and valued Liam Smith. No war was ever going to wage with that man. Roman felt that as soon as he discovered the truth about Alex, he'd get what he wanted.

Antonio approached him and slapped him on the shoulder. "You keep on believing that, buddy. I know the truth. I've known you for years, and you want to slit my throat. It's fine, but maybe you need to know what it is you want first, before you ask people to do this."

"Alex is a slut."

"I don't think she is. If so, then I'm not the kind of man she goes for. We all know the ladies drop their panties for me."

Roman couldn't help but look at Antonio's neck and think how good it would look oozing with blood.

"You know that murderous rage you're feeling right now? That's not what a guy who wants to have other men sleep with his wife should feel like." Antonio winked at him and left to rejoin the party.

Running a hand down his face, he attempted to clear his mind. Tonight was not going well.

He was running on only a couple of hours of sleep, and to be frank, he was exhausted. For the last three days, he'd been chasing a goddamn rat, one who wanted to trade their secrets for money and a safe life. It was one of their science nerds, and so far, the son of a bitch hadn't made it out of the city. The fucker had been able to make it another day. If it wasn't for his father telling him he had to be here tonight, he would've still been hunting him.

Maybe what he needed to do was stay close to home and make sure his wife fell into the traps he'd set.

So far, she had proven him wrong, and he didn't like that.

Chapter Two

For the first time since her marriage had been arranged, Alex Smith felt a little thrum of excitement. She made her way across the college grounds, found the usual tree where she had lunch, and sat her ass down.

It had been five days since she last saw her father, but last night, he'd stopped by Roman's apartment, where she'd been placed since the party, and told her she needed to get back to college.

She didn't need to argue with him because staying at home, waiting for something to happen, and attempting to find her own entertainment sucked. Coming back to school and taking her classes was a welcome relief.

The sun shone brightly in the sky, forcing her to remove her cardigan, and she slid down the tree, crossed her legs, and pulled her backpack between them. Since she'd packed herself a couple of sandwiches, a bag of chips, and some fruit, she snagged her banana and ate that first.

She was so hungry. This morning, she'd only gotten a few slices of toast. Within a few bites, the banana was gone, and she grabbed her apple to take a bite.

Keeping her gaze open, she stared across the campus grounds. It was humming with activity, and she loved that. She loved learning.

For the longest time, she wanted to go to college. Her father hadn't wanted her to. He'd offered to pay for tutors and for her to learn at home, but she refused. She wanted the experience.

He hadn't forced her to study at home through high school. She'd gone to a public school, and that had been … interesting. Bill, her bodyguard, had always been present. Okay, he hadn't been present, but after one particular day of bad bullying and sporting a black eye, Bill had followed her to school.

One quick glance toward the parking lot, and she saw him standing there, watching her. She held her hand up and gave him a quick wave.

In response, he lifted his hand. It looked more like an alien gesture, but she took it. He meant well.

Finishing off her apple, she then grabbed her sandwich.

Since being married to Roman, he'd denied Bill's presence. The man worked for her father, so he wouldn't allow the other man anywhere near her. Last night, her father told her that he'd have people looking out for her. She was going to be a target now, not just for his enemies, but also for Greco's enemies.

Personally, she'd done nothing wrong, but it would seem, in their world, they liked to make people pay for others' mistakes.

Leaning back against the tree, she slowed down her eating so she wouldn't give herself a stomachache.

She missed Bill. Missed her dad. Missed Mellie, the cook back home. That woman had a way of making her feel loved and safe.

Roman had a chef at one of his restaurants who dealt with meals. They were delivered every day at the same time. Breakfast was served at exactly seven thirty. Lunch at twelve thirty, and then dinner by six thirty. She never got a say in what was cooked. The food looked pretentious, like it had spent a lifetime attempting to win awards.

Alex hated it.

Mellie's noodle soup and dumplings and lemon cake, and the list kept on going, those were the best. Just thinking about them now made her a little homesick.

After dusting off her hands, she put her wrappings all together and went in search of the necessary trash bins. She put her trash inside and then glanced down at the time. She had five minutes to get to English class.

Glancing back toward the parking lot, she saw Bill was there. She wanted to go to him, to thank him, at the very least hug him, but she knew he wouldn't like that. Bill liked to keep things strictly professional. At least outside, in the open. When they were alone, he let her hug and sob against his shoulder.

He was like daddy number two.

Shaking that loneliness off, she headed toward English class, only to come to a stop when she caught sight of Roman. He didn't look at her, and she stepped behind one of the thick oak trees and glanced toward her husband. He was talking to a man, but she didn't recognize who he was.

He hadn't come to get her, so what was he doing on school property? Did it matter?

Roman glanced toward her, and she sank against the tree, not wanting to be seen.

Her heart started to race. Did he see her looking?

She should just make it to English. Snooping, or spying, was not for her.

Alex was about to make a break for it when fingers wrapped around her wrist, stopping her. She spun toward the person who'd grabbed her and saw Roman was there. How had he moved from across the grounds toward her so fast?

"What are you doing?" Roman asked.

She tugged at her wrist. "Let me go." She didn't want to cause a scene. Not many people were around, but there were a few. She hated bringing attention to herself.

"Why are you here?" Roman asked. "Who sent you?"

Why was he accusing her?

"I'm going to class," she said. "Please, I don't want to be late."

"Sir, I suggest you let her go."

This was Bill. This was going to be very bad.

She looked from Roman to Bill, then back again.

"Why are you here?" Roman asked.

"I have it on strict orders to keep an eye on her, to protect her, while she goes to school," Bill said.

"She is my wife. She is coming with me."

Bill stepped in front of Roman, stopping him.

She tried to tell Bill to just step aside, but he'd been given orders by her father.

"Alex, go to class," Bill said. He didn't take his gaze from Roman as he brought his cell phone to his ear. "Sir, I have Roman here, and he is trying to remove Alex from school."

She saw Roman's jaw clenching. This wasn't good. This was very, very, bad.

As she looked between the two men, Roman took the cell phone. He didn't remove his fingers from her wrist.

"What?" Roman asked.

Bill had one hand at his waist, and she knew he was getting ready to strike. Bill was deadliest when he appeared calm and collected.

This wasn't going to end well.

Roman handed his cell phone back, but he didn't let her go.

In fact, he grabbed Bill's jacket. She gasped as he slammed his head against the other man's, taking Bill by surprise and knocking him out, and then, he rested him up against the tree.

As he did so, he'd let her go, and Alex tried to escape. She took several steps away from him, but he wouldn't let her go. He grabbed her, and then they marched across the school grounds.

She didn't say anything, but fear traveled down her spine, and she felt sick. A hand went to her stomach, and she tried not to throw up.

Her father had always tried to hide violence from her as it did make her sick. She hated the confrontation, the aggression. None of it served any purpose to her, other than to instill fear inside. She wanted to run away.

But Roman dragged her across the parking lot. She attempted to dig her heels into the ground.

If she wasn't such a coward, she'd have shouted for help, but how would that have looked?

Screaming because her husband was taking her away. Was he going to beat her? Hurt her?

Her father had said it was fine for her to return to school, but the way Roman was reacting, this was the furthest thing from the truth.

He opened the car door and pushed her inside. She held on to her bag for comfort.

Roman moved around the car and then went to the driver's side. She tried her door, but he must have put the damn child lock on because she couldn't get out.

She wasn't going to show fear though. Fear was for the weak, wasn't it?

Her heart pounded and her throat felt thick. She didn't have her cell phone with her, and there was no way to contact her father for help. She was on her own.

Bill would wake up soon. Wouldn't he?

"Did you kill him?" she asked.

Roman pulled out of the parking lot, and then they were on the road. He didn't answer, and Alex hated this.

"Did you?"

He still didn't answer.

"Damn it, Bill is important to my father. You better not have killed him or else—"

"Or else what?" Roman asked.

"Or else my father will consider it a slight against him. He will make you pay."

Roman laughed. "Make me pay. The man is a fucking fool. Allowing you to go to school."

"How dare you? Just because you don't want your women to be intelligent. My father is the complete opposite. He believes all women should be treated equally."

"I have nothing against women seeking an education!" He snarled out the words.

"Then why are you taking me away? And slow down. You are going to get us killed."

She had already slid her seatbelt on, but now, she dropped her bag down between her legs and held on to the door.

"I can't. We're being followed."

Alex gasped and looked around, trying to see if there was anyone following them. At that moment, Roman changed lanes, and she saw a black car did exactly the same move. Roman changed again, and the same car did the same action.

"Okay, okay, we're being followed."

"From the moment I got to the school, that car was sat there. I thought it looked a bit suspicious, but it was there before I turned up, so I didn't think much of it. Knowing you were there, that's why the black car was there."

"They want me?" Alex asked, starting to panic.

"Are you too fucking dumb to realize that you are now a powerful woman? You are married to the Greco

Boss's son, and you are the daughter of Liam Smith, notorious crime lord. There is a target on your head, Alex."

She had no idea. "I'm not important."

"Do not be dense."

"My dad will move heaven and earth to save me, but to you, I'm nothing. I'm just a contract you can't stand." She was only stating a fact.

Roman didn't like her.

"Then you are more foolish than I thought."

"I just … my dad said it was fine for me to go to school."

"Maybe it was before you married me, but not anymore. It is not safe for you." They came to a long stretch of road, and Alex felt the hum of the car beneath her.

"Stay down," Roman said.

She had nowhere else to go.

This was the most they had talked in their two months of marriage.

He spun the car, and all of a sudden, they were facing the other car. At some point, Roman had gotten himself a gun, and he pointed it toward the car. Alex screamed as bullets hit the car.

Roman put his foot on the gas, and the car squeaked. She held on for dear life, but the noise was deafening, and she felt like she was going to be sick.

The car wasn't turning. She just knew they were going to crash.

Roman didn't veer. He didn't change direction as he stayed completely focused on the car in front of him, and panic filled her. They were going to die, and if he killed the people in the front seat of the car, they were as good as dead.

She called his name, but Roman wasn't listening

to her.

They were going to die.

****

Roman stared at the two men who were chained to chairs in the basement of one of Liam's strip clubs. Cops were upstairs, and it amused Roman that Liam conducted illegal business right under their noses, but he guessed that was the best way of finding the men who would do anything for money or sex.

Liam's man hadn't turned up yet, but he had a feeling that when he did, it wasn't going to go well. No doubt, he'd already talked to Bill, and had probably talked to Alex, who was upstairs in one of the private rooms.

Roman didn't like bringing her to a strip club. There was too much sex. He didn't want to bring her, but taking her home or leaving her anywhere else right now didn't seem logical.

She had been panicked, but what had surprised him while he'd waited for his men to arrive was that she'd secured the two men who currently sat bleeding now. Without screaming at him and without fainting.

Yes, she had thrown up, but she told him she didn't realize they were going to be trying to save their lives after she had eaten lunch. She seemed a little pissed off, but it was her suggestion to bring them here.

Was this where she lost her virginity?

Roman didn't believe for a second that she was a virgin. If she wasn't one, why did she oppose the test his father asked for?

The door to the basement opened, and then Liam advanced on him, fists raised. Roman shook him off, ready to step toe to toe with him.

"How dare you drag my daughter off campus!" Bill was right behind him, sporting a black eye.

Roman wondered if the guy had a nice nap, but he kept his thoughts to himself. Now was not the time to start a fight.

"It's a good thing I did, and look what I've got. These men were waiting for her." He'd been at the campus because the scientist he'd been after had one job to complete to be able to have the money and security he craved, and that was to build a drug.

Roman wasn't quite sure what kind of drug it was, or if it was even a drug, but either way, the only place he knew where to find a guy like the one he was after was a campus. It was sheer fucking luck that he saw these guys and put two and two together with his wife.

She should have been fucking home, where she was safe.

"Bill was there to protect her."

"Yeah? And did your precious bodyguard even notice the blacked-out car waiting for her, watching her? It fucking stuck out like a sore thumb, but he was busy watching her like some pervert."

Bill stepped forward. "I would never look at her in such a way. She is like a daughter to me."

"A daughter you're going to get killed."

"Enough!" Liam yelled, and Roman gritted his teeth.

In all his life, he had never had to step down from a fight or have so much control when it came to a man who pissed him off. His father had told him to respect Liam, to work with him, and above all else, to never make waves. This wasn't how Roman worked.

The Greco name was everything to him. Working with Liam, having Alex as his wife, it was all pushing him a little too far. He wasn't used to not striking out.

"Where is Alex?" Liam asked.

Taking a deep breath, Roman turned toward

Liam. "She is upstairs. She is the one who suggested I bring them here."

Liam nodded. "Good. She knows this is the best place to get answers."

"With cops partying upstairs?"

"Those cops are friends. I take care of them, and they take care of me. I do not have to explain my actions to you, or that most of the men upstairs owe me." He turned toward the men.

They were currently passed out.

Roman had decided to start with their nails. He found the utmost pain talked volumes. In most situations, a little pain, and men were blabbering all kinds of secrets. It was kind of embarrassing for them, but that was the way of their world.

Liam stepped forward, and he tilted their heads back.

"What are you doing?" Roman asked. He was used to working alone.

"They have the mark," Liam said and stepped back.

"What mark?"

Roman had been too pissed to get too close without beating the crap out of them. All he wanted to do was cut them up. He rather liked using his knives, and these men had thought to attack his wife. Even though he didn't particularly like Alex, she was still his wife. Under his protection, and if anything happened to her, it would be on him.

He would be a laughingstock of the Greco family.

She had to be protected at all costs, even if he didn't agree that she was part of their world. She was his wife.

"The Smirnov mark," Liam said.

This made Roman step forward and lift the man's

head. Sure enough, at the base of his neck was the mark. It was a coiled snake, the fangs dripping blood.

Roman hadn't seen that in many years. "Why are they after Alex?" Roman asked.

"Let's find out." Liam lifted the bucket of water, which was also mingled with piss. He had found another of Liam's men pissing in the bucket and said the boss liked it.

Roman didn't bother asking questions. This is one of the many reasons why he preferred to work alone or with his own men.

Antonio, Marlo, and Cash all knew the score. They knew how he worked. They were his best friends, and the only men he trusted, other than his father.

He certainly didn't trust Liam, his father-in-law. Just thinking of him like that was enough to wrinkle his nose.

The piss and water were used on the men, and they woke up with a gasp.

Now, Liam's method of torture was legendary, or at least the rumors surrounding him were. Men would rather kill themselves than face Liam's wrath.

Roman watched as Liam pulled out a knife from his jacket pocket. He unsheathed the blade. It was small.

"Why were you following my daughter?" Liam asked. He stood with his legs wide, almost straddling the man on the left. Roman watched as he suddenly jabbed the man in the chest.

A gasp, and Liam repeated the question. The man on the right just watched. With each question and jab, the man looked even more terrified.

Roman saw Liam work, and when he wasn't stabbing the man's chest, he hit his stomach, and then his thighs.

How the man was still breathing, Roman didn't

know, but his skill was … sharp, it was perfectly aimed. The man was still alive, even as Liam stepped away, and Roman saw all the blood covering the man's body. He was going to die slowly and painfully. The blood was already soaking the floor.

"Why were you following my daughter?" Liam held the knife, about to jab the man's chest, but he screamed. "Our orders were to take her!"

Liam held himself tight, ready to strike at a moment's notice. "To take her?"

"Yes, Alex Smith is an important pawn in this game. They wanted us to take her."

"Who is *they*?" Roman asked, stepping forward.

The man looked from Liam to him, then back again. "I don't know. I just know that once you get this mark, you have to do as they tell you. Our orders were to watch her, and when the opportunity presented, we were to take her."

"You work for the Smirnov?" Liam asked.

The man's lip wobbled. Liam thrust the knife into the man's neck and twisted.

"We haven't got all of our information yet," he said, angry that Liam would fucking strike now.

Liam stepped back.

The other man was dying slowly.

"I know what we're up against, and it's not pretty. I dealt with the Smirnov over twenty years ago, Roman. This is … I need to speak with your father, and I think it will be best if Alex comes back home."

"What the fuck?" Roman asked.

"It's not like you respect my daughter," Liam said. "For all I know, you could be working with them to hurt my little girl."

"You insult me. I would never work with anyone but Greco." He slapped a hand on his chest. "Alex is not in danger from me, and she is my wife."

Liam stepped close to her. "Prove it. Do you think I'm a fool, Roman?"

He glared at Liam but remained silent. This was a trap, and he refused to fall into it.

"Do you think I don't know that my daughter is still a virgin?" Liam asked. "That you have not conducted your part of the agreement? I know for a fact that I can call for it to be annulled."

Roman chuckled. "Alex would have to conduct the virginity test. I would demand it."

"To get away from you, Roman, my daughter would do it."

He didn't like this, and this time, Liam smiled. "Do you really think Alex wanted to be married to you?" Liam slapped him on the shoulder.

"Sir, Lucas Greco has arrived," Bill said.

"Good. Clean up the mess for me, Bill."

"I am so sorry, sir."

"Please, do not worry about it. We will talk later," Liam said.

Roman saw the fear in Bill's gaze, and he wasn't quite sure why, but he also didn't ask.

They walked out of the basement, and sure enough, his father was there, along with his friend Antonio and several of his guards and men. Liam shook hands with Lucas, and then they made their way upstairs, toward the bedroom where he'd put Alex.

Roman didn't want to look at his wife at that moment. He had assumed that Alex loved the idea of being married to him, of wanting to be connected in any way possible to the Greco line.

Liam didn't even knock as they stepped into the room. Roman didn't know what he expected to find, but it certainly wasn't Alex pacing the room. Staring at her now, in a pair of jeans and a t-shirt, she looked so … composed.

"Dad?" Alex asked, and she rushed forward.

This was an embarrassment. His wife didn't speak to him. She didn't even look to him for comfort, and with one glance at his father, he knew this wasn't good for the Greco name. All his life, he'd done what was required of him, fulfilled his part of the agreement when it came to his father.

"Did Roman tell you what happened?" Alex asked.

"Of course."

"I don't know what was going on. One moment we were, like, I don't know exactly what we were doing, and then bam."

What Alex said didn't make any sense to him. She didn't tell her father that he dragged her off campus, or that he yelled at her.

Who was Alex Smith? Why was her father so convinced of her innocence? How did he know that they hadn't consummated their marriage?

The only way Liam would know this was if Alex told him. She had to have.

Roman didn't buy this act. Women were always after something. All he had to do was find out what Alex was after, and once he did, he'd be able to deal with her.

"Those men were after you," Liam said. "You are in danger, and I think it's time you came back home."

Chapter Three

Alex was eight when she first learned that her father was a … bad man. Well, not a bad man, but a man who was used to getting what he wanted, and he had his own rules for getting things done.

She had woken up from a nightmare. She couldn't even remember what the dream was about, but it had scared her. Another reason why she would never watch horror movies, not even now. There was no way she was going to be scared, willingly. She'd needed to use the bathroom, and then after going to the toilet and washing her hands, she'd needed a drink. Being the big brave girl that she was, she'd gone downstairs to the kitchen to have a drink. A nice cold glass of milk, which her dad had told her would make her feel so much better.

It was halfway down the glass of milk when she saw the hooded figure in the reflection of the fridge. He'd been wielding a knife, ready to strike, and even young, she knew she should fear what was about to happen.

Her father had been there.

She later found out that her father had been watching the man sneak onto his property and had simply waited for the right moment to strike. What Liam hadn't been prepared for was his little girl, scared and thirsty, coming downstairs to enjoy a drink.

From that day forward, he was honest with her. At first, she'd been afraid, but she knew there were bad people in the world. Her dad wasn't the biggest bad person, and he cared in his own way. He told her so many stories of life on the streets, of the fears he had as a boy, and then how he used them to get to where he was today.

Alex watched as her father and her husband stood toe to toe, yelling at each other. Liam wanted her to come home, and the truth was, she wanted that as well. To come back home. Being married to Roman was … boring and difficult. This wasn't a fairytale ending. Not that she'd ever sought that.

Alex had never planned her wedding. She'd never looked through catalogs and thought about the big day. She'd thought about a future where she was whoever she wanted to be, even though she didn't know exactly what she wanted to do or be. When she talked to teachers and career advisors, they always said there was time to figure it out. To find the path she wanted to take and to let it flourish properly.

Having a big family wasn't a career, and it meant having a guy in her life, and she didn't want to be with men. She had hated guys growing up because they were mean. She'd never had the slender body or the looks that men loved.

Mousy, curvy, and quiet. That was often how she was described. Even her dad had once said that she was Daddy's little mouse. As a nickname, it wasn't sweet or cute. It was kind of gross.

"Stop," Alex said.

They didn't stop.

She closed her eyes and stepped away, pacing. That car was waiting for her, to take her away, and they were arguing.

Alex hated this. They were not listening.

She glanced around the room and didn't want to think of what actually happened here. A lamp was available. She reached for it and then threw it across the room so it hit the wall with a loud crash, breaking apart as it landed in pieces on the floor.

She breathed out a sigh of relief as silence filled

the arguing.

"Will you both stop it? Or why don't you get your dicks out and measure them? Ew, gross." She scrunched up her face, realizing what she said. She'd overheard a couple of women downstairs talking about different men, and how they were always arguing. It just dawned on her what she said. "Please, ignore what I just said, because that is … you're arguing here, and none of you have thought to ask me what I think."

She looked at Roman and rolled her eyes. "I understand why you did it. You and your … family don't believe in actually asking a woman her thoughts, right?" She turned to her father. "What do I do? What did I do wrong? You said I could go back to school. Why were they waiting for me?"

She felt tears fill her eyes, and she clenched her hands into fists.

"Honey," Liam said, and she shook her head.

"No, Dad, being the calm one right now is not going to work." She took a deep breath and closed her eyes. "I don't want to be a pain. I don't want to cause you guys any trouble, and I am so sorry, Mr. Greco, for doing that." She licked her dry lips. "What did I do wrong?"

The men looked at her. Her father gazed at her with sadness, and she wasn't sure how the others looked at her.

"You didn't do anything wrong," Antonio, of all people, said. "You're a powerful woman now. A weakness to our enemies. You're married to Roman Greco, who will one day be The Boss, and you're Liam Smith's daughter, who is a powerful man in his own right."

"Roman has said all of this, but I am no one."

Liam stepped forward and put his hands on her

shoulders. "Stop saying that, sweetheart. I was wrong about this. I put your life in danger."

"Dad?"

"Yes, little mouse."

She groaned. "What do I do?"

"You come home," Roman said. "I will protect you. I have been protecting you."

"I don't want to hide," Alex said. "I've never done that."

"Only until we find those responsible, Alex," Liam said. "And we will. It will be safe for you to do what you want."

"You can study," Roman said. "There are online courses you can take. I will talk to the school personally and have it arranged for you to do that."

She frowned as she looked at him. "Why?"

"It is what you want, and regardless of what you think, I am not that cruel."

Alex didn't believe him. She wrapped her arms around herself and stared at the room full of men. There was way too much testosterone tonight, and she knew she was nearly killed.

"Okay." She looked at her dad. "Can I … stay home tonight?"

"I'm taking you home," Roman said.

"I mean in my old bedroom." She didn't want to be with Roman. He didn't make her feel safe. She missed her old home, her old house, and Millie. The only way for her to feel strong right now was to enjoy a nice big bowl full of Millie's comfort soup. She didn't even know what was in the soup, she just knew that she wanted it.

"I'm not letting you out of my sight," Roman said.

Her father snapped back, and then they were arguing again. Of course, they were arguing.

"Fine!" Alex yelled, raising her voice loud enough to be heard. "You can stay. I'm sure my dad has plenty of rooms."

"I will stay in your room," Roman said.

He was just doing this to rile her dad.

"I don't care," Alex said, looking at her dad. "Can I go?"

"Yes, I will drive you," Liam said.

"And I'll be there." This was from Roman.

"Actually, Mr. Smith," Lucas said. "I would like for us to have a word. I think it is only fair that we give Alex and my son some time. They have, after all, had an awful experience. We can talk."

Alex wasn't in the mood to argue.

"I will be home soon," Liam said.

She went to her father and wrapped her arms around his waist, holding him close and breathing him in. Whenever she hugged him, she always felt safe and warm.

Nothing and no one could get her. No imaginary bogeymen or scary, real hooded men. Nothing. She was safe.

As with all things, she had to pull away. She kissed his cheek and stepped toward Roman, who took her hand. Antonio also followed, and then she found two other men outside.

"Alex, this is Marlo Guerra and Cash Vitale."

She held her hand up in greeting. They were his other two friends. She had seen them at the wedding, but they hadn't been introduced.

They left the strip club out the back entrance, where a car was already waiting for them. Antonio and Marlo took the front seat while she sat in the middle between Roman and Cash.

She stayed tense. No one spoke on the journey,

and she wanted to be near a window just so she could look out. To see the city passing her by, and not to be afraid of anything.

She hated feeling fear. The spiraling twist in her gut was not a welcoming feeling. She wanted it to stop.

"Are you okay?" Antonio asked, filling the silence.

"I'm fine. Thank you."

"You must be scared," Marlo said.

She shrugged and then leaned her head back, closing her eyes and enjoying the hum of the car.

"Is she asleep?" Cash asked beside her.

"No," she said. "I won't be able to sleep tonight."

She hadn't been able to sleep the night of the break-in either. Not that he'd done anything to her. Every time she closed her eyes, she had seen him coming at her with a knife.

Tonight, she had no idea if she'd get some sleep.

Enemies, plural. More than one person. And she hadn't done anything wrong other than be the person she was.

"I'm pretty sure Roman can help you with that," Cash said with a chuckle.

She tensed up even more.

Roman didn't touch her. Other than the brush of lips at the wedding, they didn't touch. Today, he'd grabbed her arm, and tonight, he held her hand, but that was all. Back home, in either his apartment or his country home, they didn't even share a bedroom. She had moved all her belongings to a spare bedroom. Being as far away from Roman as possible suited her.

"Enough," Roman said. His voice was gruff.

She opened her eyes and turned her head to see Roman looking at her.

What was he thinking? He was a mystery, and

had been since their wedding.

She rolled her head back so she was looking straight up at the ceiling of the car. What could she do to get out of this situation? If she asked for a divorce, that would put Greco and her father at loggerheads, if not outright war.

Her father would be convinced she wasn't happy. This was a giant mess.

"We're here," Antonio said.

She didn't even know how much time had passed, but as she sat up, she looked out the window.

They were parked in her father's driveway. The front door was aglow with the light shining up. She wanted to climb over Cash to get to her home, but she was the perfect lady, waiting until he climbed out of the car.

Alex didn't wait for them to follow. She rushed up the front steps, and as the door opened, she saw Millie, their cook, and she threw her arms around the older woman.

"I've got you now, child. I've got you."

"Oh, Millie, I've missed you."

"And I've missed you."

She hugged her, breathing in the scent of chocolate and cinnamon. Millie was a keen baker, and when she wasn't cooking for her father, she often baked and cooked too much and took the leftovers to the local orphanage. Alex had volunteered to go with her all the time, and that had only stopped because she was now married and expected to follow Roman around like a damn puppy.

"Your father called, sweetheart. I have everything you need in the kitchen." She looked past her shoulder. "Even for your friends as well."

It was on the tip of her tongue to tell her that

Roman and his buddies were not her friends, but she decided against it. Now was not the time to start making waves.

****

Millie liked to feed people.

And it was the best damn food Roman had ever tasted. His dad once had a good cook, but Lucas had killed the bastard for attempting to poison him. Since then, Lucas and Roman used their own restaurants to cook their food. Never the same one either.

Roman couldn't remember the last time he sat down for a proper home-cooked meal. His mother wasn't a cook.

He watched Millie and Alex. They had a bond. The older woman constantly filled Alex's plate, touched her hair, and kissed her cheek. Told her she was looking a little on the thin side. Each time Millie mentioned her weight, Alex looked toward them, but Roman only observed. The only way he was ever going to learn about his wife was to see how she handled each situation as they came. So far, she seemed to be as innocent as she claimed.

If she truly was a virgin, why forego the simple test? He didn't understand it.

"So, Millie, do you have any secrets to share about Alex?" Marlo asked.

His friends were playing their roles perfectly. Appearing to be friendly to Alex to earn her trust. To get under her skin.

"There are not any secrets to share about this one. She is a treasure, truly."

Alex covered her face. "Stop it, Millie."

"I'm only speaking the truth." Another kiss to the cheek. "Stuart asked after you again."

"Who is Stuart?" Roman asked, his interest

piqued.

"No one you'd know," Alex said. "How is he? Is he okay?"

Was Stuart a love interest? An ex-boyfriend? A crush?

Millie looked down the table. "We'll talk later."

He didn't like that. No one was going to keep secrets from him. One look at his men, and they nodded. They knew what he wanted. By the end of the night, he would know everything there was to know about Stuart, unless that was another barrier Liam had imposed. The fucking meddling bastard.

He scooped some mashed potatoes onto his fork and ate. The taste was incredible. Creamy, light, and so soft. Seasoned to perfection. He watched Alex eat. He hadn't noticed before, but she was a delicate eater. Cutting up her vegetables and sliding them around her plate to gather some gravy before taking a bite.

Millie left them alone, and silence fell across the table.

Roman continued to watch Alex, expecting her to break the silence. His previous lovers had always filled the silence with their endless, inane chitchat.

She stayed quiet.

Cash spoke up first. "So, Alex, did you grow up here?"

"Yes."

That was it. No follow up, just a simple *yes*.

Cash glanced toward him, and he raised a brow.

"Was it just you and your dad?"

She lifted her gaze once again. "I don't have any brothers and sisters."

Liam had to have trained her in some way. She avoided answering questions directly.

"It must have been pretty lonely," Marlo asked.

"Do you have siblings?" she asked.

Marlo pursed his lips. "A younger brother and two sisters."

"Were you ever lonely?"

Marlo clicked his tongue and then opened his mouth.

"I'm ever so sorry, but I am feeling really tired. Thank you all for driving me home. I hope you enjoy Millie's food." She gave them a forced smile that didn't reach her eyes before getting up and with her plate in hand, turning to leave.

Which pissed him off!

She was leaving them.

"Does she even realize what she's doing?" Cash asked.

"You mean by avoiding questions, directing the conversation toward her opponent?" Marlo asked. "Yeah, I saw it."

"Antonio believes she is innocent."

In response, Antonio rolled his eyes. "Look, you've asked us to test her, and I can tell you. I threw on a whole load of charm, and she wasn't buying it. Not one bit."

"Maybe you've lost your charm," Marlo said.

"Not a chance." Antonio picked up his glass of water and took a sip. "I have fucked every single woman you've asked me to. It's not hard, and it wasn't difficult to get into their pants. I'm telling you, Alex is different."

In the past, they had all had some fun in seeing how long their current flavor of the week would last when met with another man willing to take them to bed. Out of all his lovers, Denise was the easiest. Within hours, Antonio had her on her knees, sucking his cock and then taking him deep into her pussy.

Roman wasn't upset. He didn't love or have any

kind of feelings for Denise. She was a woman he enjoyed, nothing more, nothing less.

He dabbed his lips with his napkin and got to his feet.

"You ever thought about treating her like a girlfriend or your wife?" Antonio asked. "She might open up to a guy she trusts."

Glaring at his friends, he left the room and headed toward the kitchen. When he heard Alex talking, he slowed his pace so she wouldn't hear him.

"He must be so scared," she said.

"You know he has grown attached to you. I did worry how this distance would make him, but now, he's … maybe tomorrow you can go see him."

"I don't know how my dad is going to do that. You heard what happened today."

"I know. I know."

"This is all so nuts," Alex said. "I miss Stuart. I miss going and being with him, you know. Helping."

"I'll find a way to convince your father, Alex. For the both of you."

She sighed. "Thank you, Millie."

"Always. I will do anything for you, darling."

"I'm going to head up."

"I will serve those men," Millie said. "Don't worry."

"Thank you."

Roman hid down the long corridor and watched as Alex appeared, closing the door behind her. Since leaving the table, she looked exhausted. Like she'd just been given some bad news.

He watched as she stood, pressing her hands to her face. Her shoulders rose and fell with what he imagined were several deep breaths before she dropped her hands and then headed toward the main stairs.

Following behind her, he only made his presence known when she entered her bedroom, and he nudged her inside as he joined her. "What are you doing?" she asked, stepping back from him.

This was another thing about Alex. She never reached for his touch. Never made any excuse to put her hands on him or to be near him. She always created a distance between them.

"Who is Stuart?" he asked.

"Roman, why are you here? Millie made up the spare bedrooms. They're on the main floor. She'll show you and your friends where you're supposed to be sleeping."

"Not a chance. I sleep next to my wife."

Her eyes went wide, and then he saw the smile. Seconds later, a laugh bubbled up inside her and spilled out. "Are you kidding me right now? We never sleep together. Never." She spoke the last word slowly, as if she thought he couldn't quite keep up.

Not what he had in mind.

"You're my wife."

"Here we go again. Yes, I am your wife. In name only, and trust me, I am more than happy about that. I don't want anything between us."

He frowned. This was news to him, but then he thought about what Liam said. "You don't want to be married to me?"

"Hell no. I wanted no part of any of this."

"Is this because of Stuart?"

"What?" The frown between her brows deepened. "What the hell are you talking about?"

"Your Stuart. The one Millie is going to try to get you to see. The one you're willing to risk your life for, and his. I will not be disrespected, and my wife will not be fucking any other man than me."

"Oh, my God, can you even hear yourself? We have never had sex. We are never going to have sex. You hate me, and guess what, I hate you as well. This marriage is a complete sham and a mess."

He took a step toward her, and Alex took a step toward him.

"Are you trying to threaten me, Roman?" she asked. "Because I should warn you, I may be a woman, but I am my father's daughter. If you so much as lay a finger on me, I will make you pay."

This took him by surprise. "I have no intention of harming you or threatening you." His father had already pulled him to one side many times and stated that his marriage was an embarrassment to the Greco name.

People whispered.

Enemies plotted.

And a weakness could be found in a marriage.

"You will never fuck another man. You are mine, Alex. I will make this Stuart pay. Do you understand?"

Alex laughed. "Oh, my God. Seriously, can you even hear yourself? You don't even know who Stuart is, and you're already threatening him. He's done nothing to you."

"He is taking the attention of my wife away."

"You don't even care that I'm your wife. We're perfect strangers who live under one roof, your roof."

It didn't matter. No one would ever have a taste of Alex, only him, or at least, only him from now on.

"What you had with Stuart is in the past."

"Wow, okay. Wow. This is about the stupid virginity test, isn't it?" Her hands clenched into fists, and she raised them as if to strike, but she didn't hit him. She took a step back.

"You're unbelievable," she said. "You won't accept that I am actually a virgin, will you?"

"If you were, why not take the test?"

"Do you even listen to the words that come out of your mouth? Or are they just sounds?" She spun away from him and then stepped toward him. "In case this is lost on you, I don't like the idea of having a strange man or woman looking between my legs. The reason I didn't want to have the test is because it would be a stranger, and I was allowed to have my dad present. Do you have any idea what that would be like? No, of course not, because to you, it's just a simple test, but to me, that is an invasion of privacy. I refused, end of story, and while we're at it, and you're throwing blame my way, Stuart, the guy you want to have killed, that would make you a child killer. He's six years old. I've known him since he was three. He was found dumped in a trash bin outside of one of my father's strip clubs. I found him. I was the one who tried to take care of him, but my dad decided I was too young. So we placed the baby in an orphanage and he has never been adopted."

She took a deep breath. Roman was shocked.

"Are you happy now? Do you still want to go out and kill this young boy? He is a sweetheart, and in the last three years, no one has even cared to give him a chance. He is adorable and sweet, but he has scars. He doesn't remember anything other than me. Now, please get the hell out of my bedroom. You have no right to be here."

It was the first time Roman had ever been kicked out of a room.

He watched as Alex ignored him and went through to her bathroom, which he glimpsed right before she closed the door.

Chapter Four

Leaning against the door, Alex breathed out a sigh of relief that she was able to escape after she had let off that steam. She'd been determined not to let him get under her skin, and yet, he'd done it anyway.

Why did he have so many bad opinions of her? It made no sense unless they were all based around that stupid virginity test, which frankly was the worst thing she'd ever been asked to do. She had expected her father to demand she take it as well, and he'd surprised her by having her back. At least someone did.

Licking her dry lips, she closed her eyes, counted to ten, and then stepped away from the door. It had been a long day with far too many revelations. Someone wanted her dead or at least to kidnap her and use her against her dad. She doubted Roman mattered in this situation. If anyone had been watching them closely, they'd know he didn't care for his young bride and would probably thank anyone for *dealing* with her.

Alex stepped toward the mirror and glanced over her reflection. Her eyes were a little red from trying to hold in all the tears. Thinking about little Stuart didn't help. It was the only time she and her father had been on opposing sides. She'd hated him for taking her little boy away. The moment she'd found him and held him, she had wanted to take care of him. Her dad wouldn't let her.

The only chance she got to see him was when she was with Millie.

She had to go and see him, but with this threat now imposed on her life, she doubted she was going to get the chance.

After stepping away from the mirror, she stripped off her clothes and climbed into the shower. She turned the water on and pressed her hands against the cold tiled wall as the icy jets splashed on her skin, waking her body up like it had been in limbo for far too long. She gritted her teeth and waited for the water to warm.

She often did this as a child. It helped her to focus, especially when life seemed to be more chaotic than she could handle.

It was moments like these when she wished she had a mom. Millie was the closest thing she had, but her loyalty would forever be with Liam. Alex understood that. It was why she wished she had her mom.

For the longest time, Liam had been everything, her dad and her mom, which had been hilarious when she had womanly problems to deal with. Thinking about her first menstrual cycle and looking back on her father with adult eyes, she couldn't help but laugh. He'd been so far out of his depth that it was more a comedy show. They'd gotten through it. They had gotten through a whole lot, and she knew he missed her mother. They weren't married at her mother's request, but they were soul mates.

The moment the water warmed up, the pain slicing through her body eased. She hated thinking about her parents and Stuart. Focusing on them now helped her to deal with the other problem of potentially being killed or kidnapped.

Grabbing the soap, she lathered up the sponge and then quickly washed her body before reaching for the shampoo, followed immediately after by the conditioner. Hair and body washed and cleaned, she turned the water off and stepped out to grab a towel and wrap it around her body.

She avoided going into her bedroom by brushing her teeth and combing her hair. The length was long, and she liked it that way. Roman had asked for her to cut it, but she refused. Of course, she did. Just because she was married to him that didn't for a second mean she had to do every single little thing he asked.

She had fought on her hair and lost on so many other things. College was being taken away from her, which sucked. She loved going to classes and being a part of that way of life. It was fun, exciting. Today, apart from nearly getting shot at and ran off the road, had been exhilarating just by seeing Bill and of course studying.

Grabbing another towel to prolong her time in the bathroom, she leaned forward and let all of her hair fall forward, and then she bound her hair up.

She wasn't decent. Way too much flesh was showing, but for now, it was going to have to do. As she nodded at her reflection, it was time to face … Roman. Her husband.

She opened the door and found him standing by her desk, and of all things, reading one of her diaries.

Alex rushed over toward him, but Roman snapped the diary closed. Her father had given them to her as a gift so long ago, when she was struggling to deal with her feelings. He'd advised that she keep a diary and use it as a way of talking to … Mom. She didn't use it often, just when she needed to unload. Like tonight. Like right now.

"What the hell are you doing?" she asked, quickly closing the distance between them and trying to reach for her diary. He held it just out of reach.

"I will be taking this."

"That's my personal diary. You have no right to take people's things without asking them." She tried to reach for it, and in the process of jumping, the towel around her hair spun out of control and fell out. She couldn't contain the wince as it tugged at strands of hair before it left her locks free, which did feel good.

Alex still had one hand on the towel wrapped around her body, and she kept trying to jump up to take the diary, but it wasn't working. In the end, she let go of the towel, hoping the power of her boobs would keep it in place, and she used her hands to try to get the diary.

Roman was taller, bigger, and it was impossible. That diary was the last one she had written in. She hadn't taken it to his place because she had worried he'd find it. The last entries were all leading up to their arranged marriage, and of course their wedding, the night before, at least. There was no other entry because she'd been with him, with no way of talking to her diary.

Her towel gave way, and Alex didn't grab it immediately. The protection she had fell to the floor, around her feet.

She cried out and scrambled to get her towel, only to have Roman reach for it as well. Alex wasn't entirely sure what happened, but they somehow managed to bump heads, and she ended up on the floor, not covered, and Roman stared at her.

Panic filled her, and she scrambled for the towel and her diary. Roman seemed to still as she got both and pulled away from him.

Within seconds, it became a tug of war as Roman grabbed the diary, and she had no choice but to turn her back and immediately wrap the towel around her.

Roman had never seen her naked.

No man had seen her naked.

Her heart raced.

"Please give me back my diary," she said, keeping her back to him.

Her face was so hot. She had never been so embarrassed in her life.

"No." He stepped past her. She tried to grab his shirt, but she had no choice but to keep one hand on her chest.

"Please."

Roman turned at the door. "You're my wife, and a Greco never begs. Don't do it."

He slammed the bathroom door, and Alex gritted her teeth. She wanted to call her father, to ask him to demand that Roman give her diary back, but that would be involving her father in a pathetic spat.

Roman was just being a pain in the ass. She got it, and kind of understood it, even if she didn't completely agree with him and his asshole ways.

After stepping into her closet, she opened the drawers and pulled out a pair of shorts and a tank. It was warm, and she wished she could have head-to-toe pajamas, but that would be way too uncomfortable.

Her hair was nearly dry, and stepping out of her closet, she went to her dresser to run a brush through it. Her bed looked so inviting as she stared at it. Did she want to sink into the soft covers or fight with Roman again?

She glanced at the bathroom door and decided he had already taken way too much of her attention. Sticking her tongue out, which was completely childish to do, she stepped over to her bed, pulled back the covers, and slid right inside.

The moment she lay down and stared up at the ceiling, she closed her eyes and just basked in being back home, in her bed, away from Roman … ish. He was in her father's home, and currently in her shower or reading her diary, but that didn't change the fact she was finally home.

Roman's home and apartment were all his. His bachelor pad. His domain. Where another woman had decorated and made it the vision he wanted. She was a stranger in his home and in his world.

She didn't mind not being close to anyone all her life. Having Liam as a dad guaranteed that people weren't her friend. She lived with it, dealt with it. It was probably the only part of her life that made it easier to deal with Roman's world.

The shower stopped, and Alex rolled over so she wasn't facing him. She had no idea where he was going to sleep.

Growling, she shoved her blankets off and then climbed out of bed. The man was an insufferable bastard, and he pissed her off all the damn time.

She walked back into her closet and grabbed spare blankets and some pillows.

With them in hand, she stepped back into her bedroom at the same time as Roman entered.

"I'll be sleeping in the bed," Roman said.

"No, you're not. That is my bed, and you're not sleeping in it."

He raised a brow. "Where you sleep, I sleep."

"We don't sleep together at your place, and it's not happening now."

Roman chuckled. "You're a spoiled little princess used to getting your own way."

"And you're a brute and a bully used to taking what he wants. You're not sleeping in my bed. Simple as that."

In response, Roman eased the towel from around his waist, and Alex gasped, closing her eyes. She didn't see anything, and staring at her husband's naked body didn't appeal to her, not in the slightest.

She heard rustling, and when she opened her eyes, she saw Roman was beneath her blankets on her side of the bed, with her damn diary.

Alex wanted to scream at him. "You're naked in my bed? Your ass is, like, making an impression."

"My ass is nice and warm. There is enough room for both of us."

She glared at him and then moved toward the window where she had a few beanbags from her days of being a child and not wanting to use conventional chairs.

Nudging them together, she made herself a little bed, much like she had when she was a child, and then, somehow found a way to build a bed for herself.

It was so uncomfortable, not like before when she was so young. This wasn't her bed. It wasn't comfortable, but it would do.

With the blanket thrown over her, she got comfortable, aware of the noise the bags were making, but eventually, she got comfortable.

The light was still on, and the only sound she heard was the unmistakable sound of the pages turning.

Bastard!

****

The following morning, Roman opened his eyes to a strange room. The bed was so comfortable. He couldn't remember ever sleeping so well before in his life.

As he sat up in bed, the events of the night before came back at him. He glanced toward the ground nearby the window, and of course, Alex was nowhere to be seen. He gritted his teeth, threw off the blanket, and then checked to make sure she hadn't stolen the diary from him.

Alex's writings were sweet, innocent, and interesting. She didn't talk about every part of her life, and in the diary, it was always addressed to *Mom*. He'd started at the beginning, and by the time he was ready to fall asleep, he'd gotten to the part of her life when it had just been agreed for her to marry him.

Much to his surprise, the passage had started with

her saying she never wanted to get married.

Roman closed the book, not wanting to read further, but the main thing was that he was tired.

He grabbed the small diary and held it as he moved into the bathroom.

Alex was nowhere to be found. He used the toilet, washed his hands, and brushed his teeth with a spare toothbrush that was still sealed in its packet. Alex must have left for him.

Her politeness was … strange.

Once he was fully dressed, he made his way downstairs. A quick check on the time, and he saw it was a little after eight.

He never slept this late. Never.

Entering the kitchen, he found Millie beating something in a bowl. Did Liam ever consider using his cook to torture people? The swing on her arm was so impressive.

"Hello, Mr. Greco," Millie said. "Mr. Smith has already been down for breakfast. He wanted me to remind you that you've got to keep an eye on Alex today. He had some business to attend to. Also, your father will be coming for dinner here tonight, to discuss some important matters. Alex doesn't need to leave, as she is going to be attending the orphanage today."

"No. Alex cannot go anywhere for her own safety."

"I have never seen any harm come to that girl during my watch, and I never will. Do not think to insult me again."

His grip tightened on the diary. "I am not accusing you or trying to insinuate that you're not capable of looking after Alex. I know you are. You've been doing it for twenty-one years, but these are not your regular enemies. They have a job to do, and Alex is not just a Smith anymore."

"I'm aware of the dangers she faces, but you must also know that I am trained to take care of anyone who threatens my boss's daughter. She is one of my own, and trust me, no one would want to take me on." She did look threatening.

"Where is Alex?" he asked, gripping the back of his neck.

Millie chuckled. "Lost her already?"

"It wasn't … she was gone when I woke up this morning."

"Alex always was an early riser. She hates lying in bed. Drives her dad crazy. She's already had breakfast and yours is keeping warm in the oven." Millie looked past his shoulder. "She's probably in the sewing room. That's where she told me she'd be."

"Sewing room?"

"Yes."

He frowned.

"You do know what a sewing room is right? For making clothes, toys, creating things with fabrics and stuff?" Millie asked. The woman's voice was filled with sarcasm.

"Where would I find the sewing room?" he asked.

Millie didn't answer him. "I'll tell you after you eat breakfast." She tutted. "No wonder you needed to ask Mr. Smith for help. Even your friends haven't come down for breakfast."

"Antonio, Marlo, and Cash are still here?"

She nodded. "I saw them to their private quarters last night. They are … polite, which is more than I could hope for."

Roman stared at the woman in front of him, and he just knew she was going to be difficult. Liam's house was huge, and it would take him all day to find his wife.

The same wife who should have slept right next to him, but her stubborn ass had kept this distance between them, which did piss him off.

He sat down at the counter, but Millie didn't move away.

"We have never had the chance to get to chat, you and I, with the wedding and everything. Alex means the world to me. She is like a daughter I never could have. I've watched her grow up. I've been there when she has tripped and fallen. Bruised her knees, cut them, sprained them. I've held her when she cried for the mommy that wasn't coming home. I was there helping her after she got shot by a stray bullet, and I was there the night before she was supposed to marry you. The panic she had. I calmed her down, told her she was a fierce woman, and I am here for her now. If you hurt her, or in any way treat her like crap, then you won't have to worry about Mr. Smith finding you. I'll hunt you down and gut you like the piece of shit you are, do you understand?" she asked.

"You do know no one threatens me."

"And no one threatens Alex. I know what you're up to, with your friends. It ends today."

Roman glared at her.

"Alex is a good girl. If you were half a man, you'd see that." Millie stepped back and smiled at him. "Just a friendly reminder."

He'd never been threatened, not by a woman, and certainly never warned. Something in his gut told him that he had to tread carefully with Millie, and, he had a feeling, with everyone associated with or in Liam's employ.

Nodding at the woman, he picked up a scoopful of scrambled eggs and shoved them in his mouth. The breakfast was nice, but from keeping warm, it was a little overcooked.

After seeing Alex, he would hunt for his friends and deal with them. His plans for them to try to lure Alex into bed hadn't been discussed in this house with him. But they must have said something for Millie to know.

He finished off his breakfast, and of course, Millie still held all the power as she presented him with coffee.

Roman held the cup and had no choice but to blow across the rim as the coffee was steaming hot. Was Millie stalling him on purpose?

Was Stuart all a ruse?

Did Alex have a secret lover, and was that why she wanted nothing to do with him? According to the diary, Stuart was a sweet little boy who'd been abandoned. Alex had found him. There were several entries referring to the moment she did, which had to be in another book.

The moment he could drink the coffee without scolding his throat, he swallowed it down.

"Great, Alex is next door," Millie said.

"What?"

"Her sewing room is literally the door just after this one, opposite the dining room, and right near her father's study. Before she passed, it was her mother's, and it was only fitting that Alex got it for herself."

With that, Millie turned her back on him, and he couldn't believe Alex was so close by.

Getting out of the chair, he stepped out into the hall, and sure enough, there was a sewing room. It even had *Sewing Space* written on a black plaque right near the door.

This house was making him feel so fucking stupid. So were all the people inside it, and so far, he'd only encountered two women. What was the matter with him? He was the boss in his world. The person with all the control.

He didn't bother to knock and stepped inside. He was, in fact, surprised to see Alex there, sitting behind a sewing machine.

The room was a complete sewing room. Not a large space, but he saw a couple of different machines set up, and the walls had different sewing stuff. He wasn't sure what it was called, but there was a single word across one wall that said *notions*. Was that what it was?

Again, he wasn't sure.

Alex looked up from her sewing machine, and she stopped her actions. There was some fabric beneath the machine, and she quickly stood. "Millie has breakfast waiting for you."

"I've already eaten."

"Ah, that's Millie for you."

"What is all this?" he asked, nodding around the room.

"It's my mom's. It was my mom's space. She loved to make things. My dad told me it started out with a few toys, and then some clothes, and then, she was making clothes, badly, he said. She didn't have a whole lot of time to get good, before she … passed."

"And you sew?"

"Most of my life. Since I was a kid. Dad always thought he would have to turn this room into something else, but he could never bring himself to get rid of another memory of his … of my mom."

"So, you use it?" he asked.

"I like it here. It has some of her old notions. Her sewing machine." Alex smiled, touching the white machine in front of her. "And it has something she was working on as well." She pointed toward the dress form. "I think it was a dress, or possibly a skirt. She had these big ideas, and she sketched a lot of them down."

Alex moved from her position at the table to the small bookshelf that only had a handful of books, but was empty.

She grabbed a sketchbook and opened it up at a random page. "See."

Roman looked at the sketchbook, not really sure why he was entertaining this idea for Alex. This was boring, woman's stuff to him, but he also couldn't help but enjoy the light he saw shining in her eyes. She looked so happy. He couldn't remember her ever seeming so happy with him, or at their wedding. She'd been cold, but so had the service.

"You hate this. I'm sorry. I don't mean to bore you." She snapped the book closed.

"How did I not know about this?" he asked, pointing at the room.

"What was there to know?"

"You have never asked for one of these."

She shrugged. "It's your home and your apartment. You never wanted to know, and you told me to leave your place as it was. That it was perfectly functional."

"What have you been doing the past couple of months?" he asked.

"Reading." She moved back behind her machine. "A lot of reading. Watching some television."

"But do you want one of these at our place?"

"Our place?"

"Alex, we are married."

"We don't have to be," Alex said. "All you have to do is say the words, and we can get our marriage annulled. I even looked into it. If neither of us contests it, we can have it done so fast. You can go back to your old life, and I can go back to mine."

"Is being married to me really so bad?"

"You don't want to be married to me, and besides, didn't you once tell me I wasn't good enough for you? That women in your world were far better and didn't allow other men to touch them?" she asked.

He'd said those things to her. Roman hadn't been the best role model when it came to being a good husband. He sucked at it.

"We're not getting this marriage annulled, Alex."

She pressed her lips together. "Okay."

"Do you want a sewing room?" he asked.

"No, it's fine."

What game was she playing with him?

Chapter Five

Alex knew there would come a time when Roman wouldn't want her anymore, at least not her name. He'd never wanted her body, so she didn't have to worry in that regard. Giving him the option of an annulment was what she intended to do, weekly, if not daily. Neither of them wanted to be married to the other.

They were only doing this for their parents.

There was no point in him building a sewing room when she knew he was going to get rid of her. They would part ways soon. She hoped they did. Last night was a clear indicator that they were not suited.

After sewing together the three panels of the skirt, she searched for her concealed zip and lined it up on the edge of the skirt. She loved making clothes. The challenges of them. After finishing up the sweater she'd made for Stuart, she had gotten to work finishing the ankle-length skirt she had started months ago. It had been cut up, ready and waiting for her. Being back behind her mother's machine was a welcome relief.

Roman stood and watched her for a good thirty minutes before tutting to himself and mentioning lazy-ass friends, then leaving her alone.

"I'm heading out," Millie said, coming to the door.

She looked up and saw a smile on the older woman's face. "What's the matter?"

"It's good to see you here, working on that machine."

Alex lifted the skirt. She still had the waistband to sew down, but it was now time for it to drop on the bias. "What do you think?"

"You're going to look stunning in it," Millie said.

She loved sewing for other people, and getting to her feet, she rushed to the small wardrobe to open the doors and grab the sweater she had also finished. Millie had been complaining about the cold just before Alex's wedding.

Alex had hoped to present her with the sweater, but she hadn't been home and hadn't been able to finish it until that morning.

"This is for you," Alex said. "I know it's super warm now, but when it's cold, it's for you."

"Oh, Alex, you are a sweetheart."

"I don't like the thought of you being cold. You know. You need to keep warm, so that you and my dad can take care of each other."

Millie was slightly older than her father. Alex had once thought the two might … hit it off, but she had later learned after trying to get the two together that they saw each other more like brother and sister than as lovers. She'd asked Millie in private many years ago if she loved her father.

"Of course, I love your father, but not like that, Alex. I'm not hiding anything, but he is a great man, just not a man I would want to be a love interest."

She'd been so gutted, but the three of them had made a good family. Alex had so many fond memories of Christmas, New Years, birthdays, and just about every celebration she could think of.

The older woman pulled her into her arms and hugged her tight. "I love you, sweetheart," Millie said.

Alex wrapped her arms around her and closed her eyes. "It's just a sweater."

"I know, but I also know you, honey. You cared enough to think about me."

"Always."

"And that is what makes you special. Your dad is

so very proud of you, you know?"

"Will he be all right?" she asked.

Having breakfast with her father was a nice refreshing change, rather than eating alone in a sterile environment.

He hadn't been able to stay and chat though, making his excuses and leaving for business reasons.

"You know your father, Alex."

She nodded. "Yeah, I do." She sighed.

"Let's not frown. Stuart wouldn't want to see you frown. I've got brownies and cupcakes loaded in the van. I've also got a ton of ice cream scheduled to be delivered in about twenty minutes," Millie said. "Time to go."

Alex grabbed the sweater she'd made and wrapped in some wrapping paper. She left the sewing room, pulling the door closed as she followed Millie toward the front door, only to come to a stop when she saw who was blocking their exit.

Roman and his buddies.

She had no idea what they were doing here. "Please, move," Alex said.

"You're not going out there alone." Roman looked toward Millie. "Can't you go alone?"

"No!" Alex snapped out the word. "She's not going alone. I already talked to my dad today, and he said he didn't see a reason why I shouldn't."

Roman held up his hand, attempting to silence her and pressing some buttons on his cell phone.

She heard ringing, and then the sound of her father's voice.

"What do you want, Roman?" Liam asked.

"Alex is under the impression she can go to the orphanage."

"That is correct. I gave her my permission earlier. Enjoy, Alex."

She smiled.

"Liam, have you lost your fucking mind?"

Millie tensed at her side.

"I agreed to let my daughter go because I had her husband and three of his closest friends, who, according to my records, have the ability to protect her. Not to mention if you four dipshits fail, I know I can count on Millie, isn't that right?"

"Yes, Sir." Millie puffed out her chest, and Alex wrapped her arms around the older woman, giving her a squeeze.

"Are we done here, Roman? Unlike you, I like my daughter to thrive, to have a life, and to show my fucking enemies that I'm not afraid."

She saw a tic in Roman's jaw as he clenched his teeth. Liam had just embarrassed him. The call ended abruptly, and he looked up. She saw the anger in his eyes.

"I do not like this."

"I'm going to go see Stuart. I trust that you will all keep us safe. Besides, last night, we dealt with two of the enemy's men. I doubt they would try to attack so soon." Stepping past them, Millie by her side, she walked out to the waiting van.

As she suspected, Antonio, Marlo, and Cash took the three seats up front, leaving her, Millie, and Roman to sit in the backseat.

"You know this is reckless," Roman said.

"Would you have us all staying at home and waiting for the enemy to get bored? Is that it?" Millie asked.

"Her life is in danger."

"Alex's life has been in danger her whole life. Being your wife doesn't change that."

"It makes her more of a target."

"And yet, from where I sit, it makes her more protected. There are five people here to make sure she is safe. Do you have so little confidence in your men?" Millie asked.

Alex winced at the jibe. It wasn't a nice one.

"Stop fighting," Alex said. "I only want to see Stuart and the rest of the kids. I love them all."

"Why do you only have one gift?" Roman asked. "Do you favor one? That will make him a target."

Millie tsked. "There is a box in the trunk, next to all the brownies and cupcakes I've made. Alex has been making them kids gifts for as long as I can remember. When she wasn't studying, she was sewing. The only kid's sweater she had left to do was Stuart's. The only reason she is holding it is because he's so withdrawn. He doesn't like to get involved, and the kids know that." Millie shook her head. "Where do they make men like you? Always so suspicious."

Alex stared out the window, no longer caring to justify her actions. Roman was always going to see the worst in her. She didn't know why he felt like she was this evil person or someone he couldn't trust, but if she was being honest with herself, she was tired of it. Tired of him constantly putting her down.

The battles. It was exhausting.

The journey wasn't long, and Millie ended up shouting at Antonio to stop when they came toward a private residence.

Millie climbed out and typed in the code instead of telling Antonio and the car full of people the access to the orphanage. The gates opened, and Millie climbed back inside.

"Does this help you to understand why Liam was happy for Alex to come to the orphanage? It's protected. He would never put his daughter in any danger."

Millie continued to shake her head, and Alex just stayed quiet.

There was no reason to add insult to injury.

This was her life.

Her father had told her since she was a little girl that he would do everything in his power to protect her. That she would never know fear or pain. He wasn't accurate as she had experienced both, but each time, he'd been there to fight everyone else off.

As she climbed out of the car, the front door opened, and the moment the kids saw her, they came running. All of them wrapping their arms around her. She had spent so much time with these kids. Boys and girls. She was there when they were adopted, and she always asked her father to make sure they were happy.

She also received regular letters from kids who had been adopted, which she loved.

"Ice cream, cake, and brownies," Millie said.

The kids cheered.

"Now, who wants to see what Alex got you all?" Millie asked.

Alex's cheeks heated as they all screamed in delight, and the box she had spent a couple of months filling was held open. Millie started to hand out the gifts. Each one was labeled for each child.

Carla, a little eight-year-old girl, came to her, tugging at her shirt. "He's in the dining room. Under the table."

She smiled at the young girl and stroked her cheek. "Thank you."

The young girl's name was called, and Alex made her way inside the house. She found Stuart sitting in the middle of the table, underneath it.

Getting to her knees, she smiled at the young boy. His eyes went wide. "Alex?"

"Hey, buddy, can I enter?"

He nodded, and she crawled under the table. The moment she was close, Stuart wrapped his arms around her, pressing his face against her stomach. "I missed you," he said.

She put her hand on his back. "I missed you too, buddy. So, so much."

"They said you were taken. That you weren't going to come back."

"That's not true. I … I got married to a man, and he … he didn't know that I came here. Daddy is sorting everything out, and hopefully when it is all fixed, I can come here all the time."

It broke her heart seeing how tired and scared Stuart was. When she came to visit him every single day, he started to get stronger, confident. All that hard work had been undone.

"I made you something." She held out the wrapped sweater, and Stuart took it, staying as close to her as possible.

He tore into the wrapping, and without looking at it properly, he pulled it on. "I love it."

His arms went around her. "Don't leave."

"Not for a few hours. We have cake, ice cream, and brownies. I know they're your favorite."

Stuart held her, and she smiled, not wanting to show him her sadness.

"Or we can stay right here, and just … be safe." Being under the table always made Stuart feel safe.

Alex stared across the floor and saw several pairs of feet, and she knew they belonged to Roman and his friends. She didn't care what they heard. They all already had a bad opinion of her based off some stupid test.

They could go and suck it, not that she'd tell that to their faces. No, she was happy to stay under the table because the truth was, she was just as scared as Stuart, but she had different reasons to be.

****

Roman got to meet the little boy under the table, but it took three hours of being at the orphanage for him to come out. In the end, it took Millie coaxing him out with ice cream and brownies.

Of course, it meant that he never got to speak with Alex as the little boy was plastered to her side like a second skin. He also wore the sweater she made for him. All the kids wore them, and each one had a different design. Much to his surprise, they all adored her. The other kids accepted Stuart's fear, though, and none of them commented about how he was stuck to Alex.

They were approaching dinner, and after eating way too much ice cream, he was ready to head back, but Alex didn't want to leave.

Once again, Millie had no choice but to pull his wife away, and the guardians helped with Stuart, but he saw the pain in Alex's eyes at leaving the boy. No, not just the boy, but the whole house. The kids put on brave faces, but he saw how much they loved her.

Back in the car, Alex stared out the window, watching the house for the longest time. Millie held her hand. "We can return tomorrow," Millie said.

Alex didn't say anything. She held Millie's hand like it was a lifeline, and he guessed at that moment, it was exactly that.

No one talked.

He'd listened to Alex and Stuart when they first arrived at the orphanage. When he saw her heading into the main house, his suspicions had risen, but then he'd watched. He didn't think Alex had seen him bend down to see who this Stuart was.

The boy had been terrified, holding on to Alex

like he was going to lose her.

Antonio, Marlo, and Cash were there. None of them knew what to say.

Arriving back at Liam's house, Millie and Alex made their way inside. Dinner was expected within the hour, but he didn't see any sign of his father or Liam's car. He checked his cell phone, and still nothing.

"Are you okay?" Antonio asked.

"Yes, I'm fine."

"You don't look fine." This came from Marlo.

"I'm fine."

"I don't know, it seems to me you kind of married a … good girl," Cash said.

"This could all be an act."

"An act that didn't want to marry you in the first place?" Antonio held his hands up as Roman shot him a glare.

"Look, your words, not ours. You're the one who told us that."

Liam had been the one to tell him, as well as the few entries on her diary, which was inside his jacket.

"I'm going to get changed for tonight," he said. "My father will want you all there." He left his friends to get ready as he headed up to Alex's room. The bathroom door was shut, and he tested the door to find it locked.

Roman could break it down, but he knew Alex needed some time. She loved those kids.

Sitting on the edge of the bed, he pulled out her diary and opened to where he'd left off. The edge of the page was pulled down and neatly folded.

Dear Mom,

You never got married, and I don't want to either. So many dresses came today. Dad told me to have fun and to try them all on, but … I hate them. I hate dressing in white. I know he had to go and see ... whatever his name was, because there was this stupid, horrible, request.

The pages were smudged like Alex had been crying as she wrote.

They want to find out if I'm a virgin. Have you ever heard of such a stupid thing? It is stupid. So fucking stupid.

I'm so angry.

Dad said that I don't have to do the test. He believes that I'm a virgin. Of course, he does. He knows that I have no desire to be near boys. They're horrible and cruel, and I hate this. I don't want to marry Roman Greco. I don't want to be married to that family, but I know how important it is to Dad. I overheard him talking to Millie. She was trying to help me get out of it, and he said that it is important. He likes Lucas Greco. The man, although old-fashioned with the whole virgin thing, is a good man at his core. He wants a world where I am safe, and he feels this is the best course of action. Roman is supposed to be a nice guy, but he's not. I know he's not. I've heard what the soldiers have said about him. He's scary as hell.

A damn virginity test.

For what?

He's no virgin.

Why do I have to be?

Not that I'm not. I've never had sex. I've never kissed a boy. Never even hugged a boy unless you count Dad!

I hate this. I refuse to do it. I won't allow some strange person to look ... there. That's my place. It's my body. There are limits, even now, right?

There was no ending to the passage.

Roman slumped.

Not even kissed a boy.

When he'd kissed her in church, her eyes had been wide, and if his memory served him right, she hadn't even puckered her lips.

Why hadn't she done that? Did she not know how?

The door to the bathroom opened, and he slid her diary back into his jacket.

Alex had a towel on, and her hair fell around her in wet rivulets. "What are you doing here?" she asked.

"My dad likes punctuality, and I need to get ready."

"I don't have any clothes here for you. I can go and fetch some from my dad's room."

"No need to. I already have clothes here. While I was waiting for you this morning to finish your sewing, I organized some suits. They're in your closet."

Their marriage wasn't coming to an end any time soon, and he doubted it ever would. Everything he found out about Alex showed him this woman was strong, loyal, and loving.

Not the image of his wife he had.

His past lovers and the women in his world were anything but. Innocence was often destroyed, and quickly, unless they were young children.

She rubbed at her temples. "You're right."

Roman stepped closer toward her. "You care for that boy, don't you?"

"I care for all of the kids at the orphanage. They're all special. He was the one I found."

"He relies on you a lot."

She sighed and rubbed at her temple. "Can we not

talk about this? It's hard enough to leave them. I don't want to think of them alone at night."

"Don't they have guardians?" Roman asked.

"They do, but they're being paid to take care of them." She went to step around him, but he placed a hand on her waist, stalling her. He didn't grip her too tightly as he didn't want to startle her or make her afraid.

"Alex," he said.

"What is it?"

He stared into her eyes.

Roman had never taken the time to look into her eyes before. They were a deep brown. At first, he had thought they were cold, malicious, and that she was after whatever she could get, but he knew that wasn't true.

They were warm, filled with a great deal of love. There was a lot about his wife that he didn't know about.

He looked at her lips, and he had never noticed before how plump and inviting they were. He wanted to kiss them. To be the first man to actually take those luscious lips.

He leaned forward only to have Alex jerk back. "What are you doing?"

Roman frowned. "I was going to kiss you."

"What the hell for?" Alex shook her head and held her hand up. "No, I don't want to kiss you. I don't know what you were doing, but leave me out of this."

No woman had ever rejected him, and he was taken aback by the sudden move. This had never happened before.

Alex made her way into her closet, and not one to linger, he walked into the bathroom and pulled out her diary again. She hadn't been kissed, but she didn't want his kisses?

That made no sense. He was her fucking husband.

Slamming the book down on the counter, he

looked at his reflection, and he did appear to be a little … out of it. Roman didn't go around begging women. They were waiting for him, panting for more, and desperate for whatever he could give them.

He didn't have time to stand idly by, so he quickly stripped out of his clothes and stepped beneath the shower. The water was warm, and he needed it cold. Blasting his body, he allowed the freeze to take him over. The cold was welcoming. The moment he was done, he wrapped a towel around his waist and stepped out into the bedroom only to find his wife was gone.

Fuck!

In this place, he was always going to be one step behind her. He changed quickly, hiding her diary near her bed, where he hoped she'd never look. The small book was proving to be quite insightful, if not a little obsession of his.

He made his way downstairs, only to come face to face with his father.

"Where is everyone?" he asked.

"They're at the table. I wanted to have a word with you, in private. Can we step outside?" Lucas asked.

If his father wanted a private word in another man's house, then he knew without a doubt that something bad was about to happen, but he didn't say so.

He followed his father away from the building, near his car, and there was no one close by. Lucas clicked his tongue. "Tell me how things are going with Alex."

"She's alive. There were no attacks today."

"Liam seems to be under the impression that at any moment, when Alex asks for it, he will seek to have this marriage annulled. Is that true?"

Roman didn't want to lie to his father.

"For fuck's sake, Roman, I saw those bloody

sheets. An annulment would make you a mockery, and I would be laughed at. Our power, our reach, it would sever overnight."

"There's no guarantee she's a virgin," he said.

Lucas snorted. "Please, you think that woman in there is not a virgin? I have known Liam my whole life. I've had many dealings with him over the years, and I have also seen that little girl grow up into a beautiful woman. There is a reason I didn't pursue the test. I knew she spoke the truth."

"But you're … you don't like her."

"I'm not used to a woman who can't be controlled, Roman. Surely you can see that she is … different."

"Yes."

"Liam hasn't trapped her in a life like we do. He allows her to be her own person, within his protection, and I know it makes her a subject of gossip in our family. Liam is a powerful person. I have watched him go from nothing to controlling the streets of the city, Roman. He is not a man to be insulted. The only weakness he has is that woman in that house. He will do everything for her, and if she is unhappy in this marriage with you, and seeks an annulment, then he will do it. Even if it means soaking the streets with blood. He will."

"We will fight him."

"Roman, I know you are a Greco. My blood runs in your veins, and I know we will put up a good fight with Liam, but I could never guarantee the outcome. Our men and our women would die just because you won't make a young innocent woman fall in love with you."

"Do you want me to rape her?" Roman asked, trying not to show his anger, but it was difficult not to.

"No. Of course not. I would have no choice but to let Liam handle you, and anyone who goes against Liam is never found again. You are set to take over one day. What I am telling you to do is get Alex to fall in love with you. By doing so, you'll be able to bed her, and then any annulment cannot happen. Our families are united. We are strong apart, but together, we are unstoppable."

"You don't think it makes us look weak, binding ourselves to Liam?"

"No, it is the best and wisest decision we have made. Trust me on this."

Chapter Six

Being seated at the dinner table with Lucas, her father, Roman, Antonio, Marlo, and Cash was the most surreal experience for Alex. She sat next to her father, while Lucas sat opposite him on the other end of the table. Roman was beside her father, next to her. Opposite were his three friends.

Millie and a few of their wait staff brought out platters of food for them to serve themselves.

"You have food prepared at home?" Lucas asked.

"Yes, it has always been this way."

"And you don't find that reckless?"

Liam smiled at Millie, who was shooting dangers at Lucas. The man had just insulted her cooking.

Alex wondered if Lucas had a death wish. She wouldn't be surprised if she didn't do something awful, like not season his food.

"I have found that if you have the right allies, make friends, and don't fuck them over, they don't want to poison you. Maybe you should try it. It beats all that crap they serve at restaurants."

"There is no way I would allow my family to eat at such … places." Millie glared at him. "I'm watching you."

Lucas held his hands up. "I'm sorry. In my experience…"

"We've had people die from poisoning. My little sister died because of it," Roman said.

"I had no idea," Liam said. "I'm sorry."

"It was ten years ago, but still, you are right. I have too many enemies and certainly not enough friends."

Liam grabbed his glass. "Then let's toast to new

friendships and a future of peace."

Alex lifted her glass and joined in with the toast. There was no point in arguing with them.

"How was Stuart?" Liam asked.

"He's not … the past couple of months have been hard on him."

"I know, but he must learn to adapt."

"I still think I could—"

"No." Liam slapped his palm on the side of the table.

"Dad, please."

"That boy is not your responsibility. You are not going to take the time adopting him or having anything to do with him. That is final."

This was the only time they disagreed on something, and it sucked, big time. She stared down at her plate.

Silence rang around the table.

"Maybe I can be of some assistance," Lucas asked.

"My daughter found a kid. A sweet kid, but he's not hers. She wanted to adopt him at eighteen. From personal experience, raising a kid is not easy. Besides, you now have a husband of your own. End of discussion."

Alex had never asked for anything. She'd never caused a problem. Never made waves. She'd been the perfect daughter to him. Gripping the edge of the chair, she tried to calm herself, to remove the tension building in her body, but it just kept threatening to get out. To expel.

Anger flooded her body.

They had started talking about their work, about business as if her life didn't matter. As if what she wanted didn't even register. She wasn't asking for the latest gadget or something selfish. She wanted to help a little boy. Actually, she wanted to adopt all the children in the damn orphanage. When she was eighteen, she had even asked for a gift, the chance to do just that, but he'd refused.

She slammed her hand on the table. "What would Mom say to you right now?" she asked, raising her voice to be heard.

She looked toward her dad and saw the shock in his gaze. She had never questioned him, certainly not in front of business associates.

"Alex, we will discuss this another time."

"Why not now? You're treating me like I'm asking for the most impossible thing when all I am asking is to make a difference to children."

"Exactly, Alex. To children. Not to one kid. You want to help everyone, but not everyone can be helped. I am not going to allow you to throw your life away."

"But you're quite happy to throw it away for me?" she asked.

"Enough."

"No! No more *enough*. No more telling me to be quiet. I'm twenty-one years old, and I have already married a man I do not love, who cannot stand me. I have done everything you asked of me. I ask for this one thing, and you won't even consider it."

"You were eighteen. Raising a child alone is not easy."

Tears filled her eyes. "And here was me thinking I wouldn't be alone because I'd have my dad. Thanks a lot." She shoved her chair back.

"Alex, get back to this table."

"Screw you." She had never spoken like this. Never felt like this.

She kicked off her heels and stepped out toward

the gardens, not even caring that it had started to rain. The night was still warm, but she was done being cooped up all day.

With her heels gone, and the lights illuminating the garden, she took off, chasing away the anger building inside her.

What more did he want from her? What did she have to give?

She headed toward the back gardens. It had been years since she last came to the gardens, and only a couple of solar lights were working. Her father had built her a tree house. She used to love spending hours out in the yard, watching sunsets, reading books, doing a little hand sewing, and there was once a telescope, which had broken after a storm knocked it out of the tree house.

Alex found the steps and climbed up, not caring that her feet were sore and she'd gotten a few cuts. Hauling herself up into the tree house, she groaned as there were cobwebs in the corner, but it looked the same, only smaller, seeing as she was bigger.

The sound of rain hit the roof, and she left her feet dangling out. She just sat, trying to get as much protection as she could.

Her dad was right. She didn't know the full consequences of raising a kid, of doing it alone. He'd done it with her, but he always said it was a pleasure.

Time passed, and finally, the rain subsided, but Alex didn't want to go in and face her father. It was warm enough to stay outside.

"Are you okay up there?"

She looked out to see Roman standing on the ground, alone.

"What are you doing here?"

"Well, it looks like I'm asking a girl if I can come and join her in … what is this?"

"It's a tree house. Didn't you ever have one as a kid?"

"Nope. None whatsoever. Can I come up?"

There was enough room, so she nudged over, being careful not to disturb any cobwebs. "Come on up," she said.

He climbed into the tree house. The wood creaked beneath his weight, but as he sat down next to her, it settled.

"Did my dad send you?"

"No, he didn't send me, but he did send this." Roman held out some wrapped foil. "He said you'd know what it means."

Alex took the foil and opened it up, seeing a sandwich. It would be her father's famous guilty cheese and pickle sandwich. She loved it.

Her father rarely cooked, and he never set foot in the kitchen. Unless Millie was sick, or to cheer her up, he'd make her something.

Picking up the sandwich, she took a bite and smiled.

"Did your dad make this?"

"Yes."

"It's … great."

She laughed. "You should have seen it when he first put it together. It was amazing." She missed those days. Spending hours playing out in the backyard, when her father had once said she'd be safe, protected, and loved. "What brings you out here?"

"I don't know, sitting in your room and reading your diary seems wrong with you outside."

"You shouldn't be reading my diary. It's an invasion of privacy."

"I know you don't want to be married to me, but I think I speak for both of our parents when I say that it does have to happen," Roman said.

"You don't like me," Alex said. "I embarrass you."

"You're … different, but that doesn't mean I don't like you."

"Please, you always look angry. I get it, I'm not like those beautiful women that are passed around your families."

Roman tapped his thigh. "It's not an escort service. They don't get passed around. Marriages form strong alliances. They build power and wealth."

"And they forget about love. Women don't need to feel that, right?"

"Love is never brought into the equation."

"Have a lot of successful marriages?" she asked.

"Yes. We have zero divorce."

"Just unhappy marriages for the women?"

"You're infuriating."

"And I don't want to be married to you, Roman. I don't like you. I know you're probably sleeping with a gazillion women, and this life isn't for me." There she had said it. After spending the day with Stuart and being back home, she had come to the decision she was going to ask for an annulment.

This wasn't going to work. It was doomed to fail right from the start.

"I know what you want, Alex, and to be honest, I don't know if I can give it to you. What I can do is offer a compromise."

"Don't you want to be free?" she asked.

"No one has ever asked for a divorce or even started proceedings."

"We won't be getting a divorce." Did she have to point that out to him as well?

"You are determined to make a mockery of me,

of everything our family built?" Roman asked.

"I want to set us both free."

"And how many lives are you willing to take to get it?"

"There will be no lives lost."

He chuckled, but it sounded forced. "You heard Liam. A future of peace. The moment you request an annulment, peace will be a thing of the past. It will be the fairy tale that mothers tell their children in the hope of helping them fall to sleep at night. War will rage, and no one, not us, or Liam, can guarantee who will win. We all have enemies. Your father's are now ours, and our enemies are now your father's. We are united by blood. By marriage. Take that away, and all that will remain is war."

"You're lying."

"I'm not, Alex. Do you think I entered this marriage lightly? I did not. I know what is expected of me. One day, men and women will look toward me, not my father. I will be the Boss of the Greco outfit. It will be up to me to decide who lives and who dies. This unity is as fragile as fine china. If you want to end this marriage, then fine, but I hope you're willing to deal with the consequences and their deaths. Yours, your father's, Millie's, Stuart's, all those children's. Anyone you loved, or have ever loved, strangers, could all end up dead because you want to be free. It's not a cost I am willing to make."

****

Roman stood with Antonio, Marlo, and Cash in Liam's backyard. His father and Liam were discussing Alex's future.

Running a hand down his face, he glanced up toward her bedroom window, and sure enough, he saw the woman who was driving him fucking crazy staring right back at him.

"Did you convince her?" Antonio asked.

"I have no idea."

"What's the plan?" Cash asked.

"Simple, I've got to make her fall in love with me. I have to bind this marriage, and then, I've got to get her pregnant." His father had been clear. In fact, after his little exposé of what their annulled marriage would look like, his father had pulled him aside and warned him that his time was running out.

Roman didn't have the first clue of how he was going to make his wife fall in love with him. He didn't know anything about her, and the few little bits of detail he did know was everything he'd learned in the past few days.

"And what about our part in your plan?" Marlo asked. "Do you still want us to continue … pursuing her until you're satisfied she's a slut?"

"Yes," Roman said.

"Don't you think that is going to be a little counter-intuitive?" Cash asked. "Getting all three of us to get in her pants? To fuck her?"

"The moment she caves, I will have all the proof I need," Roman said.

"The moment you fuck her, according to you, you'll have the proof you need," Marlo said.

"If you don't want the job, then I can find someone else."

Antonio groaned. "It's not that we don't want the job."

"We know what it means if we succeed," this came from Cash.

"If you see an opportunity to pursue her, go for it. I'm not going to stop you. The moment I know the truth, I can deal with it. It will put me and my father back in fucking control over this situation, and we don't have to take orders for Smith. That's the goal. Until then, I've got some work to do."

He squared his shoulders and made his way into the house. No one tried to stop him as he walked all the way up to her bedroom.

Alex hadn't stayed in the treehouse, which he had to admit was cool. His dad had only ever taught him about fighting, self-defense, and training. Learning to take pain. Ever since he was thirteen, he had lessons every single day where one of his father's trusted soldiers would inflict pain. He had to withstand the pain, and not squeal, not cave in to the pressures. The moment he learned how to take pain, and his ability to withstand it increased, his father had then given him permission to start trying to escape.

Once he learned how to escape and fight back, he was able to prove himself worthy to his father. It was why he was always by his father's side, and his little brother, Phillip, never got the chance.

Even now, his brother struggled on a daily basis to earn his father's respect, but then, Phillip was also ten years younger. Closer to Alex's age, but also weak.

Entering the bedroom, he found Alex sitting on the window ledge, book in hand.

"It's dangerous to be by the window," he said.

"My dad has guards everywhere. I'm protected here at all times."

"Insinuating that you're not protected at my home."

She closed the book she'd been reading and tilted her head toward him. "Your soldiers are ordered to take care of you. My father orders his men to take care of his family. They're loyal to him and to me. Your men will fight for you."

"And that's a problem?"

"No, I just know I'm more protected here than at your place. Besides, we both know your family and your world hates me." She got to her feet, and Roman couldn't help but notice the curvy shape of her legs.

Alex was a curvy woman. The shorts she wore didn't hide that, and with her sitting on the ledge, with her feet up, it had caused the fabric to ride up, exposing more of her body. Even though it had been raining earlier, the air was still warm, and she wore a tank top.

One glance at her tits, and he saw she was indeed still wearing a bra. He had an overwhelming urge to feel her against him. To have her naked chest pressed against his and to touch her body. His dick ached.

He wanted her so badly. The intense sensation took him off guard.

"Did you mean what you said?" she asked.

"What?"

"Before you left. The war. The death. All of it, or were you just trying to scare me?" She held the book against her chest, and he wanted nothing more than to tear it right out of her arms and to pull her against him. She held her hand up when she took a step toward him. "I don't want you to lie to me either. Just give me the truth, and give it to me straight."

"It's no secret that our worlds don't get along. Liam is a rival. By my not … taking you on our wedding night, it is an insult."

"So you've insulted him and me?" she asked.

He closed his eyes and took a step back. For this conversation, he needed to be in his right mind, and currently, being close to her, that wasn't him being in his right mind. He was … thinking with his dick, and this hadn't happened before.

Even with the other women in his life, before he

got married. They never got under his skin. They never came before work.

"Yes and no. To many, I've insulted you, which wasn't … the plan. I don't know if you're a virgin, and it means something to our culture."

"Damn it, Roman. I am a virgin. I didn't lie, and I certainly didn't avoid the damn test to hide something." She growled, and he watched as she tossed the book she'd been holding onto the bed. "You've been reading my journal."

"I have."

"Don't you see that even with my father being very open and accepting, he has limits? He doesn't want just anyone near his little girl. I … Millie is the closest person I have to a friend. He wouldn't even let me adopt Stuart. The only reason he agreed to allow me to marry you is because he felt it was ideal for all of our futures, and apparently out of all of the men in the Greco empire or fucking cult, you were the best damn candidate."

"You cuss when you get angry," he said, and he found her rather cute.

She growled and spun away from him. "That's not helping." She tapped her foot on the carpet and shook her head. "I don't want to cause death, but I also don't want to be living my life like the past two months. I can't do it. I miss being … me. I'm not someone who stays home all day, or shops, or … I don't even know what the women in your family do."

"They keep homes."

"You have a cleaner for that."

"That's not what I meant."

She rolled her eyes. "Have you ever thought about how badly we mesh?"

"Mesh?"

"We're not suited. You're used to your life, and

I'm used to mine. I like going to college. Being free to do my own thing. If I want to spend the day in my mom's sewing room, I can do it. I can be around Stuart and the orphanage. I don't have to ask permission."

He watched as she twisted the ring on her finger.

"I've seen the women you've been with. Your mistresses, the women you've slept with. I don't look like them. I'm not … blonde, or beautiful, or slender. I'm not refined. We don't mesh."

Roman took a step toward her, then another.

Alex stepped back, then did so again, and again, until her back hit the wall, and she had nowhere to go.

Roman pressed his palms on either side of her head, keeping her in place and also making it so his body was close to hers. There was no escape, not unless she wanted to press her body flush against his.

She was trapped.

"What are you doing?"

"You keep talking about how we don't fit, but have we ever given it a try? I know I haven't given this a shot, but I've got to say, Alex, your lips are looking real fucking good right now."

"I don't know what you're trying to do."

"You don't want to cause a war or be responsible for death, and I don't want that either. It has taken us a lifetime to be strong. We need Liam, and it embarrasses me to admit that. I'm willing to do whatever it takes to keep us free. To make our streets safe."

He closed the distance, and Alex's head was pressed against the wall. She seemed to try to escape through it.

"So how about we have a little … experiment?"

"Experiment?" she asked, frowning.

"Yes, how about we see how much we don't mesh?"

"How?"

"Simple. We start with a kiss. Just some kissing, nothing too … heavy. My hands will stay on the walls. Just our lips will touch."

"Why should I believe you?"

"I've never given you a reason to doubt me before."

"And what does this experiment prove?" she asked.

At least she wasn't hitting him and telling him to get the fuck out. "We'll see how far our … meshing abilities go. If we enjoy the kiss, then we will give it time, and we will keep enjoying kissing. If it doesn't, then we will come to some arrangement that means this marriage can survive."

"I think this is ridiculous. We can just come to some arrangement where it can work. I agree with the latter."

"And you want a marriage that is completely cold and dead?" he asked. He didn't have a clue what Alex wanted, and this was a shot in the dark. There was a chance this could all backfire on him, but he was willing to take that chance. Mainly because he had orders, but also, a small slither of him wanted to taste those luscious lips.

He'd never noticed how plump and inviting they were, and if he had, then he hadn't given it a thought of actually enjoying her.

"No, I don't."

"I'm not offering you love, Alex. I don't think I'm capable of giving it. I don't even know what it is."

"I don't want love, but I also don't want … I don't want to hate being near you. If being with you means we have to come to some sort of compromise, then yes, I will … do it. I'll at least try it." She smiled at him.

He didn't know why being close to her made his dick ache. "I'm going to kiss you now," he said.

"Okay."

There wasn't much space between them, and he noticed how nervous Alex looked. "Close your eyes."

"Why?"

"So you're not judging me too early."

She smiled, but he waited until her eyes slid closed, and then he slammed his lips down on hers.

It was hard keeping his hands to himself, but he clenched them into fists where they rested on the wall.

One kiss, and he felt so fucking free.

Alex let out a little whimper, and her hands went to his chest. They didn't move, just stayed perfectly poised on his body.

Tracing the curve of her lips, he heard her gasp and felt her open to him. He plundered her mouth with his tongue, deepening the kiss. She hadn't bitten him or pulled away, and he figured this was a success.

He'd never given much thought to kissing, but Alex's lips were fucking stunning, and he found himself intoxicated with her lips.

Chapter Seven

Alex glanced across the dining room table. Last night, she kissed her husband, and this morning, he hadn't been anywhere to be found. She hadn't gone looking for him, and Millie had told her that Roman, Lucas, and Liam headed out early, so she spent the day sewing.

Tapping her fingers on her leg, she didn't have a single thing to say to break the awkward silence.

Her father had come home and ordered her to go to dinner with Roman. This was a ruse. Liam wanted to see how far the threat went, and even though he hated using her as bait, she was the intended target of whoever was after her. She had been told time and time again that his men, as well as Greco's men, were everywhere.

The restaurant was fancy, the kind designed for lovers.

Not for the first time, she licked her lips, and again, her mind flashed to the moment Roman kissed her. She didn't understand why it was constantly playing a loop in her mind. It was just one kiss. The only kiss she'd ever experienced.

There would come a time when she would have more kisses to compare them to. Even as she thought that idea, she knew it was laughable. At twenty-one years old, Roman, her actual husband, was the first and only man to kiss her. It was pitiful.

She had to wonder if other women felt this way.

"How was your day?" she asked.

"You're thinking about it," Roman said.

"What?"

He smiled and leaned back in his chair. "You're thinking about our kiss last night."

Her cheeks immediately felt way too hot. "I don't know what you're talking about."

"In the past five minutes, you've licked your lips five times, and each time you do, you look at me. You're thinking about our kiss."

"I could be licking my lips for any reason. You don't have to be the cause." She didn't know why she tried to evade the question.

"And there you go again."

"I wasn't thinking of you that time."

"So you just admitted that the other times, you were." He smiled, and Alex didn't know what to make of it. It seemed … genuine.

"Yes, okay, fine, I was thinking about …our time together. Is that so hard to believe?"

"I've thought about our kiss plenty of times."

"I doubt that."

He leaned forward, and before she could stop him, he'd captured both of her hands. "I've thought about how good your lips felt against mine. How I want to feel them all the fucking time. When I kiss you again, I'm going to hold you, feel you against me."

"Who says there is going to be a next time?" she asked.

"We are because we're going to make this work."

"You want to make this work?"

"Yes."

"Why don't I believe you?" she asked.

He chuckled and clicked his fingers for the waiter to bring them the menus. When they first arrived at the table, he'd ordered wine. She had no choice but to quickly change her order to water. He'd tried to get her a sparkling water, but she hated that stuff and asked for still instead.

"Is it hard to imagine me wanting a nice

marriage?" he asked.

"You didn't want to be married to me."

"True, but you didn't want to be married to me either. Don't forget that I read your diary, so I know all your little secrets." He stopped long enough for the waiter to give them their menus. "How about I make a proposal?"

Alex looked up at him, not exactly sure what he meant.

"I don't want to have a marriage that is … like all the ones I know. They're filled with…" He stopped talking and looked past her shoulder.

"Loneliness. Pain. Deceit. Betrayal."

"How do you know that?" he asked.

"No one talks to me. It doesn't mean I don't listen to what everyone else has to say." She shrugged and glanced down at the menu.

"Is that the marriage you want?" he asked.

"You mean to hate my husband, to dread him coming home, to be afraid to even talk to him? Yeah, sounds like a real dream." She rolled her eyes. "Of course, I don't want that." She shook her head. "Has anyone ever told you how annoying you can be?"

"I do get that from time to time," he said, smiling.

"You look way too proud of yourself."

"I didn't think I'd enjoy this." He pointed between them. "It's fun."

"I'm glad I somehow entertain you."

"You truly do, and I can safely say it is a gift."

She stared down at her menu, somewhat happy that she has been able to make him happy, which was crazy. Up until a few days ago, they never spent any time together, and when they did, whatever he had to say was critical.

"What do you want out of a marriage?" Roman

asked.

"I honestly don't know. I never thought I was going to get married, so I didn't think I'd have to come up with an ideal part of it." She sighed. "What about you?"

He held his hands up and started to tick his fingers. "I wanted a wife who was loyal. A good mother. Someone who doesn't freak out at the sight of blood. Who can … handle this life."

"Let me stop you there. I have no idea if I can handle this life."

"You live with your father."

"Only because I know what he does. I've not been … exposed to it."

"I think you're handling it a lot better than even you realize." He went back to holding her hands, and Alex didn't even realize she could have pulled them away from him.

"Why do you want this marriage to work so badly?" she asked. There had to be some other reason he was willing to keep this charade up, or to even contemplate making it work. It made no sense. She had given him an out. She hadn't realized what that out would cost and the far-reaching consequences, but she had … tried. The thought of people dying just so she wouldn't have to be married to him scared her. There was no way she'd be able to live with herself.

"The same reasons I want you to stay, Alex."

She leaned forward. "I've heard the rumors about you, Roman. You kill easily."

"I do what I've been trained to do, but that doesn't mean I want to be responsible for the death of hundreds, if not thousands of people."

"Thousands?" she asked.

"Do you think the only people who will get

injured will be our men and yours?" he asked.

She held her hand up. "Stop it. I already said I wasn't going to ask for an annulment or a divorce. I get it. If we separate, it's bad news. Why all of a sudden do you want to … make this work?"

He shrugged. "I guess I came to the realization that I don't want to hate coming home. I don't want to look at you and see how disgusted you are with me. I'm not promising love. I can never love. I'm not capable of it, but I can be a good man to you."

Alex frowned as she looked at him. Why? What? When? How? That was all that went through her mind. Part of her wanted to trust him, but another part of her, the realistic side of her brain, told her something else was going on. She'd been living with this man for two months, and they hadn't been easy.

At times, he'd been a cruel asshole. Always critical. Always pushing her like he wanted her to go running back to her father. Something didn't seem right, but she also didn't want the picture he painted. All the unnecessary deaths as well as the life living with him that she hated. There was no reason to it. At least, she didn't think so.

"Fine."

"What do you want in a man, Alex?"

She lifted her gaze to look into his blue eyes. There had been a few times over the past couple of months when she had felt his eyes held pure evil, especially when he had nothing nice to say.

Tonight, they seemed soft, almost calm and beautiful.

"I-I don't know. I've never thought about it."

"Okay, what about marriage?"

She tried to tug her hand away, but he held on to her, making it impossible for her to let go. Forcing a smile to her lips, she glanced around the restaurant. "I'm not trying to be difficult, but I never imagined getting married."

"You didn't."

"No. I never fantasized about my wedding dress, or what the big day would be, not even the guy I would be marrying. I guess I figured no man would be strong enough to get past my dad."

"I am."

"Not quite. We weren't exactly a loved-up couple. This is a business arrangement. You wouldn't have looked at me twice."

"You don't know that."

"I know to a certain extent, Roman. I've seen the women you've been with." She didn't like the thought of him being with the other women. Again, she tried to tug her hand away, but he wasn't releasing her.

Gritting her teeth, she glared at him, but he merely tilted his head to the side as if they were only having a conversation.

"You've never met the women I've been with."

"Two of them came to the wedding. I know because I overheard the women saying how ridiculous it made me look. Are you going to tell me that they weren't there?"

He cleared his throat. "They weren't supposed to be there. It's why I had them escorted away as soon as possible."

"You didn't use them? You know, to make the wedding night sweeter?" she asked.

"Did you want me to fuck you on our wedding night?"

"No." She didn't know why she'd brought up his mistresses or ex-girlfriends, or whatever they were called. "Will you please let go of my hands?"

"You're angry."

"I'm not angry."

"Jealous?"

"I don't have anything to be jealous about." She had never felt jealous. Not a moment in her life.

Roman smiled.

"I don't know why you're smiling."

"Simple, you're jealous."

"Whoever you sleep with is none of my business."

"So, in your ideal marriage, you wouldn't care if your husband was with other women."

"Of course, I would. In a real marriage, I'd want love, and I'd love him. We don't have that. We will never have that."

"How about this then? Is there a chance you like me?" he asked.

"No." She bit on her lip and glanced away as he tensed. "I'm sorry. I don't know you."

"But what you do know, you don't like."

"I don't think we should be having this conversation," she said. This was going from bad to worse. The menu lay open on the table in front of her. "Maybe we should just order."

Roman didn't let go of her hand, and even as she tried to avoid his gaze, he still stared at her. She looked around the room, trying to find an excuse to distract him, but she had no choice but to look at him, and he kept on staring at her.

His gaze was so intent.

What was he thinking?

What did he expect? They never spent any time together on the buildup to their wedding. From what people were gossiping about, he'd been with so many different women, and she was just the pitiful bought bride. The one he didn't want, and that stung a little, which she hated to admit.

****

Alex didn't like him, and Roman shouldn't care.

Many people hated him and would pay good money to see him dead. He had never cared what people think of him. Why should he? It was their problem, not his.

When it came to Alex, his forced wife, he couldn't help but … feel something. He didn't know what it was exactly. Disappointment? Anger?

Was he angry at his father? At himself?

"Can we order?" Alex asked.

"Yes, of course." He still didn't let go of her hands.

"I'm sorry if I've upset you."

"You haven't upset me," he said. The lie was easy.

"You look upset."

He lifted his gaze to hers. "Imagine being told that you're not liked."

She smiled. "You have told me."

"Excuse me?"

"When we first went to your apartment in the city. Nearly eight weeks ago now, I think. I'd done or said something, I can't remember, and you said that you didn't have to like me, but you were taking me with you."

Roman vaguely remembered the argument. Alex had wanted to visit her father, and he'd been under strict instructions to keep her by his side. So he had, and because he was annoyed with everything going on, he'd taken it out on her.

"So forgive me for being curious as to why you would want to … you know, attempt to make this bearable." She pointed down at her menu. "I think I'd like the pasta with the roasted vegetables and garlic bread."

He let go of her hand to signal the waiter.

Alex escaped, or at least one hand did.

The waiter came, and he told them their orders. He went for his usual when he was there, steak with roasted vegetables and buttery potatoes. It was one of his favorite meals. The waiter took their menus and left.

"I want us to make this work," he said. "I was an asshole at the beginning. I didn't know what to do, or what could make a real marriage, and that's on me. I fucked up, but I won't do it again."

"Please, don't worry about it," she said. "There was nothing you could do."

"There is always something that could be done." He was so fucking pissed off with himself.

Tapping his fingers against his leg, he tried to figure out a plan, or something. He had to get Alex to fall in love with him, but with no pointers as to how to win her heart, what the fuck was he going to do?

"I'd like someone I can trust," Alex said. "Someone who wants to spend time with me. Who doesn't think I'm weird and boring because I like to sew. There are times I would love a large family, but … I'm scared of the whole birthing thing. Kind of stumbled onto a documentary-type thing that showed women giving birth, and it scarred me for life."

"Is that why you want to adopt Stuart?"

"And all those other kids. Not just Stuart. I know it sometimes looks like I show favoritism, but if you came by on another day, you'd see the kids are always wanting me to help him. He's not … he's closed off, and I want him to join in. I love them all, and I guess. They're the big family I'd love to have."

"How many kids were there?"

"Between ten and fifteen children in that one house. There have been several adopted over the years, and the numbers fluctuate."

Roman nodded.

"I'd like my husband to be faithful," she said.

"Noted."

"I-I, do you think you could be faithful?"

"Yes."

She nibbled on her lip.

"You don't believe me."

"You won't have sex with anyone else?" she asked. "Even though we're not having sex?"

"Are you saying that you don't want us to fuck, ever?" he asked.

"No, I'm not saying that. Wow, this is so hard to talk about."

"Sex usually is."

She covered her face with her hands. "I don't know if I can talk to you about this."

He chuckled. "Have you thought about having sex with me?"

"No."

Now he was fucking disappointed. Women were always all over him.

Alex dropped her hands. "I feel like I should constantly be apologizing to you."

"No, it's fine."

"You don't look like it's fine."

"I'm getting used to this feeling," he said.

"Of what?"

He was paused in answering as the waiter chose the perfect opportunity to bring him some food, and he was grateful for the distraction.

For the first time in a restaurant, he wanted the

waiter to find an excuse to stay. He never liked interruptions, but right now, he would gladly give anything to be constantly interrupted.

Instead, he gritted his teeth and smiled, pretending like everything was okay. It wasn't.

How did he tell his brand-new wife that getting women was easy for him? He doubted she'd be happy about that.

Staring at her now, he had to wonder if he would be making a mistake in telling her.

Once they were alone, he stared into her eyes. She held her fork in her hand.

"I'm used to women wanting me. I'm not trying to be a dick about it. I'm just stating facts," he said.

She smiled. "I know. I've seen the way women treat you. It must be so horrible."

"I've never had to work hard to get what I want."

Alex tilted her head to the side. "And you have to work hard for me?"

"Yes."

"Do you want me?" she asked.

Now that was the question that hung in the air. Roman stared at her. Did he want to lie? What was the truth?

"Yes," he said, but his answer was to never be heard as there was a loud bang, followed by an explosion.

Roman looked toward the main entrance of the restaurant and saw three men enter, their faces covered in white masks, and his gut told him they were there for Alex.

He had to get her out of there.

Gunshots rang out.

He grabbed his wife's hand and immediately pulled her in front of him as he felt the gunshots whizz past him. Were they trying to kill her? Or kill him?

Rushing her through the back kitchen, he ordered everyone to get down. As he got to the main exits, Antonio was already there.

"Marlo and Cash followed them in," he said.

Just as they exited onto the street, he banded an arm around Alex's waist to keep her to his side. They turned down the long street, and as they did, two men advanced on them. Antonio took one, and Roman had no choice but to let Alex go as he dealt with the man.

He pushed Alex behind a dumpster, hoping it would provide her enough coverage.

Slamming his fist against the masked man's face, he took his enemy by surprise, and while he was trying to regain his balance, he was able to tear the mask from him.

Roman didn't recognize the scarred man.

"Who are you?" Roman asked.

"We're going to take her," the man said. "We're going to fucking kill her!"

Roman pulled out his knives, and as he came forward, he struck, slicing across the man's front and then his back.

The point of the knives was to take his assailant down without killing him. There was no way they could get information out of a corpse.

More gunshots rang out.

The man cried out, but that didn't stop him from charging for more.

Roman continued to slash him. His blades were covered in blood, and the street was as well.

When he came at him another time, he impaled the blades in the man's shoulders, not through any lasting damage. Antonio stumbled toward him, his face covered in blood.

"What the fuck happened?" Roman asked.

Marlo and Cash chose that moment to come out of the back of the restaurant. "We need to get you to a safe house," Cash said.

"What you need to do is tell me what the fuck happened."

Roman watched as Alex stepped out from behind the trash bin. Fuck!

He went toward her, but a single gunshot rang out, and he rushed toward her, capturing her as she fell into his arms.

Her hand went to her stomach.

"Alex?"

The pain in her brown eyes stared back at him. She lifted her shaking hands away from her stomach, and he saw the blood.

"No!" He screamed the word.

He lifted Alex in his arms and carried her toward the car.

"Roman?"

"Kill him," he said, ordering Antonio to kill the man who'd gotten a shot at Alex.

He placed Alex, who was so fucking quiet into the car, and then he rushed toward the front of the car. Roman wasn't alone. Marlo was there.

"I should drive," Marlo said.

Roman slammed the driver's door closed.

"Shit, Roman. You're in no fit state to drive."

He ignored his friend and turned over the ignition.

"Fuck." Marlo grabbed the back passenger door and was able to climb behind him.

Pushing his foot to the floor, he took off. The car jerked left and right with the speed that he was using. He didn't care.

He needed to get Alex to the hospital. Glancing at her, he saw the blood seeping into her clothes. He pressed his hand to her stomach.

"Alex, stay with me."

Marlo was on his cell phone, calling Liam. He was sure of it. Roman didn't have that time to waste.

The nearest hospital was ten minutes away. It was the longest ten minutes of his life as he pressed his foot to the gas. He lost count of the cars he nearly hit. Alex was starting to look way too pale.

"Stay with me, Alex. I'm here. Stay with me."

She didn't speak, and he saw her eyes were closed.

"Fuck, no, no sleepy time for Alex. You need to talk to me. You need to stay with me."

Marlo leaned forward, cupping her face. He'd already removed the headrest, and was able to get to her.

"Come on, Alex, wake up. You can't go to sleep." Marlo pressed his fingers to her neck. "Her pulse is strong."

"Do not let her die."

"Liam and your father are heading toward the hospital," Marlo said. "Antonio and Cash will be with us soon as well."

"Did … did we get any of them alive?"

"No. You told them to kill. Now they're just cleaning up the bodies."

This was bad. He knew that, but that fucker he'd been slashing, he had a gun, and he'd hurt Alex. She should have stayed behind the trash bins. She would've been safe there. This was all on him. He'd put his wife's life in danger.

Arriving at the hospital, he parked near the front doors and climbed out, leaving the ignition running.

Roman rounded the car until he got to Alex and

opened the door. Her eyes were still closed. With his wife in his arms, he ran into the hospital screaming. He didn't know what the hell happened next, but Alex was taken from him, and he seemed to realize he was in a private room.

"Are you okay, man?" Marlo asked.

"What the fuck just happened?" He went to rub his face, but he realized his wife's blood was on his hands.

"You threatened the hospital staff. You said if anything happened to your wife, you'd kill them all. I'm sure Lucas and Liam will handle everything you did. One of the nurses brought you here, and Alex was taken to emergency surgery."

"She shouldn't have been shot," Roman said. "That shit is on me. She can't die."

"Man, do you care if she does?" Marlo asked.

He spun toward his friend, glaring. "Yeah, I fucking do!"

Chapter Eight

Sporting a black eye, Roman waited. Liam had already been by, and now he was dealing with the hospital staff as well as the cops. Lucas sat beside him.

Still covered in blood, Roman stared at the door.

Antonio, Marlo, and Cash were all present, but they were keeping their distance. His dad was pissed at him for making the mistake of turning his back on the enemy.

"That could have been you shot," Lucas said.

"It would have been better if I was."

"Do not say that."

He turned to his father and glared at him. "My wife is in the operating room."

"There will be more wives," Lucas said.

Roman looked at his father, a little taken aback. "What?"

Liam wasn't in the room, and Lucas sighed. "If his daughter dies at the hands of our enemies, then we are not responsible and you don't have to stay married to her."

"You wanted this union," Roman said.

"I know what is good for the family, for our side, Roman. Do not be stupid and pretend you don't know what that is. We all know what it is."

He wasn't sure exactly what he was hearing. "Did you … was this … do you want to kill Alex?"

"Of course not. I'm a man who sees opportunity."

Liam entered the room. The man looked like he'd aged twenty years since Roman had last seen him. At least his fists weren't clenched, and he wasn't ready to take another swipe. "Any news?" Liam asked.

"Nothing yet."

He was starting to have doubts about his father's involvement in the attacks on Alex.

"I will go see if we have an update," Lucas said.

Roman watched his father go, and he didn't like the suspicion flooding him. It suddenly seemed way too convenient that their old enemies, the Smirnovs, were rising up. It was also a convenient time for it.

"The last time I was here when Alex was shot, I lost her mother," Liam said, filling the silence. His honesty surprised Roman. "Hitting you doesn't solve anything, and for that, I'm sorry. Alex will be worried when she sees that you have a black eye."

"A lot of shit was going down. I don't even know how or what the fuck was happening. We were about to enjoy our meal, and the next thing, masked men came into the restaurant, gunning for Alex."

"Wait a minute, masked men?" Liam asked.

"Yes."

Liam frowned.

"What is it?"

"The Smirnov men are not … they were never known for hiding their identity."

Roman looked toward his friends.

"I need to make a call," Liam said. "I will not be far."

"What's going on?" Antonio asked.

"I think my dad set up the attack," Roman said, speaking quietly.

"What?" Marlo asked.

"That's a fucking leap," Cash said.

"He just said that if Alex is killed by our enemies, then Liam cannot pull out of any deal we have with him."

"But that is still a big fucking leap to your dad being involved. He's the Boss, Roman. Even for you, pointing the finger has big fuck-off consequences."

"I know that!" He quickly lowered his voice. "Don't you think I know that? Think about it. How is it that a woman who has spent twenty-one years staying out of the line of fire is suddenly the prime target in an attack?" Roman asked.

"This isn't the first time, Roman," Antonio said. "You just heard Liam. She was shot when he lost her mother."

"Yeah, but if you look at that, it was a turf war. That had nothing to do with Liam. He got himself involved. Alex and her mother was just a mistake. In the wrong place at the wrong time. That was the deal there."

Marlo blew out a breath. "I don't like how this looks. Roman has a point."

"How? I don't think the Boss, *the fucking Boss* of the Greco line would send a hit out on his ally's daughter," Cash said.

"Then how did they know to attack the restaurant? The right one," Marlo said. "And your father, he's shown his dislike of Alex many times. She speaks her own mind and often does what she wants."

"He didn't like that she wouldn't take that stupid test," Antonio said.

"Fuck, that does make a shit load of sense," Cash said. "Then we're all fucked. If our Boss wants her dead, what do we fucking do?"

"Alex doesn't deserve to die," Roman said. He didn't want to think of her dead or dying. "We have to protect her."

"How?"

"I need to … talk to Liam," Roman said.

"If you even imply that your dad is responsible for this…"

"I'm not going to imply it's him, but what I am

going to do is suggest it's an inside job," Roman said.

He looked toward the door and saw the doctor approach, just as Liam had as well. Roman stepped toward the door and opened it as the doctor finished talking. Liam shook his hand.

"What's going on?" Roman asked. "What's happening?"

"I'll talk to him, Doctor," Liam said.

The doctor gave him a grim look. He felt his stomach start to twist. A grim look wasn't good. What did that mean?

Alex couldn't be dead.

He turned to Liam, and the older man sighed. "Alex sailed through surgery, but it is always the next twenty-four hours that are most worrisome. She is not out of the woods yet, but he is hopeful."

"Can I go and see her?" Roman asked.

"Yes, we both can go and see her."

Liam put a hand on his shoulder, but Roman didn't care as he was squeezed tightly. They moved down the long corridor, going through a double set of doors and moving toward the private room.

He stepped into the room and listened to the machines beep. There were none on her mouth and face. A couple on her fingers, and she had something on her arm as well. He didn't know what it was.

Liam let him go, and he watched as he grabbed the base of the bed, squeezing the metal bar tightly.

"I swore I'd protect her. I held her mother in my arms as she was dying, and she begged for me to take care of Alex. To love her. To make sure she never knew pain or sadness, and I fucked up."

"Alex is alive."

"She was shot," Liam said. "I knew agreeing to the marriage with you was a big mistake."

"It's not. We're strong together. You know that."

"Then how come this is the only other time she's been shot?" Liam asked. "The two times I take my eye off the ball, this happens. She's never leaving my sight again. I'm never allowing her to go."

"Liam, you can't do that. Alex wouldn't want that."

"She didn't want to ever get married, but I asked her to."

Roman stared at his wife, and she looked so fucking small and fragile. He hated hospitals with a passion.

"She's strong, and we will make it through this, together."

"Don't give me that crap, Roman. I know you didn't want to marry my daughter. She's not good enough for your little ideal world."

"You're wrong. Alex and I are going to make it work. I'm not turning my back on her." Roman walked toward her and took the chair beside her bed. He sat down and reached for her hand. She was unresponsive, but he didn't care. He was going to hold his wife's hand and never let her go. "She'll come back to us, and then I'm going to show you that we're going to be good together. I'm good for your daughter."

Liam didn't say anything.

Silence fell between them. The only sounds in the room were those of the machines and the commotion of the nurses outside.

He stared at his wife and prayed that his fucking father hadn't done this. Alex didn't deserve to die. She was a good person. Sweet. Kind. She had been born to the wrong man, that was her only fault.

Roman could imagine her with a bunch of kids running around at her feet. Smiling. Happy. Safe. He didn't like where the thought took him.

There was only one man who was going to be coming home to her, and that was him. Alex was his.

She was his wife. And he would go up against his father if he had to.

****

"It's not Roman," Lucas said.

"What about his three friends?" Liam asked.

Lucas shook his head. "I'm not sure." He'd stepped out of the hospital to make a call. "The security footage is being delivered to my house."

"Masked men?" Liam asked.

Lucas had to agree with the man. "I don't like this. Someone is trying to fuck with us, and they're using an old enemy to do it." He and Liam had been trying to figure out who it was that could have put the call out to take Alex. Today's attack was a step-up, attempted murder. If it hadn't been for his son, Alex would be dead. "But it has to be someone close. Someone who knows Alex and Roman's movements. Only a small circle of people knew he was taking her to the restaurant."

"Fuck!" Liam yelled the word, startling some people who were walking past. He didn't apologize. "Nothing can happen to my daughter. Nothing."

"I swore to you that I will protect you."

"Your son is going to suspect you," Liam said.

"Good. I need him to be on alert. If they come after Alex, they'll come after him, and it will only be a matter of time before chaos floods our streets again. I will not let that happen." He'd already lost one child because of it.

Pretending to be the enemy was not the best idea. His son may get it through his mind to attempt to overthrow him, but what he needed most was for his son to get his fucking head back in the game.

Someone close to them was fucking with them. Prepared to start a war, and Lucas knew there were many casualties in battle. He'd nearly lost everything years ago in his quest to be on top.

He glanced over at Liam. His … friend had also experienced loss and pain. They both knew what coming together meant, what being united meant. Neither of them wanted to see their children suffer because of them.

It was why they had agreed to meet up. Why they had spent many hours learning to trust each other and finally coming to the agreement that the only way forward for them was through family.

Lucas wouldn't fuck that up.

Regardless of what his son, or anyone else thought, he adored Alex. When she refused to take that virginity test, it had annoyed him a little. He was always suspicious, especially of women, as they had tried to fuck him over in the past. Alex wasn't manipulative. He had asked for a private word, and she had said to him that she didn't feel comfortable having strange men or women between her thighs.

He believed her.

Roman wasn't a good man. Lucas hadn't been able to raise a good man. He had to raise his eldest son to take over, to be in charge, to be feared. It was going to take one hell of a woman to deal with him, and he knew Alex and Roman would have a rocky start, but they would find each other, eventually.

Who was trying to fuck up his plans?

****

Roman hadn't left Alex's side. Liam rarely left. When his cell phone went off and he needed privacy, he stepped out of the room. Lucas visited often as well.

Alex's private room had a small bathroom, and that was where he went. The nurses and his friends brought him food, but otherwise, he kept his ass in the chair, only getting up for bathroom breaks.

The first twenty-four hours came and went, but Alex didn't wake up. The doctor didn't seem overly concerned.

Roman didn't like this. He wasn't a doctor, but people shouldn't just stay asleep. They should fucking wake up.

Reaching for her hand, he pressed a kiss to her knuckles. At least she felt warm to him. "Alex, babe, you need to wake up."

He didn't like where this was going. With every hour that passed, his suspicions about his father grew. "I know you didn't want to be married to me, and that is okay. It is fine. I don't care. You can hate me. That's fine as well. I can deal with everything, but you've got to give me a chance. Not waking up, you're not giving me a chance to show you that I can be different. You've got to wake up," he said. "Even if it is to just prove that I'm not a good enough husband. Alex, please, wake the fuck up."

She didn't flutter.

No sign.

No movement.

"She'll wake up when she's ready," Millie said, startling him.

He turned to see the older woman, the cook, stepping into the room. "Millie," he said.

"You care for her." Millie frowned. "I didn't see that one coming."

"I … I … she…"

Millie stepped toward him. He didn't let go of Alex, but he stood up.

She placed a hand on his arm. "It's good to care for people."

"She doesn't deserve to die." That was all he kept

thinking and feeling.

She offered him a smile. “I agree. Alex is a tough one.” Millie stepped away from him and moved toward the opposite end of the bed. “She has always had this fire about her. Don’t get me wrong, she is a wonderful child. Always was.” Millie touched her other hand. “She never made waves. Even when Liam annoyed her or wouldn’t let her stay up. Alex doesn’t like to be afraid, and she would try to watch these horror movies. She’d do it to try to prove that she’s not afraid. Of course, she was, and she’d spend so many nights wide awake and afraid. Liam had to ban her.” Millie chuckled. “I remember Alex saying that she stopped watching them because he told her to but not because she was afraid. Always so strong. I hate seeing her like this.”

Roman didn’t know what to say. “I don’t love her.”

“But you care for her.”

“I don’t want to see her get hurt.”

“You don’t know Alex,” Millie said. “And I’m guessing you don’t even know what love is. Maybe what you should do is give yourself time to see what the two are like. To learn to love?”

“I’m … not capable of it,” he said.

“Everyone is capable of love, Roman. Even you. Even Liam. Everyone is capable of love.”

Roman went to say otherwise, but he felt Alex’s hand twitch within his grasp. “Alex?” He stared at her eyes, and then looked down at her hand.

“What is it?”

“She squeezed my hand. I felt it. Alex, I’m here. I’m here,” he said.

Her hand squeezed his.

“I felt it too,” Millie said. “I’ll go get a doctor and Liam.”

Millie left the room, and Roman stood up, placing a hand by her head, staring down into her eyes.

Alex opened her eyes, and he looked into her deep-brown depths. "I was never afraid," Alex said.

"Then I guess you and I are going to have to watch a horror because I don't believe you."

She smiled and then groaned. "Do I want to know what happened?"

"You were shot," Roman said. "We were having dinner and the restaurant was attacked."

Alex nodded. "I remember."

"Are you in pain?"

"No, not … a little, maybe. I'm not sure." She sighed.

The hospital door opened, and Roman had no choice but to step back and allow the doctor to get to work and check over his wife.

He was so fucking happy that she hadn't died, but now, he had to focus on keeping her alive.

****

"I hate hospitals," Alex said.

She had been trying to leave for over a week. The doctor had requested to keep her in for observation. The bullet didn't cause any lasting damage, and he believed she would make a full recovery.

Everything was fine.

Yes, she hurt, and there was a brand-new scar on her stomach, which was bound up, and the dressing was changed daily, but even the nurse was impressed with her speedy recovery.

"Everyone hates hospitals," Roman said, bringing in the wheelchair.

Everyone had been surprised that Alex followed the orders of resting. What they didn't realize was that she knew the key to getting out of this place was to rest.

The more rest she took, the faster she healed and could go home.

Roman moved to her side and helped her into her wheelchair. He hadn't left her side since she woke up. According to Millie, he'd been by her side while she was asleep. Alex didn't know what to say to that. Roman was her husband, so it made sense he wanted to be by her side, but the full extent of his care to her, that did surprise her.

She sat down on the wheelchair, and Roman stepped behind her, grabbing the handlebars and pushing her out of the room. There were a lot of flowers from his friends, his father, and her father, everyone hoping for her speedy recovery.

"I promise if you get the agreement to allow me to leave, I will be the best patient ever."

"You're being the best patient here in the hospital."

"Anyone ever tell you that you're a pain in the ass?" she asked.

He chuckled. "I've often been told that I am."

She folded her arms and leaned back in the wheelchair. They made their way toward the elevator, which was free.

Roman reached over and pressed for the ground floor, which would take them toward the private hospital gardens.

"Why are you here?" Alex asked. The elevator doors were not clear, so she couldn't look at him.

"You're here."

"Did you … the men, didn't you get one?"

"No. They didn't make it."

"Oh."

"Yeah. Don't be afraid though. We will figure everything out. You have my word," he said.

"I believe you." She rubbed at her temple.

"Do you have any enemies?" Roman asked.

"Not that I know of."

"I figured as much."

The elevator doors slid open, and he pushed her out into the main area. Like all the other times before, it was so busy. She looked left and right, and there were so many people. This was one of the many reasons why she hated coming here. A quick glance around the room, and she saw so many people in different states of distress. It was heartbreaking. People were worried, panicked, annoyed, and in pain.

Roman didn't linger, and the moment they were out in the fresh air, she felt better. She spotted Antonio, Marlo, and Cash up ahead.

They gave them a wave, and Roman pushed her toward the table where a coffee and a plate of food waited for her.

She noticed there was no other food. "Are you guys not going to eat?" she asked.

"Hospital food," Roman said, wrinkling his nose.

Alex rolled her eyes. She was hungry. She took a sip of her coffee and then shoved a giant fry in her mouth. The food wasn't great, but it was food. She missed Millie's food.

"How are you feeling?" Antonio asked.

"Fine. I want to leave the hospital. I'm fit as can be."

Marlo and Cash laughed.

"You're not leaving yet."

"People leave the hospital all the time with wounds far worse than this. Why do I have to stay?" she asked.

She wanted to stamp her foot and slam her hand against the table, but she did fear it would harm her chances of getting out sooner.

The doctor had stopped coming to her room. There was only a nurse assessing her injuries now. She didn't see what the big deal was. It was time for her to come home.

"The doctor wants to check on your recovery," Roman said.

Alex noticed the way Antonio, Marlo, and Cash looked at him.

"The doctor hasn't been to see me for two days, Roman. I'm good to go, and I bet he has cleared me to leave."

"You're not leaving."

"What is the big deal?" Alex asked. "I hate being here."

"It's safe for you here," Roman said.

She opened her mouth and closed it. Taking another sip of coffee, she stared at him and realized what he hadn't been saying. "The threat is still out there."

"At this hospital, your dad has plenty of men in place. I'm always here. We can monitor who gets close to your room. You are safe."

His friends wouldn't look at her.

"I … I can't stay here, Roman. I hate it here. There has to be some other place I can go."

"I can't guarantee your safety anywhere else. You're staying here, and I can protect you."

She slowly ate the food on her plate, taking her time and trying to think of some way of getting out of the hospital.

"You must hate it here as well," she said.

"I do, but I am willing to do whatever it takes to keep you safe."

She rolled her eyes. "This isn't safe. This is … this is biding our time until I'm attacked again." She wasn't trying to make light of what happened, but staying in the hospital wasn't going to help.

"I'm not putting your life at risk."

"I want to talk to my dad," Alex said. She held her hand out. "Please let me borrow one of your cell phones."

No one moved.

"Alex, this is my decision."

"And your decision is crap. I need to speak to my father."

She still didn't get a cell phone.

"Fine. If you won't help me, I will find someone who will." She glanced down at her chair.

Roman had put the brakes on, but because she'd been playing the role of a good student, she didn't know where to remove the brakes.

She gritted her teeth and then looked up. "I know a place where I can be safe. That's in a secure place. No one will find me. No one will think to find me."

Roman folded his arms, and she knew he was going to shoot it down.

"Where?" he asked.

"The orphanage. Think about it. No one but us needs to know, and possibly my father. Perhaps your dad," Alex said.

"No. My father doesn't need to know."

"My dad will want to know," Alex said. "We can't keep him in the dark."

"What makes you think the orphanage is a good idea? People go and visit."

"Yes, but I can blend in. I'm always there. People don't know that I'm Liam's daughter, and it's one of dad's privately owned buildings. He helps to invest money there, but he doesn't do so openly. It's private. For the safety of the children, and also for me, seeing as I volunteer there all the time, even before I found Stuart," Alex said.

"It sounds like a good plan," Antonio said, sounding a little reluctant.

"It's a bad idea," Roman said.

"I would never put those kids' lives at risk."

"It's not about that. How can you … rest and recover if you're surrounded by kids?" Roman asked.

Chapter Nine

Roman hated this idea.

Liam had loved the plan.

Antonio, Marlo, and Cash were not fans of it either.

Liam's men were already placed in secure locations around the orphanage. The people employed were on Liam's books. No part of Greco touched this place. Only he and his friends knew about it.

His dad was aware of a little boy named Stuart from the dinner that had ended in disaster, but that was the extent of it.

He stared at the garden where Alex sat in the wheelchair as the kids each ran toward her, showing off another prized picture. He saw how desperate they were to hug her, but he'd taken all fifteen kids to one side and told them all how important it was that they allow her to recover.

None of them had pushed.

Yet.

Even Stuart was on his best behavior and joining in. He had to take him aside and ask him to be big and brave for Alex. The little boy had been afraid of him, but Roman talked to him, man to man.

"Dude, I dump women the moment they start talking kids, or even hinting at not using a condom. You're here in serious relationship central," Antonio said.

Roman rolled his eyes.

"Alex was right. This place is not directly associated with Liam. Even though it's close to him, there are no connections at all. It's the safest place for her to be."

Roman knew Liam was looking into the security footage, attempting to find the assholes responsible for putting the hit out on Alex.

While Alex had been in the hospital, Roman had been alerted to another call, putting a price on Alex's head—alive. She had to be taken alive. It was why he'd kept her in the hospital. Three people had tried to get to her. All of them had failed, but as attempts had been made to hold the people intent on killing her, they'd taken some kind of poison and killed themselves.

The bounty on her head wasn't a lot, so the people making the attempts were amateurs. Whoever was trying to fuck with them was low level, or they didn't have the appropriate funds to take them on.

This brought him to another confusing part of all of this. His father was rich. Money wasn't a problem. He could funnel money to any person, hide the actual transaction, and have a professional kill Alex.

The more he thought about the restaurant, the more confused he got. If his father wanted Alex dead, he wouldn't have it done sloppily like that. It would be clean. Their enemies would struggle to be caught.

"You're glaring," Marlo said.

"Something doesn't feel right," Roman said.

"I heard that is the first sign of love," Cash said.

"Fuck off with the love. I don't love my wife. I'm just … I'm taking care of her. I'm doing what my father asked of me," Roman said. "I'm getting her to fall in love with me."

"The same man who would be happy to see her die?" Antonio asked. "That's a bit odd, don't you think?"

Roman ran a hand down his face. "Something doesn't add up in all of this. Think about it."

"I am thinking about it," Marlo said. "All of this is a bit of a stretch. Your dad, Alex, do you think Liam could be involved?"

"No," Roman said. "He loves his daughter. He would never, ever, put her in harm's way. What does he have to gain by killing her?"

"Freedom?"

"If he pins it on your father, an all-out war," Cash said.

"Yeah, but look at who is doing the attacks. Supposedly the Smirnov Bratva, right. An organization that was nearly wiped out years ago. Their old enemies. Dad wouldn't allow people like that to rise up. You've got to think about the logic on this one." Roman started to pace. The kids were all on the grass with Alex, and he had her in his sights at all times.

The staff were also near her, keeping an eye on the kids.

"If Liam was going to attempt to pin it on Lucas, then he would make sure it was the Greco mark, not an old enemy. It can't be him, and I don't see him attempting to kill his daughter. He wouldn't do that."

"So we're back to your dad again," Antonio said. "And what he said to you in the hospital room."

"Yeah, which makes no sense, because forty-eight-ish hours before, he was telling me to make Alex fall in love with me." He gritted his teeth. The answer was right in front of him, he just couldn't quite reach him.

"If he was going to kill Alex, seeing as there was already a hit put out on her already, why would he tell you, in private, to make this marriage work?" Marlo asked.

"Exactly."

"So we rule out your dad," Cash said. "Which brings us back to square one. Who would want to kill Alex?"

Roman looked toward his wife. The smile on her face was infectious. She'd only been with the kids a couple of days and the color was back in her cheeks. She looked so happy. He loved seeing her like this.

He hated hospitals, and keeping her in one had been difficult.

"We have no one," Roman said. "Alex is … she's not…"

"There has to be someone. We're overlooking, or we're not looking close enough," Antonio said. "What about an ex-lover?"

Roman frowned and looked at his friend. "What?"

"Think about it, the moment your dad told you, you were engaged to be married, you stopped visiting your women. You ended things abruptly. Some of the women you were seeing, they liked all the pretty things you had."

"They're not killers," Roman said.

"I don't know, Denise looks like she'd be pretty pissed if someone messed with her money pot," Cash said.

"She was all about the money," Marlo said.

Roman chuckled. "So what we're saying is an ex-lover of mine, who knew of the Smirnov, has arranged to have my wife killed and potentially start an all-out war because of my dick?"

"Some women can be quite possessive," Antonio said. "Maybe she or they didn't like being passed over for Alex. Let's face it, we've all heard the rumors. None of the women believe she is good enough for you."

Roman shook his head. "None of them could have done this, okay? I paid them a huge settlement. They have no reason to even think about Alex."

"Apart from the fact they think she's getting your

dick."

"I'm not talking about this anymore. It's not helping."

"We've got to exhaust all angles," Marlo said.

What he needed right now was to be near Alex.

After stepping off the porch, he walked all the way toward her. Several of the kids were near her as he approached, and all of them rushed back to their little easels to start drawing again.

"You look angry," Alex said.

"It's nothing."

She looked past his shoulder, and he didn't need to turn to know she was staring at his friends. "Trouble in paradise?"

"I don't know, you tell me. Boys and girls, I'm going to take our precious patient for a little stroll," Roman said, going behind her wheelchair. There was a chorus of okays and a few boos, that eventually turned into okays. Not that he'd stop doing what he was doing to appease them.

"Is everything okay?" Alex asked.

"Just trying to figure out who is trying to kill you."

"Ah, good thoughts."

"It's not funny."

She held her hands up. "I know. Trust me. I know. This isn't fun for me either. My classes have stopped. I can't do anything. Being around the kids is awesome though. They're a good distraction."

"Do you love kids?"

"Yeah, I do. Do you?"

"This is the first time I've been around them."

"Don't you have siblings?"

"I do, but I didn't spend any time with them. Since I'm the eldest son, Dad focused on me and told me

I didn't need any distractions when it came to learning what I needed to take over. There was no time to get close to anyone. It was just me."

"That's sad."

"I never missed what I didn't have."

"I always wanted a brother or sister," Alex said. "When I got too lonely and Millie was too busy and Dad was as well, I'd put all of my teddy bears around this small table I had. I'd name them all. I even had a chart that told me their name, what they did, if they were good or bad."

"And if you had a brother or sister, you would've been able to boss them around."

"I was never bossy. Even teddy bears can be so bossy when they want to be." She tilted her head back and smiled up at him, which he found utterly adorable.

The grounds were beautiful. Liam had outdone himself in picking the perfect location for the kids. From what he heard, an orphanage in the city, on Liam's turf, had burnt down. All the kids had been saved, including their guardians. As a boy on the streets, and building up his reputation, Liam developed a soft spot and created an opportunity for these kids. The house was stunning. The people vetted and constantly checked. Liam put a lot of anonymous funds into this place.

He also figured this was Liam's way of apologizing to Alex. If he wouldn't allow her to adopt or take on these kids, then he was at least going to make sure they were cared for. Liam truly only had one weakness, and it was the woman in front of him. They came to a stop at some benches, and Roman put the brakes on the chair to take a seat opposite her.

"I thought we were going for a stroll?" she asked.

"We are, and we're going to enjoy a few minutes of peace and quiet."

"Not handling being cooped up in one place?"

"It's not that. I'm trying to scramble my brain for people who'd want to see you dead."

"Why not expand the search to all people that would like to see you and my dad suffer? You've got a lot of enemies."

Roman leaned forward, staring into her beautiful brown eyes. "I've thought about that, but there are so many different ways of hitting back at us."

"I know you're right. I have to wonder if this is an attack on my dad, more than it is on you."

"How do you figure that?"

She tilted her head to the side and rolled her eyes. "Come on, Roman. I mean absolutely nothing to you. We don't have that kind of marriage. Outsiders can see it. We're not close. You wouldn't care if I died. I mean nothing to you. My dad, I know I'm his whole world. If I die, it would send him on a warpath."

Roman stared at her as she looked away, closing her eyes and tilting her head back toward the sun.

"I would care," Roman said.

"Why?"

"You're my wife."

"And?"

"I have a duty to protect you, and regardless of what you think, I don't hate you." He wanted to take her hand, but he also didn't want her rejection, not right now. "We haven't given this a real shot. For all you know, we could be amazing together."

"Even though you've said you don't do love."

"It doesn't mean this can't be the best damn thing we've both had before." Roman put his hand on her knee, needing to touch her. He couldn't quite explain it. "I wasn't happy with you being in the hospital. I hated seeing you look so … helpless."

"I got through it."

"I'm not going to allow you to ever get hurt again, Alex. No matter what."

****

Alex sat in bed, reading the same lines of her book and not having a clue what they meant because all she could think about was Roman.

What was his game?

She accepted that they meant nothing to each other, but he seemed determined to bridge this gap between them, but she didn't understand why.

A knock sounded at the door, and she called for whoever it was to come on in. Antonio entered, and she closed her book. "Is everything okay?" Alex asked.

Roman had to leave a couple of hours ago, just after dinner. She got the opportunity to help with the kids. They had a set routine of how bath times worked, and to encourage them not to mess around, she organized a movie night, complete with popcorn. Sitting in the large cinema room, surrounded by kids, she had loved every second of it. Hearing them laugh, squeal with delight, and then gasp in shock at a small twist. It was an animated movie, but they loved it.

Afterward, it was teeth brushing and tucking in.

With Roman not around to boss her, she was able to get out of the wheelchair he insisted she sit in, and she'd helped tuck the kids into bed. The pain was on a manageable scale. She rarely took any pain medication because she hated how drowsy it made her.

"Yeah, everything is okay. I bought you some hot chocolate," Antonio said. "I figured you could use some company."

She quickly glanced at the clock and saw it was approaching midnight. "I'm going to be going to sleep, soon. Very soon."

He smiled. "I know when I'm not wanted."

"I don't think you should be here. It's not appropriate."

"Look, Alex, I care about you. I don't want to see you get hurt."

"Don't worry. Roman has already said the same thing himself. Only he's told me he's not going to let me get hurt again."

"He has?" Antonio asked.

"Shocked, huh? I'm sure he's just spilling words out of his mouth. You know, the whole word-vomit thing." Just like she was doing right now to get him out of the room. Tapping her fingers against the book, she saw him staring at her. "What is it?"

"Do you care about Roman?" he asked.

She nibbled on the corner of her mouth. "I don't know how to answer that."

"I care about Roman. I love him like a brother. He has my back, and I will always have his. He's never really gotten close to anyone before. Especially not a woman."

"I don't need to hear this." She didn't like the feeling curling in her stomach at the thought of Roman with other women.

Antonio placed his hand on her leg. "That's what I'm trying to tell you. He's never like that with other women. They have always only held one place in his life and that was to entertain him in the bedroom."

"I don't need to hear this."

He groaned. "I'm not saying the right thing here."

"I don't know, telling me that my husband used women for his own pleasure. I do think that is a great start." It wasn't. Not even close.

She felt a little sick. And she didn't like the bad taste in her mouth. Was this jealousy? Why would she feel this way about a man she had no feelings for? It made no sense.

She hated it.

"I'm not good with words. I never have been."

"I think it's best that you go," Alex said.

"Roman doesn't know what it means to care, even when he does. He says that he doesn't have feelings for you, but I saw his face when you got shot, Alex. He cares, in his own way. You've just got to give him time. Give him a chance."

Antonio removed his hand and got to his feet.

She watched him, curious what his game was, but he left without another word.

Taking a sip of the hot chocolate he'd brought her, she was pleasantly surprised. It was sweet, just the way she liked it, with just the right amount of chocolate. It was … delicious.

She took another sip and stared at the door.

There was no way she was going to cave that easily. Roman had said he didn't love her, that he might one day care about her, but she was a job to him. An order. Their marriage was a contract of peace and of loyalty, nothing more.

After finishing off the hot chocolate, she threw the blankets back. Rather than go and immediately brush her teeth, she grabbed the cup and made her way downstairs toward the kitchen.

The house was so silent, a complete contrast to when the kids were up. It had been an exciting couple of days for them, at least that was what she was told. She adored all the kids here and with her present, she noticed little Stuart had started to come out of his shell, which was good.

Placing the cup in the sink, she stared into it at the drying remnants of hot chocolate in the bottom. She refused to leave it for anyone else, so she grabbed the scrubbing brush, turned on the warm water, and cleaned the cup.

After she placed it on the drainer, she found a kitchen towel and got to drying it. Millie would often get her in the kitchen growing up, helping out with chores. Teaching her what it was like to run a house.

"One day, this is going to be all yours. You're going to need to know how to run things smoothly."

Alex doubted that she would own her father's house. She always pictured herself somewhere else, like this place. Her father's place was so large, and the rooms so empty.

"I thought I told you that you needed to rest."

She spun around at the sound of Roman's voice. "You startled me." She stared at him, seeing his hair was a little damp from being outside. They had no choice earlier to bring the kids inside as the sunshine had turned to a sudden downpour, and it had been raining most of the day.

The kids were gutted as Roman promised them a round of baseball. He'd even insisted Marlo, Cash, and Antonio would help.

With how wet Roman looked, she figured it was still raining.

"You're supposed to be resting."

"I am all rested out."

He took a step toward her, and she rolled her eyes.

"You keep doing that," he said.

She placed the cup back in its place, in the cupboard just above her head. When she moved, Roman was already there, trapping her between the counter and his rock-solid body.

"I keep doing what?" she asked.

"Rolling those pretty eyes."

She was not going to focus on the fact he said her eyes were pretty. "You keep saying the same things, Roman. How is … everything?" she asked.

"Fine. Your dad misses you and told me to tell you that he is doing everything in his power to make it safe, and so am I."

She nodded.

He was so close. The shocking blue of his eyes startled her. They were … intense, beautiful, and she couldn't look away.

Licking her dry lips, she tried to think of something to say, anything, but the silence was so deafening, and her heart started to race.

"I missed you," he said.

"You were gone for a few hours."

"And yet, I spent most of those hours thinking about you. Wondering what you were doing."

"Helping with the kids. Watching a movie. Sitting reading a book in bed. Not very exciting."

"But you had a blast?"

"Yes."

"You love being around those kids," he said.

"Yes."

"You're an amazing mother."

The compliment took her by surprise. The kids felt like her own. She loved them so much.

Alex couldn't help but drop her gaze toward his lips. They were so close, and they seemed almost inviting at that moment. The early days of their marriage a couple of months ago, his lips were stern, constantly set in a disapproving line, but now, they looked … kissable.

They had shared one kiss, two if she counted the kiss on their wedding day.

Why did she suddenly care about his lips? How

they might feel again on her lips.

Roman cupped her cheek, and she couldn't help but gasp at the sudden contact.

"I'm going to kiss you, Alex."

"Why?" A word that seemed to be in her vocabulary a lot just lately.

"Because I want to."

She didn't get time to question him as he suddenly slammed his lips down on hers and kissed her. No, devoured her.

This wasn't a chaste kiss, or a gentle, sweet locking of lips. This was possession, fire, and passion. The kind of kiss she read about in a few of the romance books she talked about. The hand on her cheek moved toward the back of her head, holding her in place as he took her lips.

She placed her hands on his waist, not sure what to do with them, feeling a little out of place and not completely herself. Then as he deepened the kiss, his tongue tracing across her mouth, she gasped.

Like before, Roman took full advantage, plunging his tongue in her mouth. He closed the distance between them, and then she felt the hard ridge of his cock against her.

A whimper escaped her.

"I need a glass of water."

The interruption shocked her, and she jerked back. Opening her eyes, she saw Roman staring at her.

"Dana, sweetie," she said. "Are you okay?"

"I'm thirsty," Dana said, and she put her hand up, laughing. "You're in love."

Alex refused to look at Roman. She couldn't believe she had been caught making out with her husband by this little girl. She grabbed a glass and quickly filled it with water, then handed it to Dana. The little girl took it and drank it all in one go.

"Is that better?"

Dana nodded.

"Would you like me to put you back to bed?" Alex asked.

Dana nodded and held her hand out. The little girl was eight years old and had been found alone in an apartment. They believed she had been there for at least a week. Her mother was later found in the back alley, a drug overdose.

She held Alex's hand tightly.

"I'll help," Roman said, coming to Dana.

Much to Alex's surprise, he lifted her up onto his hip and carried her upstairs to bed. Dana wrapped her arms around Roman's neck, holding him tightly.

"Are you my new daddy?" Dana asked.

Roman stopped, and Alex saw him tense.

"It's getting late," Alex said.

"Are you going to be my new mommy?" Dana asked.

"We'll talk about this later." She forced a smile to her lips, even though her heart was breaking inside.

They made it to Dana's room, and saw Evie, the other girl, was fast asleep.

Pulling the blankets back, Roman eased the little girl down onto the bed, and Alex tucked her in.

"I want you as my mommy and you as my daddy. Everyone says we're going to be a big family." Dana wriggled in the bed, and Alex watched her, worried that her staying here was giving the kids the wrong impression. She would love nothing more than taking care of the kids, but her life and future were out of her control.

Leaning forward, she kissed Dana on the head, and then stood, leaving the room.

Roman was close behind her. "Are you all right?"

"Yeah, I'm fine." She was the furthest thing from fine.

"Everything is going to be okay. We'll find the person responsible for hurting you. The one who gave the order."

"I don't care about that. I love these kids, Roman, and you saw that. You heard her. I don't want to be the one responsible for breaking their hearts, and I know deep down, I am going to be." She shook her head. "I need to go to bed."

She had to sleep, to be alone to think.

"You know, there's nothing to say we can't … be here for them," Roman said.

Alex had already started to walk away, but at his words, she turned toward him. "What?"

He shrugged. "I like being here. They're good kids."

She shook her head. "Don't do that. Don't give me hope like that and certainly don't give it to these kids. They trust us, and I'm not ever going to let them down." She tucked some hair behind her ears, needing to do something with her hands because, for the first time since her father had told her *no*, she felt hopeful. "You need to think about it, to be sure that you know and understand what you're offering."

She looked at him one more time, and then she turned on her heel, escaping back to her bedroom to try to calm herself. Between the kiss and Roman's potential promise, her mind was a riot of emotions. None of which she could make a whole lot of sense of. There was so much happening, and she was terrified she wasn't going to be able to catch up.

Chapter Ten

"That's a pretty good picture, kid," Roman said. He hadn't quite mastered the art of knowing who was called what. If he was honest with himself, he wasn't sure if he was any good with kids, but he had five of them around the table with him.

It had been three days since he brought up adopting them completely with Alex. His dad had told him to find any means necessary to win Alex over, and this place seemed like a solid plan. There was also a tiny slim part of them that was starting to adore the kids and enjoy their company.

He never thought he'd enjoy dealing with a bunch of screaming brats, but he did. They were a lot of fun to be around. Growing up, he never had the luxury of sitting there and coloring in pictures or drawing.

However, at the ripe age of thirty-five, he was finally getting the chance to do that. What he wasn't doing was drawing what he knew. The kids didn't need to see death, blood, and destruction. All they needed to know was rainbows and houses, and well, he drew a big fuck-off rainbow with every single color he could get his hands on.

The kids loved it, and he was rather impressed with it.

Antonio, Marlo, and Cash took it in turns to escape, to return to the harsh reality of what was going on outside. To many, nothing had changed. Liam was on a warpath, and so far, he had tortured and killed many enemies.

The Smirnov Bratva was a pointless lead. The only thing that had survived of them was their insignia, which could be inked anywhere. He knew in his gut his father wasn't responsible.

It just didn't add up.

And now, the family was starting to get suspicious as he and Alex had missed multiple events in the past few weeks, including an engagement party. Their presence was being missed.

His dad had already talked to him, and in a couple of weeks, he and Alex were supposed to make a big entrance at another party. One to celebrate Lucas and Liam's union. The plan was to use him and Alex as bait, but also to see if anyone showed any signs of wanting her dead.

It was a risk.

He didn't like it.

Hated it.

But Liam had also agreed to it.

The event would be heavily guarded. It was the party of the year, and they were supposed to show a united front. He'd told Antonio, Marlo, and Cash about it, but he had yet to speak to the woman herself.

Not that he was afraid to tell her. He had no reason to be afraid.

She couldn't turn him down, and if she did, her father would get involved. Damn it, he didn't want her father to get involved. This was already bad enough.

"Ice cream," Alex said, calling out to the kids.

All coloring was forgotten as the kids ran toward the kitchen. All except one. Stuart, who approached him.

"What's up, buddy?" Roman asked.

Stuart stared at him and then, much to Roman's surprise, he crawled up into his lap. For the longest time, they just stared at each other.

"I like you," Stuart said. "You make Alex smile."

Roman didn't know what was happening.

"I like you too."

"Do you like Alex?"

"Yeah, I do."

"She's an angel," Stuart said.

The little boy startled him further by throwing his arms around him and hugging him tight before climbing off and leaving.

Roman wasn't sure he'd lived it until he looked up to see Alex approaching. She held an ice cream cone. "I thought I'd save you one," she said.

He took the ice cream from her as Alex lowered herself into the chair that had been occupied by one of the boys minutes before.

"Thanks."

He looked at the ice cream.

"Stuart likes you."

"He does?"

"That's his little … acceptance. You got a hug. He likes you."

"I think he was looking out for you. Making sure I treat you right." He watched as Alex flicked her tongue across the soft ice cream. She gave him a smile. "He's a great kid."

"How come … no one adopts these kids?" Roman asked.

"Adoption is quite hard. Some people don't pass the required tests. Then, of course, you have parents who are looking for a specific kid. If they don't meet what they want, they don't get picked. It's a brutal process. I hate that the kids have to go through with it."

"They're amazing," Roman said, and he meant it.

"They are. I hate having to leave them."

For now, she didn't have to worry.

"Is this yours?" Alex asked, picking up his picture of a multi-colored rainbow.

"It sure is."

"I like it. This should go on the fridge with all of these pictures." She put the picture down and went back to licking her ice cream. He could think of many other things she could be doing with her tongue.

Did she even realize what she was doing?

He doubted it.

"I've got to talk to you about something," he said.

She stared at him and continued to suck on her ice cream, and he wanted to feel those lips wrapped around his dick.

"There is an … event," he said. "A party. Our presence has been missed, and well, our fathers would like us to attend in a couple of weeks, but what they want is for us to appear … close."

"Close?"

"In love. Like the last few weeks we've been together."

"Don't they know I've been hurt? Injured?"

"No, they have been able to keep it under wraps," Roman said. "No one knows." It was a miracle they'd been able to keep it quiet for this long.

Locking Alex away had helped though. The men who had been placed at the hospital were the most trusted. They were known for getting the job done without saying a fucking word.

"Isn't that dangerous?" Alex asked.

"They're hoping to either draw out a suspect or rule out everyone associated with the Greco family."

"That does make sense. So I'm bait."

"No, we're bait. I'll be by your side the whole time."

"Sounds like fun."

"The only problem," Roman said.

"What?"

"The in-love part. Liam and my dad said that it

has to be real. It has to be … authentic."

"Roman, I don't think I need to tell you that it's going to be impossible to do that. You don't believe in love and we're not an in-love couple."

"Which is why I figured we've got two weeks to at least act it. We can't be indifferent to each other. We act like a normal couple, and to help, Marlo, Cash, and Antonio have agreed to help us. We will be training with them."

"Training? Are you kidding me? Training to be … in love. Don't you think that sounds crazy?"

"The main training will start when the kids are in bed. We'll be using the basement to practice."

"That's just great. Using the basement where it's the main port of horror in all scary movies."

"Which you don't watch to help your dad?" he asked, trying to lighten the mood.

She chuckled. "Yeah, he doesn't like me watching them, so I don't."

"And not because you're afraid."

"No, I'm not afraid. Don't you think this is a bit ridiculous?"

"It sounds it, but I'll do whatever it takes to keep you safe, even if it means undergoing training from three men."

Alex held a finger up. "Wait, how can they be our teachers in this? Are they in love? Have they ever been in love?"

"They're the closest ones that have been. I don't trust anyone else, Alex. They're the only ones who can help us."

"Then I fear we are doomed."

He agreed.

The plan was to try to help his cause in making Alex fall in love with him. The guys knew they had to keep them close, force them to look at each other, and there were going to be a lot of parts Roman didn't know, but the guys promised him that they'd help him.

With how important it was for Alex to fall in love with him, he'd put an end to his plan for his friends to try to get her into bed. He didn't like how it made him feel anymore. The thought of any of them touching Alex, kissing her, stroking her body, feeling how curvy and perfect she was, it filled him with rage. He just couldn't handle anyone else touching her or wanting her.

She was his.

The kids began to make their return, and Alex stood to make room for them back at the table. She rounded the table and stood behind his.

The only sounds to be heard were the licks and the hums of approval. Who knew that an ice cream cone could silence children?

It was nice. Sweet music to his ears. The only time the kids were this silent was in the middle of the night.

He often found himself lying awake, trying to hear a sound of anyone threatening his woman. The moment they found the person responsible, Roman was going to deal with him. Liam was under the impression that he was going to get the chance to deal with him, but not on his watch.

This man had fucked with the wrong woman.

"What are you guys drawing now?" Alex asked. She placed her hand on his shoulder and leaned over.

He didn't want her to move away. The simplest touch felt like so much more. What was happening to him? Why did he care so much about Alex?

He had hated her for the longest time. No, not hate, just not liked.

Damn it, she was messing with his head, and he

needed to get his shit back into the game.

"Doggies!" Stuart said.

Alex sighed. "I wish we could get a dog for you guys, but I've been told time and time again, the answer is no."

Roman filed that piece of information for later. The kids started to draw a dog, and Alex attempted to step away, but he captured her wrist and pressed a kiss to her inner wrist. He didn't want her to leave.

What was wrong with him?

He wasn't dependent on a woman. He never felt this way, but when it came to Alex, she was fucking with his head.

****

The basement wasn't so bad.

Several years ago, Liam had donated the money to get it decorated and to turn it into a hangout room for the kids. Just another room for them to enjoy.

Sitting on the sofa in front of Marlo, Cash, and Antonio, Alex started to feel like it was more of a horror movie as they kept looking at her, and she felt so out of place. She didn't know what to say or do.

They just stared at her and Roman as they sat on either end of the sofa. A nice large gap between them.

"This won't do," Antonio said. "You need to sit closer together."

"Noted," Roman said.

"So do it now." Marlo held his hands out and waved them in front of him, pointing for them both to get closer together.

"I don't think we need guidance for this. How hard can it be?" Alex asked.

"When you both came down here, you took the furthest space possible together. If you need to convince a roomful of people staring at you like you're under a microscope, every single little detail of your actions is going to be watched," Cash said. "From the way you both look at each other. So, Alex, you need to get out of eye rolling. That is a serious mark against you."

"Thank you," Roman said. "I told you, you do it all the time."

She rolled her eyes. She just couldn't help it. "He did that on purpose to see me fail."

"And he did it so easily."

"Roman, you're not free from error either. You glare, way too much. A man who glares shows disapproval."

Alex couldn't resist sticking her tongue out at him, and of course, Roman glared. This time, she burst out laughing. "I'm so sorry, but there was a time you looked scary but now, I think you're super cute."

"It's the rainbow," Roman, Antonio, Marlo, and Cash all said at the same time.

To Alex, Roman had lost that scary edge, which wasn't a bad thing. At least, she didn't think so. He was cute and adorable, sexy, manly, and she was so going to stop there. She had never thought of Roman as sexy and manly. Cruel and mean at times, but never sexy.

She had to get her head back on straight. "Let's take this seriously," Alex said.

This was a job for them. They had to be tutored in the art of appearing to like and love each other. It wasn't something she should be turning into a joke, no matter how funny it seemed.

Hands clasped together, she stared at the three men who were watching them.

"This is good," Antonio said. "Being able to laugh at each other and with each other, it is a good sign."

"Think of our audience," Roman said. "Half of

the people there hate each other."

"We know that," Marlo said. "But you're not trying to sell an arranged marriage anymore. With your disappearance, you're adding a whole different spin. You're the rare couple who fell in love after an arranged marriage."

"Hold Alex's hand," Cash said.

Roman took her hand, holding it as if they were strangers.

Cash tutted and approached, arranging their hands so that their fingers were locked together.

"To sell this, you've got to look comfortable touching each other. Alex, stop tensing. Roman, don't glare. You're holding your wife. The woman you're supposed to love. The one you're protecting and showing the world you want," Cash said.

Alex stared off into the corner.

Antonio clicked his fingers. "Stare at each other."

She glared at him and then turned to Roman. "Do you feel this is stupid?" she asked.

"Yeah, I do."

"Keep on staring at each other," Marlo said.

She looked into Roman's eyes, which were so pretty. Her mouth suddenly felt dry.

"What are your plans for tomorrow?" Roman asked.

"I was going to do a game of baseball, but you have banned me from any physical activity."

"You're not doing anything strenuous yet," Roman said.

"You know I feel fine."

"I see you're sometimes in pain, Alex."

"Now kiss her," Cash said.

They both jerked away and turned to their teachers.

"What?" they said at the same time.

"And that is our problem right now," Cash said. "You can randomly talk to each other, and forget you're holding hands, but what you both need to do is to get over this barrier. Regardless of what you both think, I bet you're attracted to each other."

Alex wanted to deny it.

"Roman, your dick is a perfect indicator if you're liking her or not, and Alex, your tits harden. There, I said it," Antonio said. "I've seen the way you both look at each other, and there is an attraction between you. If you would only put aside all of this other bullshit that is going on, you'd be able to work on that."

"We need to give them homework," Marlo said.

"You'll be sharing a room and a bed from tonight onward," Antonio said.

She wanted to refuse and was about to, but they continued with their list of homework.

"Wherever possible, you touch. I don't care where it is, but you touch each other," Marlo said.

"And you have to kiss," Cash said. "That's nonnegotiable. In fact, as your teachers, I say you are going to do that now!"

Alex jerked toward Roman, a little taken aback. "You cannot order us to kiss."

"Be grateful we haven't ordered you to fuck," Antonio said.

"Line!" Roman yelled.

Antonio held his hands up. "We're trying to help you two, remember? We all know what the parasites are like. We don't want ugly-ass rumors to spread."

Alex could only imagine what it was like. She turned to Roman, and instead of waiting for him to make the first move, she grabbed his face and pulled him close.

Slamming her lips down on his, she kissed him.

Her experience in his department was limited to the few kisses she and Roman had shared.

At first, it was just proving a point of being able to kiss Roman in front of these men. Then his hands moved to the base of her back, and slowly, they started to travel up, to sink into her hair. She liked his touch. The feel of his hands on her, and she didn't want him to stop.

She pulled away, a little taken aback.

Roman's gaze captured hers, and without another instruction, he cupped her face and pulled her back for another kiss. His lips were highly addictive.

In the distance, she heard someone clear their throat, but she was enjoying the kiss a little too much.

Roman once again traced across her lips, and this time, she was prepared for it so that when she opened her mouth, and he plundered inside, it didn't take her by surprise. Stroking her tongue against his, she tasted the hint of coffee.

All too soon, the kiss came to an end, and she immediately stood, hating that they had an audience.

"This is the end of the lesson?" Alex asked.

"Same time, tomorrow."

Without a backward glance, Alex moved to the stairs and ran up them, not stopping until she rushed through the house and went to her bedroom.

One glance at the large bed, and she knew Roman would be joining her.

She had already changed and wore her pajamas. As if on cue, Roman followed into the room behind her.

"Do you have a preference for what side of the bed you like?" she asked.

Back at her father's home, she'd avoided sleeping in the same bed as him, but it would seem she wasn't going to be that lucky this time.

"Either side. I don't care."

Alex nodded and took the side nearest the door. Pushing the blankets back, she slid inside and felt a little nervous.

Roman cleared his throat. She kept her eyes closed as she imagined him removing his clothes, preparing to climb into bed.

When the bed moved, she couldn’t help but tense up. This was going to be an awful night’s sleep.

Neither of them spoke.

Alex opened her eyes and stared across the room, not that she could make much of anything out. It was dark.

“I’m sorry about the guys,” Roman said.

“They’re trying to help.”

“Can I at least look at you?”

It was on the tip of her tongue to tell him no but decided there was no point in being difficult at this time. They were both in the same bag here.

She rolled over. It was still dark, but she could make him out as he was close.

“How are you feeling?”

“Fine. You?”

“You don’t have to lie to me.”

“I’ve never shared a bed with anyone,” she said. “At least I haven’t been forced to.”

He laughed.

She noticed he didn’t have the same problem. They were two different people.

“Have you ever fallen in love?” Alex asked.

“No.”

“What about the women you were with before?”

“Alex, I didn’t live like a saint. There were women before you, but since we’ve been together, there hasn’t been another woman. We’re supposed to be getting closer, and I don’t want to make this difficult by dwelling on what happened before."

She nodded. "Right, of course."

Roman touched her cheek. "They didn't matter. I wouldn't care if they lived or died, but with you, I care. It matters to me."

****

"Do you think Roman even realizes he is in love with his wife?" Antonio asked, sipping the beer he'd snuck into the house.

He'd been able to have his day out, and he'd enjoyed the pleasure of three women. Being around kids, he'd needed to feel like a man, and well, three women sucking at his dick and doing nothing but pleasuring him had been welcome. Back here, surrounded by kids, he missed the chaos of the regular dealings of the Greco name.

"No," Marlo said.

"And he's fucking stubborn about it," Cash said.

"At least he's stopped us from trying to win her over," Antonio said. "I don't think Alex is like that though."

"Agreed." Marlo pointed his bottle toward him. "She always seems nervous around us, but not because we're a temptation to her."

"Roman's not used to being near an innocent woman. Look at the women before her. Especially Denise." Cash sipped at his beer.

"I like her," Antonio said.

"Denise?" Marlo and Cash asked at the same time.

"God, no, that woman is a fucking vulture. No, I'm talking about Alex. She isn't afraid of Roman. He can't just walk all over her. She has a fire inside her. I think she's his match, but he's too damn stubborn to realize it." Antonio shook his head. "We've got to help bring them together. Roman will be a lot happier if he's in love."

"We don't know that," Marlo said.

"Look at how he is here."

"This is fucking nightmare central," Cash said.

"So many fucking kids," Marlo said.

"And yet, look at Roman. I saw him smile at a kid. He loves them, guys. You've seen it. I know you have. Alex is good for him. They're good for each other, and we have a duty as his friend to make sure he doesn't fuck it up." Antonio had been by Roman's side for as long as he could remember. They were as close as brothers. All of them. He knew the kind of shit Roman had to put up with. The intense training, the lack of love, and even the modicum of comfort. Lucas Greco needed a strong son, and to do that, he did what he thought was best.

Roman was a monster. He was cruel and fair, and he did what he had to do. But it had come with a cost.

Little by little, Antonio had watched his friend slowly disappear. Only with Alex had he seen the old Roman, the one who enjoyed life, who took his responsibility but also knew how to have fun. He was starting to come back, and if it meant he had to push Alex and Roman together, then he was going to do it. What he needed to do was make sure Roman didn't fuck it up.

Chapter Eleven

"Put your hand on her waist," Antonio said.

Roman placed his hand on Alex's waist, and she immediately tensed up.

"I'm sorry. I'm sorry." Alex let go of him and stepped back.

"It's fine. We can go again. I'll keep touching you until we get this right."

Her face was bright red, and she turned toward him, putting her hands back on his shoulders.

He touched her waist, and she twinged.

"I'm not used to dancing."

Roman knew what she was really saying. She wasn't used to being held by a man. Once again proving her innocence and making him feel like an utter bastard.

"You know what," Marlo said, "we need to bring some music in to play." He turned the stereo on, and a dance number started to play. He clicked his fingers and began to swing his hips. "And you just have to let the music come to you."

"I don't dance," Alex said.

"Come on, Roman," Cash said. "You know how to dance."

"The glare! Bad point to Roman."

A chart was hung on the board, and each time he glared, he was struck with a bad point. If Alex rolled her eyes, she got a point as well. So far, he was the one with the bad points as he kept on glaring. Alex had a few eye-roll moments, but not enough.

She stood there, stepping from side to side, and her hands were so tense by her side. "I have no idea what I'm doing."

Roman laughed, and then he started to dance,

feeling the beat of the music as he swung his hips. "You have to relax. Here, let me show you." He took hold of her hands and spun her around so that her back was to him. "Close your eyes."

Alex shut her eyes, and he moved her so that her ass was nestled against his hips. He had to grit his teeth and concentrate as he felt the warm heat against his dick. That morning, their first sleeping together in a bed, he'd woken with Alex snuggled against his chest. He had his arms wrapped around her, her face was on his chest, and her leg was nestled between his.

He'd never slept against a woman before. Alex was his first.

When she told him last night, he'd wanted to admit the truth to her, but he also didn't want to … he didn't know what he wanted to do, but he'd kept the truth from her.

He'd fucked plenty of women, but he never wanted to give them the impression that he wanted more from them. Roman always left.

Alex was the first woman he'd slept with, all night long. The first woman who'd ever snuggled up against him. And he'd fucking loved it.

Placing his hands on her hips, he started to sway her body. She was tense to start with, but the music loosened her up, and he had no choice but to put a little space between them because he was getting harder by the second.

Alex was his wife. He should already be fucking her, and yet, he hadn't crossed that line with her, not yet. He wanted to, so badly.

It had been a long time since he'd taken care of his needs.

The music suddenly stopped, and Marlo, Cash, and Antonio looked pretty happy with themselves.

"Alex didn't tense one, and you've got your hands on her waist," Antonio said.

The moment they pointed it out, she tensed up and stepped away from him.

"I think we can leave it here for tonight," Marlo said.

"Not yet, kiss," Cash said.

Roman wanted to hit them all hard, but instead, he pulled Alex against him and kissed her lips. She softened against him instantly.

His dick wasn't softening though. He needed to go and take care of that.

"Homework," Antonio said. "I want you to look at each other without your clothes on."

"What?" Alex asked as Roman glared.

"Another point."

"What the hell, Antonio?" Roman asked.

Another strike was put by his name, and then Marlo and Cash both put a point next to his name, but that wasn't fair. The glare hadn't stopped.

"Now I think you're being unfair," Alex said.

"You're still glaring!"

"What do you expect?" Alex asked. "You're asking us to get naked with each other!"

Antonio sighed and looked toward Marlo and Cash. "I should explain everything, shouldn't I?" He didn't wait for an answer. "You are husband and wife. I was there to witness the tradition of the bloody sheets, yet we all know that you two have not slept together. I bet even strangers would put a bet on whether you guys have fucked or not. You're going into enemy territory, keeping her injury a secret. You need to look like you've been so loved up, and you're training for that. Staring at each other naked, that's what couples do. You need to be comfortable with each other with your clothes fucking on, and you can't even touch each other unless there is a distraction of music. We're on a countdown. You're married. Act like it."

This time, Antonio was the first one to walk away.

Roman looked at Marlo and Cash, and they shrugged but followed Antonio out of the basement.

"Is it me, or did he sound … right?"

"He sounded right," Roman said.

"I'm starting to hate this basement."

"You and me both." He couldn't be naked in front of her, not with his hard dick. He had to take care of that first.

"I'm going to head upstairs," Alex said.

"I'm coming."

This was different from last night. They didn't have to do their homework, but Antonio was right, like always. Why did he have to be right?

Closing the basement door, Roman tried not to look at her curvy ass, but with the way it swayed in front of his face, he wanted to grab her, to press his face against the lush curves. They made it into the bedroom, and as soon as he closed the door, he made his excuses and escaped into the bathroom.

Roman didn't linger. He immediately removed his clothes, being careful as he lowered the zipper across his dick. The moment he was free, he released a sigh of relief and stepped into the shower.

The sudden cold blast of water was supposed to help calm his arousal, but his cock was still rock hard. He stayed under the water, waiting for it to heat up, and in the process, to cool the fire in his blood, but nothing helped.

Wrapping his fingers around his hard length, he groaned as in his mind, Alex flashed. Her beautiful smile that he'd seen on her face so much since she'd been here. Within seconds, he thought of her completely naked and pressed all against him. He imagined her whispering the sweet words, ordering him to fuck her, to take her.

Roman wanted to feel her body and touch her. In the last few weeks, that was all he'd been thinking about. To have her body pressed against his and to be free to touch her whenever he wanted, without fear of her being scared of his touch.

His balls started to tighten, and he felt the stirrings of his orgasm. It had been a long time since he'd taken care of matters with his own hand, but as he came, he gritted his teeth, trying to hide the grunt of his release.

Keeping his eyes closed, he allowed his sanity to return, and the moment it did, he finished washing his body, ran some shampoo through his hair, and then turned the water off before stepping out.

He grabbed a towel and wrapped it around his body.

One glance in the mirror, and he saw he looked a little flushed, but that could easily be explained by his shower.

He moved into the main room and saw Alex sitting on the edge of the bed.

Roman paused.

She wore a pair of pajama shorts and a tank top a couple of sizes too big for her.

"Hey," she said.

"What's the matter?"

"It's a tiny stupid thing, but I've never, I mean, it's, ugh … I've never failed on homework before." She turned away from him and lifted her hands toward her face. "I know this is stupid, and your friends are not exactly teachers, but what if they're right? It sounds so stupid, but what if they are right?"

"Alex, you don't have to do anything you don't want to do. Antonio was just, in all honesty, I don't know what he was doing, but you don't have to get naked for me." He wanted her to, and he couldn't understand why he wasn't all over this opportunity.

"Do you not want to see me naked? I could totally understand that."

"I've already got over a dozen marks for glaring. I'm not going to lose more points for being blamed for not doing homework."

"You just said it didn't matter. They're not teachers."

"But we are married," he said.

"So? A lot of couples have absolutely nothing to do with each other."

"Do you want that?" he asked.

"I'm happy to live like it if I have to."

"That doesn't answer the question."

Alex had turned toward him, and she groaned. "I don't know what to do. I've never been given homework like this before, and to be honest, I would normally tell my dad."

Roman released the knot on his towel and let it fall to the floor.

There he was, completely naked for her to see. The Greco emblem on his chest, just above his heart. He had a couple of pieces of ink as well, some on his arms, a few on his back. Mindless pieces that had caught his eyes.

"Does this answer your question?" he asked.

She hadn't covered her eyes.

"Now, I'll get the A star and you'll get the F."

"Hey! That's not fair."

He put his hands on his hips. Never in all of his life had he been in a situation like this. Being tutored by his friends to appear closer to his wife. Waiting for her to get naked and also anticipating it.

Roman wanted to see her completely naked for his gaze.

Alex gripped the waistband of her shorts and shoved them down his thighs. Next, she grabbed the top and eased it off her head. Then, she stood before him, bare, proud, and fucking stunning.

Only, she covered her body or at least attempted to with her hands.

"You don't have to hide from me."

"I've never … this is the first time… I've never been naked, okay?"

"I'm not going to hurt you."

Far from it.

Alex was … she was curvy in all the right places. She had nice juicy thighs, thick, like he could grab hold of them as they were wrapped around his waist as he pounded inside her. He wanted to feel them. She possessed full hips, nicely rounded, as was her stomach, a slightly small waist, and large tits.

Her body looked soft and fuckable, and he wanted to take her. Even though he'd taken care of his dick a few minutes ago, he wanted her again, really badly.

****

"You really are a virgin, aren't you?" he asked.

Alex's face couldn't get any redder. She couldn't believe he'd ask her that.

"Seriously? I'm standing here naked and that is what you're focusing on."

"I assumed you lied."

"I told you the truth," she said.

"I still thought you lied."

"Do you have a hard time trusting people?" she

asked.

"Alex, I'm used to people lying to me. They always do to get what they want. I'm always assuming people are lying to me."

Roman wasn't supposed to appear human, or nice, or for her to feel sorry for him in any way, but he was doing it right now. "I promise you that I won't ever lie to you," Alex said.

"Don't make promises you can't keep."

"I've never lied," Alex said. "Even when you've asked me if I've wanted to be married to you. The answer was no. I didn't want to ever get married. If what you say is true and everyone has lied to you in the past, then I make it my vow and promise to you, as your wife, I will never lie to you."

"Never?"

She shook her head and then agreed. "Never. I'll always tell you the truth."

"Would you like me to fuck you right now?" Roman asked.

Her eyes went wide, and she couldn't help but look down at his enormous dick. She assumed he had a tiny one because his attitude was so sucky, but it would seem Roman was blessed. Not only was he good looking, he also had an amazing dick.

"Er, I, er, I don't know how to answer that."

Roman took a step toward her. "It's simple. You and I are going to have sex, eventually. Would you be opposed to sleeping with me?"

This wasn't fair.

She promised him she wouldn't lie.

Sex was a huge step for her, but seeing as she said she wouldn't lie, she said, "Yes, I would like to, but not right now."

He was so close as he took another step.

Why was he closing the gap between them?

Her mouth felt a little dry.

"Why not now?" he asked.

She tilted her head back to look at him.

"I'm not ready," she said.

Roman reached out and touched her face, cupping her cheek. At first, she tensed. "One day, I hope you won't flinch against my touch."

"I don't mean to. I'm not used to men touching me."

"Men won't be touching you, Alex. Just me." He put his other hand on her face, and she watched him, wondering what he was going to do next, curious about his next move.

Only his hands on her face were touching.

She opened and closed her hands, not sure if she should touch him or not.

"I'm going to kiss you," he said.

"Okay."

"If you need me to stop, tap my back." He let her go, taking hold of her hands and placing them on his back. "Like this." He showed her how to stop him. It was a simple tap to the back.

"I can do that."

"Good."

His hands were back on her face, and she stared at him, waiting.

Slowly, he lowered his head, and then they held themselves still, their breaths mingling.

"I can't believe this is happening," she said.

"Me either. When did your lips get so … kissable?"

She didn't have time to answer because he slammed his lips down on hers, silencing any protest from her, and she moaned his name, but it got lost in the kiss.

Alex didn’t move her hands from his back, and she slowly trailed them up his body, sinking into his hair.

Roman’s hands moved as well, sliding into her hair before gliding down her body. When he grabbed her ass and hauled her against him, she was a little taken aback by the sheer force of him. Then he started to move her back, and Alex followed his lead.

The back of her legs hit the bed, and Roman slowly lowered her down.

She tensed up.

“I’m not going to fuck you. I promise. You’ve got to trust me. I won’t … hurt you.”

Alex nodded, and he started to trail his lips down her body, taking her by surprise as he went to her neck. There was a slight stubble on his face, and as he teased her neck, the sensations rushed through her body, taking her by surprise at the sheer pleasure. She had never felt this way before.

She whimpered his name, and he flicked his tongue across her pulse before gliding down her body. When he came to her breasts, Alex didn’t know what to do. Should she stop him or let him keep going?

As his lips touched across one nipple, stroking over the nub, Alex cried out his name, arching up and not wanting it to stop.

The pleasure shot straight between her legs, taking her by surprise. She pressed her thighs together, trying to ease the ache building within her.

Roman’s hand went to her thighs, slid between, and eased them open.

Alex followed his lead as she wasn’t quite sure what to do and what to say.

Roman was everywhere. She didn’t want to say no either. Was she crazy for giving in to this man? She felt so.

His tongue trailed down the path between the valley of her tits and moved to her other nipple as he devoted his time to teasing that one.

"You have amazing tits," Roman said. He cupped both of them in his palms, kneading the flesh, and she stared down at him as he pressed a kiss to each rounded breast. "Did you know I've thought about these?" he asked.

"What?"

Roman chuckled. "You're so fucking innocent, aren't you? My sweet little virginal bride."

"Roman?"

"Don't worry, I am going to wait. You'll stay a virgin for now, but I'm going to show you what I can do to you." He started to slide down, kissing across her stomach.

Her body wasn't perfect. She had lumps and bumps, and until marrying Roman, she hadn't cared what they meant. It was her body, and she loved herself just the way she was. Growing up with Millie and her father, they had never made her feel ashamed of the fact she liked food. She was okay with exercises, but she much preferred to spend her time in front of her sewing machine or chasing after kids. Her dad had a full gym back at home, but that had no appeal to her whatsoever.

Running at nothing, toward nothing, wasn't something she wanted to do, and she doubted she ever would.

"Trust me, Alex," he said.

He kept on asking her to do that, and she was trying.

Roman moved between her legs, and as he did, he had no choice but to spread them open. She stared down at him, waiting, curious as to what he was going to do next. She was innocent, but she had a curious nature, and so she knew what sex entailed. She would be lying if she said porn didn't arouse her.

It had.

She'd been curious about sex, had wanted it, but she also didn't want to lose her virginity to anyone. All her life, she'd been nervous around boys. She had no idea why, but she was never comfortable with them. Her dad had often said the time would come when she'd find the right man to be with.

She had never found anyone she wanted to be with.

Roman's hands moved up the inside of her thighs.

"And I bet you've never been touched like this before," he said.

"That's what a virgin means, right? Untouched."

"You never let a boy touch you?" he asked.

"Never."

"Not even to kiss you."

She gasped as he pressed a kiss to her pussy. "No."

The tips of his fingers grazed over the lips of her sex, and she gasped his name as he opened her up.

"Then let me take care of you and show you that there is nothing to be afraid of."

She wanted to tell him there was everything to be afraid of, but then his lips and tongue were on her body, and the pleasure was … she couldn't believe she had lived so long without knowing what this felt like. The instant hit of sensations traveled through her whole body, sparking something inside her.

Alex nearly jerked off the bed at the force of it.

Roman's hands moved to her ass, and he started to work the flesh. Even that added to the sensation of what he was doing between her thighs.

"I've got you, Alex. Let go. Trust me."

His tongue lapped at her clit, stroking across her nub, and then he sucked her into his mouth, and she couldn't control herself. She cried out his name and arched up, feeling this pull within her body. It was coiling tighter, almost instant, and she knew she was heading toward something amazing.

She had given herself orgasms before, but nothing ever prepared her for this.

Within a matter of seconds of him touching her pussy, Alex found her release, and she came hard, fast, taking her completely by surprise, but Roman didn't stop. He held her at that pinnacle, not letting her come down, and it was almost too much.

The heat and pleasure radiated out, and she couldn't stop it, not once it started. She had no choice but to lift up and tap him on the back as she couldn't take anymore.

Roman was true to his word, and he stopped the moment she asked him to.

Collapsing to the bed, she took several deep breaths. Her body still shook a little from the aftershocks of her orgasm.

"I'm sorry," Roman said.

Alex turned toward him, startled. "What?"

He placed his hand on her hip. "You heard me."

"Why are you apologizing?" she asked.

"I thought you were lying."

"You still didn't believe I was a virgin."

He shrugged. "I guess I didn't see the big deal in the test."

"There has never been anyone."

"And now that you're mine, there never will be anyone else."

"How do you know that?" she asked. "I could

have any lover I wanted."

"No," he said.

She knew from that voice and that tone that any man she tried to take as a lover would end up dead. "I wouldn't do it," she said, rolling her eyes.

"I'm telling Antonio about that one."

"And I'm telling him about the glare you're giving me." Alex glanced at him. "Do you need me to … ugh?" She had no idea what she was doing, or how to ask him if he wanted her to give him an orgasm.

Roman took her hand and pressed a kiss to her knuckles. "Already taken care of," he said.

"It is?"

"I had no choice but to handle it in the bathroom."

"You were … masturbating?"

He chuckled. "Damn, you're cute. How come I've never noticed this before?" he asked.

"I can't believe you were doing that."

"It wasn't part of the test but just thinking about seeing you naked was enough to drive me crazy."

Alex rolled onto her side, staring at him. "Will you take any … lovers?" she asked. She bit her lip as she stared at him.

"Do you want me to?" he asked.

She shook her head. "No."

"Then I won't."

"But, what if I don't … you have desires."

"And when the time comes, you'll be ready to deal with them, Alex. If you don't want me to take lovers, then I won't, but you've got to promise me that you're going to be ready to allow me to have you. To not hold back and to not be afraid," he said. "I'll take my time with you. I'll love you. I'll be everything you need me to be."

"Okay," she said, and knowing he wouldn't take another woman, she felt … better. Roman belonged to her now, and she was his, and that felt right to her.

Chapter Twelve

Alex had gotten the all-clear from the doctor. There was no damage inside, and her stitches had completely healed. Roman kissed around the small bandage on her stomach the other night, and he watched her now, chasing after kids.

They were all having a lot of fun, and he couldn't tear his gaze away from her. She looked so happy and at peace, and to him, that was beautiful.

"Do you love her?" Stuart asked, coming to sit with him.

This little boy would randomly come and sit with him. He was a cute kid, and if Roman was being honest, the longer he spent at the orphanage, all the kids were starting to grow on him.

He liked being around them. Even at breakfast and at dinner, when they were all arguing about what they wanted to eat. Millie would randomly visit with baked goodies, and he'd started to develop a sweet tooth.

Did he want to lie to the kid?

"I don't know what love is," Roman said. "Do you?"

Stuart sighed.

He found it cute that he tried to seem tough, worldly even.

"Yeah, I know love," Stuart said, in his adorable young voice. Words that he shouldn't be able to speak, but he knew Alex and the other kids had a play in helping this boy. "Alex makes you feel love."

"What is love though, kid?" he asked. "You can't touch it or see it."

Stuart pursed his lips. "You're wrong," he said after several seconds had passed.

"I don't think so, kid."

The young boy smiled. "Alex. You can see her. She is real. She loves a lot, and you can see it. When she hugs me and kisses my cheek, I feel it. Alex is full of love."

Roman stared at his wife and knew the kid was right.

"You're right," he said, ruffling his head.

"You love her, but you don't realize it yet. Alex has a way of making you love her."

"Oh, yeah, how does she do that?" Roman asked, and he couldn't believe he was listening to a kid for advice.

"She doesn't give up on you, and she doesn't force it." Stuart got to his feet, and much to Roman's surprise, he hugged him tightly before running off to join in the fun.

Alex tapped out, laughing and a little out of breath.

Roman held up a glass of fresh water, and she came toward him to take it and sip at it.

"Thanks. It has been too long since I've been chasing after kids," she said, hand on hip.

"You should be taking it easy."

"The doctor gave me the all-clear. I do not need to worry, trust me."

"I worry, and I don't want you to hurt yourself."

"I won't, I promise." She sat down beside him. "I saw Stuart coming to say hi. How was he?"

"I honestly don't know. Is that a good thing?" he asked.

She started to laugh. "Stuart's a good kid. He doesn't trust easily, but he gave you a hug. That is a big thing in his world. It means he does trust you, a little." She held her fingers close together.

"Ah, just a little though."

"You don't want to push it," she said, laughing.

"You love all of them, don't you?" he asked.

At first, he thought it was just Stuart, but he came to realize she loved all of them. They were a part of her life. Stuart just needed a little extra help, but she was here for all of them, and what Roman liked was that they all adored her.

"Yeah, I do. They're good kids. I wish I could give them what they want."

"And what's that?" he asked.

"A family. Parents. You know, the security of knowing they're being taken care of."

"You can have that," Roman said.

"I can't, my dad, he said I can't do it."

"And you're with me now, Alex. I'm not your dad, and if you want us to have these kids, and to help raise them, then I don't see why we can't," Roman said.

Alex turned toward him, her eyes wide. "Don't do that," she said.

"Don't do what?"

"Don't make promises you can't keep."

"Let me look into it. I'll make the arrangements, and we can adopt them, give them the proper life you want. You know, all of it," he said.

Roman didn't even know where this was coming from, he just knew he wanted her to be happy, and the only way to do that was to give them all a chance.

Alex threw her arms around him and hugged him tight. "Thank you."

He wasn't doing this to gain her trust or to make her love him. Roman was being honest, and if he was being entirely truthful, a little selfish.

His father would throw a fit over what he was about to do, but he had a valid reason. By his own orders, he had to make Alex fall in love with him. He was just getting what he wanted in different ways. There were no limits to what he could do to make her fall in love with him.

Alex pulled away and pressed a kiss to his cheek. He watched her go. She wore a skirt this time, and an oversized shirt. There was a slight wind that would show off those glorious curves, and it reminded him of the other night, of having her naked body in his arms. They hadn't had any more lessons from Antonio, Marlo, or Cash, as he'd been called away to speak with his father and Liam.

They were running out of possible leads, and he saw Liam was starting to panic. He was used to being one step ahead of the enemy, not floundering in an ocean of monsters all around him.

He was usually the biggest monster around.

Roman didn't have a clue who it could be, but he wasn't going to risk Alex's life. They had to find the person responsible, and fast.

****

"You seem happy," Millie said.

Alex looked up at her oldest friend and gave her a hug. "I am."

"No night terrors?"

She shook her head. "None."

"That's good. I guess being surrounded by kids and having Roman and those three handsome men around you can help take the nightmares away."

She rolled her eyes. "Very subtle."

Millie held her hands up in mock surrender. "What?"

"Nothing is…"

"You were going to say happening, but seeing as you stopped, I guess that would be lying."

"I can so lie."

"Badly. We all know the truth about the horror movies," Millie said.

Alex smiled. It was a long-running joke between her and her father, so that couldn't be an awful lie, not if her dad was aware of it.

"I don't know what is happening. We're not arguing or fighting, so I guess that's good."

"There's this smile and a twinkle in your eye, Alex. Does that mean…" Millie's gaze roamed down her body, and Alex rolled her eyes.

Since Antonio had pointed it out, she realized she did it a lot. "No, it doesn't mean that. Roman's different here. For one, he's not a complete and total asshole. He's nice, and we're getting along."

"But?"

"No buts, I don't think. We're in a good place."

"It took your life being in danger for you to find a good place."

Alex laughed. "Yeah, you could say that."

"You know, I trust your instincts, but when it comes to Roman, you have always been a little hesitant with him. Why?"

"He's a stranger to me, Millie."

"I know he is, but do you have no feelings for him at all? He is the first guy I've ever seen you openly dislike. You don't give him a chance at first. Why?"

Alex glanced out into the yard. The kids were lying on the grass, soaking up the sun. Roman had brought them all beach towels and sunglasses. They couldn't make the trip to the beach, but he could help bring the beach to them, which also included a sand pit.

She didn't know how he'd gotten to do that in the past couple of hours, but he had. The kids loved him.

"I didn't know him, and every time I tried to get

to know him, he'd be mean, and he didn't have time for me."

"For fuck sake, Alex, leave me the fuck alone."

"That doesn't look right. You look like a fucking Victorian maid."

"Do I look interested?"

Alex thought over the two months they were married. It wasn't easy. Roman never had a nice thing to say to her. She knew deep down that he didn't want to be married to her.

"I knew he had other women. I overheard them at the wedding, and when he had no patience with me, and I was getting things wrong, I guess I just decided that I wasn't going to allow myself to fall for a man who wasn't ever going to be mine."

"Honey."

"Mom and Dad had something, Millie. I know I wasn't old enough to see it, but the photos he has of her. I know he's taken lovers, but none of them mean anything to him. He's never had another girlfriend. Never been happy like he was in all the pictures with Mom. I grew up seeing them, and that's what I wanted. Is that wrong?"

"No, baby, not wrong. I just wished your dad knew what he was doing. At least Roman is seeing things differently now."

Alex looked toward the window and shrugged.

"You're having your doubts?"

"I don't trust as easily as I think I should." When it came to Roman, she wanted to trust this side of him, but she had caught the way he'd been looking at her. It was subtle, but it was like he was trying to work her out. She had to wonder why. Between offering to adopt the kids and talking about a future with them, not to mention how his friends seemed to be intent on forcing them together, something didn't sit right with Alex.

Was Roman forcing her to have feelings for him?

She had started to have feelings for him, and that was what scared her. He was breaking through her defenses so easily.

What if this was all a game? Why would he change after two months of being one kind of guy? It made no sense.

"Have you ever thought that he didn't know what you were like, but now that he does, he's smitten and wants to get to know you on a deeper level?" Millie asked.

"I'm sure you're right."

But again, the niggle of doubt entered her mind, and she couldn't push it away. It was there, rooted in her mind, not giving up or letting go.

****

"This is progress," Antonio said, pointing at them.

They sat close together, holding hands. The moment Roman sat down, he'd moved closer to Alex, and she had done the same. Their knees were touching, and their hands were locked together.

Roman was worried about looking at her.

Today had gone so well with the kids. They'd been excited about him bringing the beach to them. Some had complained there were no sharks, but he considered that a good thing, seeing as sharks meant death. Several of the guys and even a few of the girls were fascinated by sharks and would often be watching them on television, especially documentaries.

He had to find them all new hobbies.

The guardians were still in residence and had been the whole time, and he'd left them alone to go find Alex, to let her know he had a lawyer looking into the adoption process, when he heard her talking to Millie.

She suspected him.

Alex wasn't stupid, and he was fast coming to realize that. He hadn't had a chance to talk to his friends about what he'd overheard. This wasn't good for him.

Liam had raised a very astute daughter. He couldn't be angry because the truth was, his feelings toward her and his actions were mixed.

He was trying to get her to fall in love with him at the order of his father. The adoption, licking her pussy, and enjoying spending time with her, that was real. Roman also knew why she had her doubts. He hadn't been a very nice guy to her in the beginning.

His anger should have been directed at his father and Liam, but instead, like a fucking idiot, he'd directed it at his wife.

The first couple of months of their marriage, he hadn't said anything nice to her. He'd not had the time for her. He'd done everything he could to ignore her. But what he hadn't done was cheat on her. There were no other women. Just Alex.

Not even his hand.

Sex had been the furthest thing from his mind as he'd been dealing with Liam and all the new problems having a new tie to the Greco name incurred.

"We're good students," Alex said.

Antonio nodded and took a seat.

He waited for Marlo and Cash to stand up, to give their orders.

Nothing.

"What's going on?" Alex asked.

"We've been trying this for a week now, and we've come a great deal, but we've been talking," Marlo said, pointing between himself, Cash, and Antonio. "And we don't think we're the ones who can help you guys.

You two need to want this. We've given you all the pointers to help. The constant touching, kissing, dancing, and just being in each other's company, but the rest of it has to come from the two of you. And we can't do that for you."

His friends got to their feet, and then they started to walk toward the stairs. "We'll be in the kitchen if you need us," Cash said.

And like that, he was alone in the basement with his wife.

"Wow," Alex said.

"Yeah, wow."

They were still holding hands and still sat close to each other. Roman didn't have a fucking clue what to do.

"We have one week to get this right," Alex said.

"No, we don't," Roman said. "Look at how far we've come already. I don't want us to put too much pressure on ourselves. There's no need to." He forced a smile to his lips. "We'll be ourselves next week. There's no reason to panic."

Alex frowned. "That's a new … tactic."

"Not a tactic. I don't want to play a role to anyone else." Roman let go of her hands and got to his feet. He watched as she stifled a yawn. "And you're tired."

"I'm fine. I'll do whatever you need me to do."

Again, she tried to stifle a yawn.

"Go to bed, that's an order."

She rolled her eyes again.

"I'll put that down on the board."

She chuckled, and he looked toward the board at their names as well as their weaknesses. Roman walked over and rubbed it all off.

Making his way to the main house, he closed the basement door and found his friends in the small study, sipping bottles of beer.

"Sneaking it in again?" Roman asked.

"Someone has to. There is no hard stuff here but a can of soda," Cash said. "Want one?"

Roman shook his head. He stopped drinking beer years ago. He was a scotch man himself.

"Alex suspects what we're doing," Roman said. "What I'm doing."

"Which part?" Antonio asked.

"Manipulating her to fall in love with me," Roman said.

"How?" Marlo asked.

"I don't know how she knows, but I heard her talking to Millie today."

"Oh," Cash said.

"Yeah, oh. I can only guess that Liam has taught her to be cautious of everyone and everything."

"You're her husband. Can't that be a good enough reason?" Marlo asked.

"You'd think so, only I don't have the best track record when it comes to Alex. I wasn't exactly a prince in the early days." He sat down on the edge of an old, worn chair.

"So, what's the plan?" Antonio asked.

"I don't have a plan. I don't know what to do."

"You've got to keep doing what your dad told you to do," Marlo said. "It's important for everyone that this marriage works. It has been close to falling apart several times."

"I know."

"Why don't you just fuck her and get it over with?" Cash asked.

"I'm not going to force her. She's not ready." Roman ran a hand down his face.

"If you guys don't convince the Greco line, we'll

never find out who tried to kill her," Antonio said.

"We will. Alex and I, we'll make this work." He got to his feet and made his way out of the room.

"Is there a chance you could be falling for her?" Cash asked.

Roman was only in the doorway. He glanced back at his friends, and the truth was, he didn't have an answer to that question.

He left them alone and made his way up to his bedroom where Alex was already lying in bed.

At first, he thought she was awake, but as he moved further into the room, he saw she was fast asleep. He stepped close to her and stared down at her face. She was a beautiful woman. One of his exes had said she looked mousy, but he didn't see that. She was lovely.

His mother had described Alex as that. Roman had figured it was a way of saying she wasn't beautiful or ugly, but in between, but he knew now what his mother meant. Alex was a lovely person. She was sweet, kind, and everything their life chewed up and destroyed.

He didn't want to be responsible for ruining her life.

Teasing back a stray curl, he wished it would be so easy to turn his back on her, but it wouldn't be. In the past few weeks, Alex had gotten beneath his skin, and he feared there was no way back from that. He had gotten a small taste of lovely, and it was enough to make him addicted. To yearn for more, to beg for it.

Alex was his.

He couldn't let her go.

Not now.

He needed her.

****

"What is all this?" Alex asked.

"The kids are out on their day trip to the museum,

and we're all alone," Roman said.

Alex was so disappointed that she couldn't go. Of course, the kids had offered to stay home to be with her, but she refused to let them miss such an amazing opportunity and had demanded they all go and bring her back knowledge.

This left her alone with Roman, Antonio, and Marlo. Cash had left the house.

Roman poured some bottled water into a champagne glass. He'd set up a little picnic for them on the grass.

With no kids running around them, they didn't have to worry about any potential collisions or stampedes of feet.

"And what is all of this?" Alex asked.

"This is a late celebration of the fact you got out of the hospital. You have recovered, and we're on course for an adoption."

"You do know adoption takes a long time," Alex said.

"Yeah, it does, to others who don't have the Greco name."

She shook her head. "You're not doing anything illegal, are you?"

"No, not at all. I'm making sure my wife gets what she wants."

"Is it what you want?"

"I never considered myself father material, but I think those kids are going to teach me quickly."

She took a deep breath. "You're sure you're making the right decision? Your dad will be pissed."

Roman shrugged. "I'm taking care of my wife. He's going to be pissed regardless. He likes to make all the decisions."

She held her glass up to him. "To meddling,

controlling fathers."

"I will toast to that." They clinked their glasses together. "I thought Liam wasn't so … controlling?"

"He's … not, but he is. He likes to think he gives me the freedom to make my own choices, but to be honest, he has always pushed me to where he wants me to go. Taking over this place was what I truly wanted to do. To give those kids a family, but he told me I was too young to know what I was doing. I guess that was the first time that I realized he was controlling. Then, of course, was the dinner date where he told me that he had a proposition for me. Within three hours, I was engaged, and my life changed forever." She sighed.

"I was under the impression you wanted the marriage."

"We were both lied to and manipulated." She took a long sip of her drink and held it up for more.

"Wow, Mrs. Greco, at this rate, you will be properly hydrated."

She chuckled, and he filled her glass with water. "I will do the proper lady way and only take a sip."

Alex gave him an example, and he bowed his head to her.

They both chuckled, and it was moments like this that Alex had to doubt her insecurities. This wasn't forced or fake. To Alex, this felt natural. There was no one around. His two friends were in the games room, which Roman, Antonio, Marlo, and Cash had all set up.

The peace and quiet was nice.

The only problem with it was when she was reminded of why she was here. "You know, my life has always been in danger. Being my father's daughter and all, but I never realized just how much it was."

"I'll protect you."

"Don't you think it's a little … strange? That you

have to protect me?"

Roman shook his head. "I've been fighting my whole life."

"You mentioned how controlling your dad was. I assumed it was just because of the wedding, and you guys have arranged marriages all the time, don't you?"

"We do."

"But that's not what you meant when you said your dad was controlling?"

"No, it wasn't."

"How is he controlling?" she asked and then held her hands up. "You don't have to tell me."

"It's fine. I'm the heir to his empire. To all of this, and he needed to make sure that I was ready. He couldn't have a weak son take the helm, and so, from as young as I can remember, it has been one test after another."

"Test?"

"Yeah, stupid stuff, like telling me not to take the cupcake, and if I took the cupcake, I'd face the consequences, but to not take the cupcake would also have consequences as well."

Alex frowned. "What?"

"If I took the cupcake, I was disobeying his instruction, and that was bad. If I didn't take the cupcake, I wasn't being a leader and taking what I wanted."

"You were in a no-win situation."

"I was," Roman said.

"You were."

"Yeah, what I did was ask for the cupcake. That was what I needed to do. I was then showing my dad respect and still going after what I wanted. That's what he wanted."

"How long did it take you to figure that out?" Alex asked.

"I did it on my first try." Roman sipped his water. "But that is what started it all. Dad said I have an inbuilt alpha role. He's always talking about that shit. How there are some men who are alphas, leaders, and others who are betas and designed to take orders, like my brother."

"Your brother, Phillip, right?"

"Yep."

"Have I met him?"

"Yes, you have met all of my brothers and sisters."

"And you're not close?" she asked.

"No."

"Why not?"

"It doesn't pay my father for his children to be close."

"So have you all been competing for his attention or to be better than each other?" Alex asked.

"No. We don't have to. As my dad said, there's no competition. I'll be the one in charge, the boss, and everyone else will learn to fall in line."

"That must have been tough," she said.

"Not really. As you can see, I was never close to any of my siblings. Most of my life I've been training and preparing to take over. To lead."

Alex didn't like it. The life he spoke of was one of loneliness. "I'm sorry."

"Why?" he asked.

"It sounds lonely. You were all alone."

"Alex, I wasn't alone. I had Antonio, Marlo, and Cash. You want to know what we all have in common?" he asked.

"You're all firstborns."

"Anyone ever tell you, you're a bit of a pain-in-the-ass know-it-all?"

She smiled and rested her head on his arm. "It

would seem only you get to tell me that."

"Damn straight."

Why did this feel good?

Roman took her hand and locked their fingers together, and to Alex, it felt like the most natural thing in the world.

Chapter Thirteen

"I don't know if I can do this," Alex said.

Her hand was a little clammy within his. The limousine that had come to pick them up was slowing down, about to enter the gates of his father's mansion.

This wasn't the house where he grew up. Lucas Greco had a lot of suspicions and paranoia, so the home he entertained his people in was not the same home he lived in. Although there were often a few close-knit events at his main home, they were never the ones for such large gatherings.

"Your father is going to be there. I'm there. Antonio, Marlo, and Cash are going to be there."

Alex turned to him. "That's not helping."

"What's the matter? If you're afraid someone is going to attack you…"

"No, I'm not afraid. I don't, us, getting this right tonight. I don't want to be responsible for potentially killing people, Roman."

He took her hand within his and kissed her knuckles. This had to be the first time in his entire life that he'd ever truly been close to a woman. Really close. Kissing, snuggling, going to bed together without sex, talking about pointless shit. He'd never done that with any woman.

"We've got this. I'm going to be by your side the entire night. You don't have to worry. I promise you."

The limousine came to a stop outside of the house, and he stared up at the main doors. Soldiers were placed all around the house, and he spotted several up on the roof. This was standard procedure for any event, but even still, it made him a little nervous about the threat held against his wife.

"You're right. I'm being silly. We've got this. We've totally got this."

And she still took in deep breaths.

"What are you most nervous about?" he asked.

"Getting this wrong, flinching away from your touch. Panicking. I'm not used to being in the spotlight. I'd rather be back home, watching a movie with the kids, or, you know, lying in bed."

Roman placed his hand on her thigh and slowly started to tease up her leg. It had already been too long since he last touched her. Each night that he'd come up to bed, Alex had been fast asleep, so he had no choice but to take care of himself in the bathroom. Otherwise, he would've made a total fool of himself.

"What are you doing?" she asked.

"Do you need me to relax you? I can stroke this pretty pussy, get you nice and wet, and not let you come. You'll be so relaxed and begging for me to take care of it later." He cupped her face with his other hand, his thumb tracing across her full lips. "And you'd enjoy it. I know you liked having my tongue on your pussy, Alex."

"Roman?" She gasped his name, and he couldn't resist taking possession of her lips and kissing her hard and deep.

It had been too long since he'd felt those lips against his, even though it was just that morning.

Did Alex even realize they'd gotten into the habit of kissing each other? It wasn't a passing kiss of strangers either. Each time was more passionate than the last. He looked forward to feeling her lips on his, and as he kissed her now, he didn't feel her tense once. She'd stopped flinching away or trying to avoid his touch. She was slowly starting to accept him.

He could feel it.

This wasn't a victory to him, though. This was

something else. It was like he needed her to want him, to be just as desperate to be in his company as he was to be in hers.

"Roman," she said, moaning.

"Tell me you want it."

"I don't think it's a good idea."

"Why not?"

"Because once you start, I don't think I'll ever want you to stop."

He growled and then reached for her hand to press it against his hardening cock. "Feel what you do to me. How desperate I am for you." He groaned, resting his forehead against hers.

"We better go inside."

"Yes."

Neither of them moved. They both panted.

He didn't want to give her up. His cell phone rang incessantly in his pocket. "I'll lead," he said.

After opening the car door, he stepped out, making sure to button his jacket and smooth it out to hide the outline of his erection. He wasn't a fucking schoolboy, but she made him lose control.

Once at her side of the door, he held the door open and presented his hand for her to take, which she did with a smile at him.

They had practiced this in the basement a few times. Alex had to get used to looking at him, and the first couple of times they tried it, her face was always bright red.

Staring at her now, he saw the fullness of her lips, and she looked so beautiful. The gown he'd ordered accentuated her curves. It wasn't drab or dull. The color was a shocking red, a sign of passion. The neckline curved around her tits, pushing them together and showcasing the fullness of them. The gown tapered in at her waist, flared out over her hips, and of course, there was a gorgeous slit in the side. When she walked, it teased at her juicy thick thighs.

Her body was beautiful, and even now, dressed, he wanted to see her naked again. In fact, Roman wanted the time to explore her beautiful body. To get to know every single part of her and to learn what made her ache, what made her pussy soaked.

There would be time for that.

Roman was determined to be patient. To go at Alex's pace. This was completely unheard of. If the capos beneath his father knew he hadn't bedded his virgin wife, and hadn't taken her regularly, they'd consider him weak. He'd be a laughingstock of the Greco line. His father might even disown him if the news ever got out.

With Alex's lips so red and swollen, they shouldn't suspect a thing. By the end of the night, he planned on everyone believing he was infatuated with his wife and couldn't keep his hands off her, which was entirely true.

The doors were opened and he nodded at several of the soldiers. The moment they entered the main house, several people were already lingering, including Antonio, who came toward him.

He placed his back toward Alex so that he could whisper to him. "Denise, Scarlett, and Charlotte are all here, Roman."

Gritting his teeth, he forced a smile to his lips so no one would suspect anything. "How the fuck did they get an invite?"

"I have no idea, and they're not talking, but they don't look good, Roman. Keep her to yourself."

Antonio stepped away. "Alex, we meet again."

He held her hand and pressed a kiss to her

knuckles.

"A pleasure, Mr. Testa," Alex said.

Antonio winked at her.

"It's a full house," Antonio said.

"Then let's not fuck this up," Roman said.

Instead of holding her hand, he let her go and wrapped his arm around her waist, keeping her by his side.

Alex glanced up at him with a smile and a twinkle in her eye. How had he not seen this before?

They headed into the main hall, and he saw his father had gone all out in the decorations. Three large, crystal chandeliers welcomed them, all of them aglow. Pieces of priceless art hung on the walls. A classical band played on the main stage, and he clocked a mic as well, which suggested there would be a performer later.

Keeping Alex to his side, he was aware of the stares coming their way. He didn't look or observe them, at least not openly. Glancing through the room, he spotted Marlo and Cash doing the rounds, watching.

Alex patted his chest, and he leaned down as she was a little shorter. "What are we supposed to be doing?"

"Just mingling, enjoying ourselves. The usual," he said.

"Ah, I get it."

"I want you to laugh as if I had just made a funny joke."

She gave a soft giggle as he pulled away, and to help along with the charade, which was no longer the case for him, he gripped the back of her neck and locked their lips together.

Alex didn't tense. She placed a hand on his cheek, and he knew people were staring. They would be the center of gossip in no time. All he had to do was keep this up and move around the room, watching people.

He had a feeling the one responsible for Alex's life was in this very room. What he didn't have was the proof. Just a damn hunch, and he hoped he wasn't wrong about his father. That Lucas Greco himself wouldn't take the only woman Roman loved—no, cared about. He didn't believe in love.

"Alex. You can see her. She is real. She loves a lot, and you can see it. When she hugs me and kisses my cheek, I feel it. Alex is full of love."

Stuart's words quickly came back to him, and he tried hard to ignore them.

He didn't believe in love. Love was for the weak.

Standing up, he kept his hand at her waist.

A waiter came toward them, holding glasses of champagne.

"Can my wife please have some water?" he asked.

The waiter nodded, leaving the room.

Alex gasped. "You do realize that people are going to suspect I'm pregnant, don't you?"

"Wouldn't you rather it be that than the fact you can't handle your liquor?" he asked.

She rolled her eyes, and it was the first one of the evening.

"I'm going to count that as a one, and for me, it's a zero."

"Oh, please, you will have an angry glare on your face by the end of the night, I guarantee it." She winked at him, and he couldn't help but chuckle.

However, the laughter soon died on his lips as he caught sight of Charlotte heading their way, and he wasn't about to have his wife be confronted by an ex-lover, and all of the women in his life were exes. He had nothing to do with them.

Keeping a firm grip on Alex, he led her away

from the potential chaos. She was going to enjoy the evening and not deal with any jealousy.

You want her to fall for you.

You want her to trust you.

It didn't matter what he wanted, not anymore. He only cared about Alex and keeping her safe and happy.

****

Alex's face hurt from all the smiling. She didn't know how people did this. Her face ached so badly.

They were all strangers, and she had yet to see her father. Also, she got a sense that Roman kept on leading her around to avoid people. Every now and then, she'd clock a woman heading their way, and he'd somehow move them away.

He was an expert avoider, or so it would seem.

She already recognized the women though. They were his ex-lovers, and it made her curious as to who invited them to the party.

After they had been at the party for an hour, Lucas announced that there would be dancing. Men and women were coming together, and Roman moved her to a small, secluded alcove.

"Mr. Greco, what would anyone say?" Alex asked.

"How are you? Do you need us to leave?" he asked.

"Leave? Have you found your culprit?"

"No. I can't, no one seems to be intent on talking to us."

"Oh, I don't know, Charlotte, Denise, and Scarlett, is it? They seem intent on approaching us."

"You know … about them?" he asked.

"Yes, I do. One of the capo's wives, I can't remember her name, she pointed them out at our wedding. I don't mind, but I doubt they're the ones who want me dead. If so, wouldn't they have made their move?"

"Antonio, Marlo, and Cash hinted that they might be the ones responsible. A jealous lover."

"It's a lead, isn't it?" she asked. "Do you want to go and check it out?"

"No, I want to dance with you." He took her hands and led her onto the dance floor.

Alex followed him, and as he let go of her hands, she placed them on his shoulders, staring at him. "You're nervous," she said.

"I'm not nervous."

"You look it."

"This was supposed to be easy."

"How did you figure this was going to be easy?" she asked. "And I'm not judging."

"I suspected whoever was responsible would come and talk to us. So far, no one is talking to us. No one is singling us out or asking about the past few weeks."

For the first time since she'd known him, Alex saw that Roman seemed worried. "You're concerned?"

"Alex, your life is in danger."

"Wouldn't that set you free?" she asked.

"Don't say shit like that, okay? You've already been hurt once on my watch. I'm not going to let it happen again." He pulled her close, and she tilted her head back.

"You don't know me, Roman."

"What if I want to get to know you?" What if I want to learn everything about Alex Greco, my wife. The woman who likes to sew and study, and read. The woman I can't stop thinking about, even when a room full of screaming kids are around me."

She smiled.

"Screaming kids that I want to adopt with her, and help raise, to give them a family, because the truth is, I don't think I've ever had one. The same woman I'm a little jealous of because I know she knows more about … everything than I do."

His confession took her by surprise. Her heart raced.

"I think you need to go and talk to the women you were with before, and clear your friends' superstitions."

"I'm not leaving you," he said.

"My dad is heading our way," Alex said. "He will keep me safe."

Right on time, Liam was there.

"Roman," he said, holding his hand out to shake.

She saw how strong they were both holding their grip, and she couldn't help but roll her eyes, and the instant she did, she wanted to kick herself. Two, nil. Roman still hadn't glared, and this time, she did glare for him.

"I have some suspects to go deal with," Roman said. "You won't let her leave your side, will you?"

"No," Liam said. "I will keep my daughter safe."

A tension lingered, and Alex sighed.

Roman pressed a kiss to her lips. "I'll be back."

And she knew he was going to want to talk about what he said.

"You don't look happy," Liam said the moment Roman was gone.

"I am happy."

He put his hands on her waist. "There is a rumor that you might be pregnant. Roman specifically asked for water for you."

She chuckled. "Wow, gossip does travel fast."

"No babies?"

"No babies."

"How can you be sure?"

"Dad, come on, if I was pregnant, and I even suspected, I'd tell you, okay?"

"Good. I was starting to worry that I wasn't your favorite person, and I was hoping for some grandchildren."

"You might have … fifteen of them soon enough," she said.

"Alex."

"Dad."

"I know what Roman is trying to do, and I hope Lucas puts a stop to it."

"Why?" Alex asked. "Why are you so against those kids?"

"They're not yours. They're not your flesh and blood."

"So you believe that you only should take care of those you what, give birth to? Have a direct link to your sperm?"

"Family is important."

Alex thought about Roman. Staring past her dad's shoulder, she caught sight of Lucas Greco. He had a young model on his arm. Alex vaguely recognized her from some magazine she'd flicked through not too long ago in the hospital.

"Family is important, but it's not made up of blood, Dad. It can start that way, sure, you have a set of parents, but family is also a feeling. You could be raised in a family but not be a family." Alex pulled away from him. "I can't believe this. This is why you stopped me three years ago, isn't it?"

"Roman has a lot of responsibility. Lucas will remind him of this," Liam said. "You and Roman need to focus on what is good for the two of you."

"No," she said. "What you want me and Roman to focus on is what is good for you and Lucas Greco. It's not about me or Roman. It's about the two of you."

"Alex." He went to touch her, but she pulled away.

"You are causing a scene."

"No, I'm going to the bathroom. You're the one causing a scene." She turned on her heel and moved away from him.

All her life, she accepted her father for everything he was, and yet, he couldn't accept her for what she wanted. He saw children who were not born of her as strangers. At the moment, they were strangers because he refused to get to know them, but how could he turn his back on them?

Everything was so messed up.

Stepping out of the main hall, she looked for the bathroom. In the end, she had no choice but to ask one of the soldiers standing on guard for the direction of the bathroom.

It was on the second floor, to the right.

She walked inside and found that it was empty.

After going to a stall, she closed the door, flicked the lock into place, and then turned toward the toilet. Once she'd put the lid down, she stood on it and then sat her ass on the back of the toilet seat, keeping her feet on the lid.

Resting her elbows on her knees, she collapsed into her hands and groaned. Arguing with her father always made her feel queasy. It wasn't a good feeling.

She wanted to cry. If she did, that would smudge her makeup, and she had worked hard to make it look just right. She blew out a breath and tried to calm her nerves, to focus on what was important.

Millie had warned her when it came to those kids,

her father and she would never see eye to eye.

She tensed up when she heard the door open and close.

"I don't know about you ladies, but Antonio is looking so good tonight. I didn't even care that Roman was there."

Alex frowned.

"Oh, please, Charlotte, you were trying to get Roman's attention just as we were."

Alex could only assume these were Roman's ex-lovers, and she had locked herself in the bathroom. If she let herself out, all that would do was alert the three women she was there. She didn't want a confrontation.

After talking with her dad, all she wanted was to be left alone.

Why didn't the universe see that?

Life was so unfair at times.

"Yeah, I wanted to get his attention to see that he was, you know, completely done with me. He told me to never call him again, but you know Roman."

"No, what I know is that Roman is the king, and his friends are just like, they're not as important. If I can get a meal ticket with the big guy, then that is who I am after."

"Damn, Denise, that sounds so bad."

"I want money. I want security, and if the guy has a big dick, then that is just a bonus, and we all know what Roman is like in bed. He is fucking amazing. I am going to miss him, but I tell you, his wife, what is her name?"

"Alex."

She didn't have a clue who was talking. Their voices all sounded the same.

"Yeah, Alex, that's her name, she is a rare woman."

"What do you mean?"

"We've just talked to Roman, girls. Come on, you can't tell me you don't see it."

"See what?"

"Roman's in love. Now, I am jealous because that means no one is going to get that big dick of his, apart from his wife, but I'm actually happy for him, you know? Arranged marriages are supposed to suck, and when I first saw her, she looked a little uptight. Roman couldn't stand her, and now, he'll do anything to protect her. It kind of makes me want to stop going for married men and find a man for myself."

They seemed to go a little quiet, and Alex was shocked.

Whoever it was thought Roman was in love with her. That couldn't be possible.

Could it?

Climbing off the toilet, Alex moved to the door and stepped out, only, she came face to face with a masked man who shoved her back hard. She hit the metal door, and pain shot up her back.

Hands went to her hair and lifted her, so she used her hands to attempt to block the blow that landed on her face.

She thrust her leg up and tried to kick him. She hit him somewhere in the leg, forcing him to stumble back.

Pain radiated from her back, and as she got to her feet, she was too slow in the damn heels and dress as he grabbed her and threw her across the room, toward the sinks.

A scream fell from her lips as she was thrown, and her head hit the glass mirrors. The impact smashed one of the mirrors.

Her assailant came at her, but she grabbed a shard

of glass. As he went to touch her, she sliced right across his hand. He growled. “You fucking bitch.”

She didn’t recognize the voice, but she also heard commotion.

“This isn’t over. You will fucking die.”

The bathroom doors opened and Roman ran in. Her assailant took off, and she didn’t get to see where he went as Roman rushed toward her side. Dropping the piece of glass, she collapsed to the ground and shook as Roman came to her.

Antonio, Marlo, and Cash were there, as were Lucas and Liam, but tears filled her eyes, and the only person she wanted was Roman.

Wrapping her arms around him, she held on to him tightly, not wanting to let him go.

Chapter Fourteen

"We're no closer to finding out what happened," Roman said.

The moments after the attack, Lucas Greco had ordered his home to be put on lockdown. No one could get in or out, but it didn't matter. Roman knew the bastard had already made it out and alive, which pissed him off. They had checked the security videos. Seconds after Alex entered the bathroom, the feeds were turned off. No one knew who it was, or if he had been waiting for her.

"Roman, it's okay," Alex said.

They all stood in Lucas's office. Marlo was inspecting Alex's head. The doctor had already given her the all-clear. She might have a concussion, so tonight, Roman had to keep waking her every so many hours.

Marlo had been tasked with removing pieces of glass that were in her hair as he was the only one who had been trained to do so.

"No, it's not okay," Roman said. He turned toward Liam. "You were supposed to be watching her."

"I was, but in case you didn't notice, men cannot follow women into the bathroom. It is unseemly, or so I've been told." Liam looked toward Lucas.

"I had complaints that you were randomly inspecting bathrooms."

"You think I don't know when people are going to attack and the best places to do it? This means whoever did this heard our argument," Liam said. "The fucker is close, I can feel it."

Roman's hands clenched. Whoever it was had them fucking chasing them. Alex could have died.

He'd been passing the bathroom when he heard

the commotion, and it was only because he recognized Alex's voice, her pained scream from the last time she was shot, that he knew she was being attacked. He needed someone to hit, badly.

No, he needed someone to fucking kill.

And so far, they had let everyone from the party leave as they didn't have a reason to keep them. After checking everything, each guest leaving the building had been asked to present their hands. No one showed signs of bleeding. The piece of glass Alex used had been taken and was currently being transported for testing. They didn't know if it would be viable though.

Alex said she had cut him, but she didn't know if the blood on the glass was hers or her attacker's.

Everything had gotten so fucked.

He ran fingers through his hair and paced the length of the room.

"You took one heck of a hit," Marlo said.

"Tell me about it."

"We know the guy is strong," Cash said. "That's new."

"Of course, he would be strong," Lucas said. "He's messing with the Greco and Smith alliance. Only a fool wouldn't be strong enough to take us on."

"Not necessarily," Antonio said. "Alex's attacker could be foolish, but he has to be smart."

"No, anyone who dares to attack my daughter is foolish. They must know I will kill anyone who ever threatens her," Liam said.

"Of course, they know, and that is what they're counting on. Whoever is doing this, Alex is the primary target," Antonio said. "I think the main threat is the Smith and Greco alliance, and this just confirms it."

"Because whoever it was that attacked at this party knows of the Greco and Smith alliance. They had perfect opportunity to take out Liam and Lucas themselves, but instead, went after a woman," Roman said. "We knew she was the target."

"And we only looked at the cameras in front of the bathroom. Why not check the cameras in the main hall, as well as the corridors, of the whole house?" Antonio asked.

"Do you have any idea how much time that will take?" Lucas asked.

"Alex's life is in danger now," Liam said.

"And let's not forget my attacker is injured," Alex said.

"We've already checked everyone."

"He left out of the bathroom window, didn't he? That's the exit, right?" Alex asked. "He still had to get in, so why don't you check all the faces in the hall to the ones who left? Someone might be unaccounted for."

"That's still going to take time," Lucas said.

"And my life has been in danger for months. Roman will protect me, and I know Antonio, Marlo, and Cash will protect me. Whoever it was didn't know where I've been hiding all this time. The attack was desperate. Just before it, Roman's ex-girlfriends were in there, talking."

"Did they say anything to you?" Roman asked, stepping toward her.

Alex stood and shook her head. "They didn't know I was in there, so whoever my attacker is, he had to have stayed close. As much as I love playing detective work, I think it's time for me to get out of this dress and shower."

Roman was surprised when she didn't go to her father. She offered everyone a goodnight and made her excuses.

"I have to go," he said. He didn't bid anyone

goodnight.

"I will handle her," Liam said. "Your father wants to talk to you."

Roman wanted to tell Liam that Alex was his wife, and if she needed help, he would be the one to do it. Tonight wasn't the night to start a damn war though.

He looked toward his father and waited.

"Marlo, Cash, Antonio, leave us," Lucas said.

One by one, they left, and Roman was left alone to deal with his father.

"I am doing everything I can to keep her safe. While she was with me, she was exactly that, safe."

Lucas held up his hand. "I trust you, son."

"Tell me now that you are not responsible for this," Roman said.

"Do you have any idea who you're talking to?"

"I know who I am talking to, and I am asking, no, I am demanding. You hinted at Alex's death being the perfect opportunity to get out of this arrangement. I need to guarantee that you're not the one pulling the strings."

"Roman, I like Liam Smith. He's a hard-working asshole. I've liked him for years. I watched him after his woman died. At first, I didn't see what the big deal was since he hadn't married her. She was just a piece of pussy, but I saw his devotion. I knew that the only way to guarantee our security and safety was to one day unite our families. He's not mafia, he's not family, but he is as good as any mafia and family. I would never do anything to jeopardize that. I also happen to like Alex."

Lucas shook his head, and Roman had no choice but to believe him. It was as he suspected all along, a ruse.

"You will not go through with the adoption of those kids," Lucas said. "I have had our lawyer cease in the pursuit."

"No," Roman said.

"No? Do I need to remind you that I am your fucking boss!"

"And as my boss, you have ordered me to make my wife fall in love with me, and that is exactly what I am doing. Alex is not wowed by money, power, or violence. She is wowed by feelings. By acts of kindness. You knew this when you had me marry her, and the only way to her heart is to give her what her father never could, what he refused to. Those kids are her loves, and by adopting them, I will guarantee her love for me, and when the time is right, she will have my babies."

"They will never be Greco blood," Lucas said.

"I don't give a fuck whose blood they are. They are amazing and loyal kids. If you ever took the time, you would see that."

"You are going soft."

"Or maybe I see the bigger picture in this scenario, Dad. To win Alex, I have to put everything in. If you want to keep Smith, then this is what you're going to have to do, regardless of if you like it or not."

"I don't recall agreeing to you pissing me off," Lucas said.

Roman chuckled. "I'm your son, it's my prerogative to piss you off. Can I go now and take care of my wife?"

"Yes."

"And will you put the lawyers back on the case?"

Lucas sighed. "It is already handled. You and Alex have some paperwork to sign, and then those kids are yours and your responsibility."

"Maybe you should stop by, come and meet our family," Roman said.

"That's not going to happen."

He stared at his father. "It is if Liam ends up

stopping by. It'll be good relations," Roman said.

Roman nodded at his father and then left the office.

His friends were waiting, and he couldn't keep the smile off his face.

"I don't even know what that look means anymore," Antonio said.

"It looks like victory," Cash said.

"I have no idea either. I don't even want to guess."

"I just adopted fifteen kids."

"You know, most men would be terrified of that," Antonio said. "Are we sure Roman didn't get his head thrown against some glass, rather than Alex?"

At the mention of Alex's attack, the smile fell from Roman's lips. "Alex."

He took the stairs, ignoring his friends, and went straight to the bedroom where his father said they would be staying tonight. They couldn't return to the house, not until they were sure there were no bruises on Alex. He didn't want to worry the kids.

Liam stood outside of the door, tense, hand poised at his waist, where Roman knew where his gun was.

"The room was clear," Liam said.

"How come you're out here?" Roman asked.

"She asked me to leave. My daughter and I, we're not seeing eye to eye at the moment. She is being stubborn."

Roman smiled. "She is very stubborn, but I believe that is how you raised her."

"I raised her to see sense. Not to act irrationally."

"I will take it from here."

"Take care of her, Roman," Liam said.

"I will."

He entered the bedroom and saw the red dress was on the floor.

During her attack, some of it had torn, and the glass had also destroyed it.

Roman picked it up and tossed it outside of the bedroom door. Cleaners would deal with it. He snapped the lock into place and then made his way into the bathroom, where Alex was.

"Dad, I need privacy."

"It's me," he said.

"Oh." She had put her hands in front of her body in an attempt to hide herself.

"Can I join you?" he asked.

There was a long pause.

"Yes."

Roman stripped out of his clothes, leaving them on the floor, and he opened the door to the shower to step inside.

Alex's back was to him.

There were a few cuts on her shoulder, but in the time it had taken Marlo to get the glass out of her hair, they looked to have scabbed over.

He moved up behind her and put his hands on her shoulders, where there were no marks. "I'm sorry I wasn't there," he said.

"You couldn't have done anything."

"I could have. I would've killed him. Snapped his neck."

"And what if he was a messenger?" Alex asked. "We would've been no closer than we are now. At least he's injured, and I can't believe I said that. How horrible does that make me?"

"The man wanted you dead. Hurt you. You are entitled to say whatever the fuck you want, and whoever has an issue with it can deal with me."

He'd gladly wipe the floor with anyone who dared to say bad shit about his wife. Roman pressed kisses to her shoulders and trailed up toward her neck. "Guess what?"

"I'm not good at guessing games."

"My dad just tried to talk me out of adopting our kids," he said.

"And?"

"All we have to do is sign some paperwork and then those kids are ours, Alex."

She spun in his arms and took him completely by surprise as she threw her arms around his neck.

He was even more unprepared for the kiss she gave him, but he was a man of action. Wrapping his arms around her waist, he pulled her in close and sealed his mouth to hers.

Sinking one hand in her hair, he trailed the other down toward her ass, drawing her against him. He tried to be the good man, to keep his dick in control, but this was impossible. Against Alex, all he wanted was to fuck her, and as she rubbed herself against him, that was exactly what he was going to do.

****

Alex felt the hard ridge of Roman's cock pressing against her stomach. He was long and thick, and an answering heat filled her pussy.

She didn't know when women were ready for their first time. If it was a feeling, or the kind of guy, or the moment, but after hearing his exes say that he loved her, and feeling him now, she knew this was the moment.

At the way he touched her back, stroking down toward her butt and gripping the flesh tightly within his grasp, she let out a moan, not wanting him to stop.

He pushed her up against the shower stall, and a small gasp escaped at the coolness of the tile on her back.

Roman's hands went to her face, and he pushed her hair out of the way, stroking it back behind her ear.

She placed her palm flat on his chest and stroked down. Alex didn't know where she found the confidence to touch him, but it was there as she wrapped her fingers around his length.

"Fuck, Alex," he said.

"Am I hurting you?"

"No, it feels so fucking good to finally have you touch me."

She licked her lips. "Roman?"

"Yes."

"I … I want you. I want this, all the way, tonight."

"Alex, you were just—"

She stopped him from saying the a-word by slamming her lips on his. She didn't need him to tell her she was attacked. She was there and had the small little cuts to prove it. Not to mention the aches.

"Please," she said.

Roman stared at her, and she held her palm still wrapped around his length.

"Not in the shower," he said seconds later.

"Not in the shower." She agreed with him.

He turned off the shower and took her hand.

Alex followed his lead, a little surprised as he grabbed a towel and took her into his arms, drying her body.

"If at any time you want me to stop, you say so. Got it?"

"Yes." She wasn't going to tell him to stop. She wanted this. Wanted him.

Roman held her hand, leading her into the bedroom. The dress was nowhere to be seen, and Alex was grateful. Then, as Roman's arms wrapped around her, she didn't care. Everything else left her mind, and all that she focused on was his touch, his kisses, and his body.

He felt amazing.

Roman's hands started at her waist and slowly trailed up into her hair. He held her against him, kissing her lips. All too soon, his lips moved to her neck as his hands roamed. Both went to her ass, squeezing the globes tightly within his grip.

"I think you have a thing for my ass," she said, moaning.

"Believe me, I do. I can't get enough of this curvy ass." He gave the cheeks another squeeze, and then he pushed her down onto the bed, following her. "Let me make this good for you. I want you nice and wet before I take you."

"I'm all yours, Roman."

"Good. Remember that," he said.

She didn't ask him what he meant, but he trailed his lips down her body. He paid close attention to each of her nipples, sucking them into his mouth and using his teeth, not to cause pain but just to give a hint at what he could do.

Alex gasped as each nip and stroke went between her thighs and seemed to make her pussy pulse with a fresh wave of release. She wanted him. So badly.

Roman kissed down her body, and he grabbed her knees, spreading her legs wide. As his tongue danced across her core, she cried out his name, lifting up. The sensations were so strong, and they rushed through her body. Roman's fingers teased the flesh of her pussy open, keeping her wide, and he slid his tongue back and forth across her clit.

She was so close. It was almost embarrassing as she couldn't control her body, and she came, hard, screaming his name and not wanting the pleasure to stop, but it was also too much for her to handle.

She didn't think she could survive, and then Roman moved up between her spread thighs. She stared up at him, the aftershocks of her orgasm still rippling through her body.

"Are you ready?"

"Yes."

She had no doubt this was what she wanted.

Roman reached between his legs, and she felt the tip of him as he slid against her, bumping her clit and making her cry out before he slid down, poised at her entrance.

This was it.

In one hard slam, Roman tore through her virginity, taking it for himself. The pain was instant, and his invasion took her by surprise.

She clenched her hands into fists, which also caused her pain. From holding the piece of glass tightly in her first, she had caused herself an injury as the glass had embedded into her hand. She had a bandage on her palm.

Roman's arms wrapped around her, and he held himself perfectly still within her, but his gaze was on hers the whole time.

Her vision blurred as tears filled her eyes.

"I've got you, Alex. The pain will go, I promise."

She knew the pain would go. She had finally given herself to Roman, to her husband. To the man she had once promised she would never give anything to.

He wasn't who she thought he was. Roman was so much more, and now, they had children together. The future she had always wanted but thought she was never going to get was nearly in her grasp, and she had a husband as well. A man she knew she was finally falling for.

The real Roman. Not the man he showed the rest of the world. But her Roman.

The pain started to lessen, and Alex stared at him, seeing the concern on his furrowed brow.

Ever since the attack, he'd been earning points for the glare. It had been a continuous glare, but to make him laugh, she had attempted to blink to gain him more points.

"I'm ready," she said.

"I don't want to hurt you."

"It's not hurting anymore, Roman. I want to feel you. I want this." She started to rock her hips, trying to convince him that this was exactly what she wanted.

Roman rested his hands on either side of her head, staring down at her. "If this hurts, I'm stopping."

He slowly started to pull out, and Alex was a little nervous that it would hurt and that he'd stop. There was no pain.

As he slid out of her, she felt this pulse of pleasure. It took her by surprise, and he groaned.

"Fuck, Alex, I only have so much control," he said.

She put her hands on his ass. "Then lose control."

He slammed to the hilt inside her.

They both cried out together.

One of Roman's hands went to her thigh, lifting her leg over his hip. He held on to her as he started to fuck her, going deeper. The sounds of their lovemaking echoed throughout the room, and Alex didn't care. She felt another answering pulse within her core, and she knew she was getting close to an orgasm. Could almost feel it, so close to the surface, ready to explode.

Roman changed the angle, tilting his hips, diving deeper, and thrusting harder. "I'm not going to last."

She watched him, seeing the strain in his neck as he tried to hold back, and Alex met his pace, thrusting her hips up toward his and feeling him go harder within her.

He growled her name. Then his cock pulsed, and she knew he was coming.

She lay beneath him, watching as the pleasure rushed through him.

At the last moment, he dropped down and slammed his lips down on hers, kissing her hard.

Roman didn't move. His cock stayed deep within her as he kissed her.

She wrapped her legs around him, and when Roman pulled back, she smiled at him.

"Hello, Mrs. Greco," he said.

"Hello, Mr. Greco."

"That was amazing."

"And I told you I was a virgin."

"I need to learn to trust you more often."

She giggled and shook her head. "I can't believe we're talking about this."

"We're going to need to burn the sheets," Roman said.

"How?"

"I'll handle it. Don't worry." He dropped a kiss to her lips.

"Do you want to go again?" she asked.

His cock pulsed inside her.

"You're not sore?"

"I am a little, but I really want to do that again." This time, she didn't expect there to be any pain.

Roman groaned. "Why do I feel I have awakened a monster?"

"Because I think you have."

"I don't have a problem with that."

****

“You have let the adoption process continue?” Liam asked.

“Yes.”

“And you think this is wise?”

“We can’t stop it. It has already gone through.”

Liam sighed and sat down in the chair, sipping at his scotch. He didn’t like this. “I never wanted Alex to get involved with those kids.”

“And once again, I’m sorry that she has had to. I don’t think they will ever suspect anything.”

“That those kids are the abandoned bastards of your capos?” Liam asked.

He had discovered the truth when Alex had found Stuart. It had pissed him off. He’d been tempted to allow his daughter to adopt the young kid, but when Stuart was instantly placed in the secluded home, it hadn’t taken Liam long to put two and two together. It was why he purchased the place.

At the time, Lucas and he hadn’t formed an agreement, and there was no fucking way he would put his daughter at risk. He had no choice but to take responsibility for those kids, and so, he made sure the home was secured and the necessary funding was available to them.

Finding Stuart, purchasing the house and grounds, and then funding the orphanage was what put himself and Lucas on the path to an alliance.

What he had hated was using his daughter. Alex was never supposed to be part of the bargain, but Liam and Lucas had known that any agreement between them wouldn’t be binding without putting the people they loved in place.

Alex and Roman, their firstborns. To Liam, his only child, and to Lucas, his firstborn son and precious heir.

"Be careful, Liam. I had to do what was necessary to protect them. They are Greco blood," Lucas said.

"No, they're no one's blood," Liam said. "Abandoned, left for dead, and in some cases abused. I know the backstory of all those kids." And he had no choice but to modify the details so Alex would never know. His daughter wasn't stupid. With the marriage and attacks, she hadn't continued her questioning about the orphanage.

Liam knew it was only a matter of time before she discovered the truth.

He had to wonder if Roman was even aware of it. He doubted it. Roman was an interesting man. Loyal to his father, but in the past few weeks, he'd shown a loyalty to Alex, which surprised Liam.

Roman wasn't a man easily brought down by a woman, and in the early days of their marriage, Liam truly believed he'd fucked up in getting his daughter to marry Roman. Now though, he had to wonder if he did, in fact, pick the right choice. He saw the look in Roman's eyes. The possessiveness. It was the same within his own over his own woman. Only time would tell if Roman got this right with Alex or not.

Chapter Fifteen

Alex's laughter was infectious. Roman held her down and began to stroke his tongue across her body, turning those giggles into sweet moans. They hadn't left this bed since last night and had already skipped breakfast for sharing time with each other.

"That feels so good," she said.

After sliding a hand down her body, he pressed his palm between her thighs. "How about now?" he asked.

He had already packed the blooded sheets away. For some reason, he couldn't bring himself to completely get rid of them. Alex had never been lying to him. She was a virgin. Everything she had told him was the truth, and he knew that now.

Alex shook as he stroked his fingers across her swollen clit. Her teeth sank into her bottom lip, and she tilted her head back to release a moan. The sound filled the room, and it made him ache to be inside her. Especially when he dipped his fingers down, traced around her sweet cunt, and then plundered them inside her.

She began to rock against his fingers, and he pulled them out to push them back inside her, fucking her.

"Does it feel good?" he asked.

"Yes!"

"How good?"

"Please."

"Do you want me to stop?"

"No, please, don't stop."

"Then beg me, Alex. Beg me to make you come. Beg me for my cock." He pressed two fingers inside her, twisted them, and then, used his thumb to lightly tease her clit. He felt her tighten around his digits. Shake. Her moans filled the room, his name spilling from her lips.

"Please, Roman, please, make me come. Please, I want it."

He smiled. "Good girl," he said.

Moving down between her thighs, he spread her open and quickly replaced his fingers with his tongue to lap at her pussy. Taking her clit into his mouth, sucking it before soothing it out with his tongue.

After licking down to her opening, he circled and then started to thrust, fucking her. He caressed up her thighs, going to her hips, and capturing her waist, and then he moved her onto her knees.

"Roman?"

"Trust me."

Cupping her ass, he spread the cheeks wide and stared down at her tiny little puckered anus. His gaze didn't linger there but went straight to her sweet cunt, which was so wet, it glistened, begging for his dick.

He grabbed his length and traced between her pussy lips, bumping her over sensitive clit, which was exactly where he wanted her.

With a moan and the way she jerked a little in his arms, he knew she was far enough gone.

He placed the tip at her entrance and watched as he pushed his cock inside her. Alex took him. Moan for moan, and she was so fucking tight, it felt like she was squeezing his length like a damn vise. He couldn't focus. Once he was several inches within her core, he grabbed her hips and slammed the rest of the way inside.

Roman held himself still for several beats, feeling the rippling of her pussy as she got used to his length. To help distract her from any possible soreness, he reached between her thighs and got back to work stroking her clit.

She was so close. He brought her to the edge but held her captive there, not letting her fall, but just keeping her right on the point, ready to fall into the abyss of pleasure.

Returning to her hips, he held her and began to fuck her. He started slow at first and then built, thrusting inside her, taking her deeper and making her want it. Every time he wanted to tease her just that little bit more, he went between her spread thighs and worked her clit.

Each time, he brought her just to that edge but didn't quite let her have her release. He loved the way her pussy rippled on his cock. The sweet sounds of her moans as they filled the air were precious to him. He didn't want them to ever stop.

Running his hands up her body, he moved them to her tits and held the plump beauties in his palms, massaging them and pinching the tips before holding her hips again and pounding inside her.

He wasn't going to last.

His release was so close that he could feel it tingling in his balls. Holding himself still within her, he went back between her thighs and stroked her clit. Within just a few gentle touches, Alex came, and he had no choice but to close his eyes, to concentrate as it was sheer torture around his dick.

So tight.

So wet.

So fucking good.

Roman didn't want it to stop, but he felt his needs riding up. As he returned his grip to her hips, he fucked her harder, pounding into her pussy. With each withdrawal, he saw her release painted on his dick, and that was all it took for him to slam balls deep and release his cum deep inside her womb, filling her up and making her his. Wave upon wave of his cum flooding her.

When it was over, he didn't pull out, wanting his

cum to stay right where it was supposed to. He'd never been with a woman without a condom. Being lazy with his sperm was a lesson his father had taught him at a young age. He always bagged it, but now, with Alex, he didn't have to.

She was his wife.

His life.

"Wow," she said.

"Yeah, wow."

"I had no idea it could be this way. Is it always this way?"

He wrapped his arms around her, kissing her shoulder. "Not always."

"What does that mean?"

"Sex can be amazing, but it's not always. You and I, Alex, we click."

Alex tilted her head back, but with how he held her, she couldn't move out of his grip, and he wanted time for his cum to stay within her, to fill her up, to keep her as his.

"We do?"

"Don't you feel it?"

"I guess."

"We can make this marriage work, Alex. You and me." He ran his hand down her hips and then up toward her breast, cupping the flesh in his palm. "It's like your body has been made for me."

She groaned. "We're going to have to go down for breakfast eventually."

"Eventually, but not right now." He let go of her tit and cupped her face to kiss her. "We can stay here for as long as we need to."

"What about getting back to the kids?" Alex asked.

Roman sighed. "I know, I want to get back there

as well and tell them the good news, but I don't think that's a good idea."

"Because of the attack?"

"Alex, babe, you have a black eye and several cuts."

"You're right. I don't want to worry them." She gave him a sad smile. "But I can't wait to tell them the good news. I've always wanted to adopt them, and now I can."

Roman wanted to see her smile. He was being honest with her, though. He didn't want to stay in this place, but until they worked out all the details of who attacked her, they couldn't leave. Alex's face also wouldn't be good for the children as they'd worry.

He wanted to take her someplace safe, where no one else would hurt her, but he knew that was impossible until he found the man responsible for it.

****

Alex giggled as Roman pulled her away from the house and toward the small forest.

"What are you doing?"

"You need a break from hiding from your father," Roman said.

"How did you know?"

"You weren't there at breakfast."

Alex placed her finger on his mouth. "You were the one keeping me busy with breakfast."

"And then there's lunch."

"I seem to recall you were also doing the same at lunch."

They hadn't been able to keep their hands off each other, and Alex couldn't deny that she wasn't a little bit … happy. Roman was sweet and attentive, and amazing in bed.

Roman tucked her against the tree, tilted her head

back, and then kissed her. One of his hands sank into her hair, and the other started to move down toward her pussy.

"Someone might see."

"No one will see, Alex. I've got you covered, I promise."

He took possession of her mouth, and Alex couldn't contain her moan, not when he lifted her skirt. Then his palm pressed against her core, making her whimper.

"You're already so wet for me."

Roman grabbed her panties, and she jerked from the force of his yank as he pulled them off her body.

It was so unexpected, but it felt so good.

He shoved them into his pocket, and then his palm went between her thighs. All thought left her. His fingers moved between her slit, stroking against her clit before delving down inside her. He began to pump, moving in and out, and all she wanted was to feel him inside her.

Roman pulled out and pressed his fingers on her clit, and she had no choice but to hold on as sensation after sensation flooded her body, taking her breath away and making her want him even more.

"You look so fucking stunning," he said.

Another whimper fell from her lips.

"I need to be inside you. I don't fucking care."

Her skirt was pushed up, and Roman spun her so she was pressed against the tree, tilting her ass, and then she heard the sound of his zipper.

Seconds later, he pressed his cock against her core, and this time, they both groaned. The sound filled the air, escaping on the short breeze. The air was damp and yet fresh at the same time as it hadn't had some rain.

Roman's hands slid beneath her shirt and traced

up her body, cupping her tits. "Do you have any idea how much I fucking love your body?" he asked. "I can't get enough of it."

He hadn't said anything, but the fact they'd fucked at least six times in the past twenty-four hours was also a given.

He was insatiable, and if she was honest, she was pretty much the same. When it came to Roman, she couldn't get enough of him, which made no sense at all, seeing as for most of their marriage, she'd hated him.

Maybe people were right, and there was a fine line between love and hate.

Roman started out gentle, always making sure she could take him. Allowing her to become accustomed to the feel of him, but as she did, he stopped being gentle and fucked her hard. She had no choice but to hold herself away from the tree as he pounded inside her.

He let go of her tits, and then his hand was between her thighs, teasing her clit, stroking her, rubbing it.

The fire burned in her body, and she tried to contain her moans, but it was impossible. She was so close, so desperately close, and then she felt her release and called his name as she came.

Roman wasn't far behind her.

Her name was a growl, taken on the breeze like his name had been.

"That felt so fucking incredible," he said. "I couldn't wait another second, I had to have you." He pressed kisses against her neck, licking at her pulse.

"I can't believe we just did that," she said.

"We're going to have to get in all the practice now. When we're alone with the kids, that is going to be an impossible task, or so I've heard," Roman said.

She laughed. "You're already thinking about

what our sex life is going to be like when we're back home?"

"Aren't you?"

Alex held up her thumb and finger, holding them close together. "A little."

"I'm thinking about it a lot. I feel there are going to be a lot of bribes in my future." He kissed her neck.

She had started to notice that Roman was never in a rush to … move. Not after he'd come, and she had to wonder if that was because he liked being inside her? Did he? Or was she reading too much into it?

"You know, we haven't had much of a honeymoon," he said.

"Do you think now is a good time to think of one?"

"I can't think of a better time than now to think of one."

She loved the way his hands roamed over her body. Each touch set her on fire, making her ache for more of him.

Alex never thought they would be like this. She wasn't complaining as this felt amazing to her, real, the truth.

At the sudden sound of his name being called, Alex sighed.

"Fuck."

"Did you sneak out to be with me?" Alex asked.

"Yeah. Being around our dads all day is fucking exhausting. Count yourself lucky."

"I'm in a house I don't know, bored."

"It could be worse," he said.

"How?"

"Besides the obvious, you could have no husband trying to fuck you every single chance he got," Roman said.

He eased out of her and slowly pressed the skirt down. The moment she stood up, Alex felt his release spilling from her.

Roman cupped her face with both of his hands and tilted her head back. "I'll see you soon."

She nodded.

He pressed his lips together, but this wasn't a sweet kiss. It was possessive. The kind that made her close her eyes and think of Roman, naked, taking her.

"Think of me."

She had to make a quick trip to her bedroom, take a shower, and change, and there was no way she was going to stop thinking about him.

Roman took her hand, leading her back to the main gardens. It was Antonio who had come for him.

The other man smiled at her, giving her a wave. She simply held her hand up. Antonio, Marlo, and Cash had always been a little too familiar with her. It was why she tried to keep her distance from them. They made her a little uneasy.

Heading back into the house, she kept her head down, convinced everyone who looked at her already knew the truth about what she and Roman had done. They all knew what had happened.

She was sure of it.

Arriving at her bedroom, she went straight to the bathroom, humming to herself as she turned on the hot water to the shower. She didn't waste any time, removing her clothes and stepping into the shower.

The moment she was beneath the hot water, she tilted her head back and gave a sigh of relief.

It felt good.

She quickly washed her body and between her thighs. With her hair already wet, she quickly shampooed her hair, and after rinsing, she turned the water off.

Grabbing a towel, she stepped out of the shower. She took another towel to wrap up her hair, heading into the bathroom.

She went to the closet and quickly rummaged through the clothes, settling on a dress with a cardigan. Before she left, she picked out a couple of items of underwear, lifting them against her body and then moving back into the bedroom.

She placed them on the bed and frowned when she caught sight of a single file laying on the bed.

Had Roman been back to the bedroom?

Reaching for the file, she frowned when she caught sight of the title of the orphanage her father had been investing in for years. The kids.

She opened it immediately and sat on the edge of the bed, reading through the few documents that were there. They weren't adoption documents though.

Alex frowned as she looked at birth certificates. There were exactly fifteen certificates, but each one she looked at, she turned over, and there were other names on the back. Names she recognized because they had been at her wedding.

Under all the documents was a sheet. A printed-out copy of the children who had been there before, their adoption status, and their real parents' names.

The kids were … she couldn't bring herself to even say it, nor think it.

After pulling off her towel, she put on the dress, needing to confront Roman about this.

Was that why he was willing to adopt those kids? They were part of his family?

Did her father know?

Had this been a plot from the start, and how could anyone give up their kid, especially if they knew who it was?

With her dress on, Alex left her cardigan and grabbed the file, determined to get an explanation for all of this. Her heart pounded as she made her way down toward the main office, and then she froze as she heard raised voices coming from the study.

The door was partially open.

Had someone left it that way?

How could this be possible?

"We don't have time for games, son. Alex needs to fall in love with you and give you children. I allowed you to have that fucking adoption process. Now you give me what I want," Lucas said.

"Alex is falling in love with me, but it is going to take time. As for … the other, I'm working on it."

"Working on it. The key to getting a woman pregnant, Roman, is to fuck her. Not to give her fifteen reasons to be exhausted, or are Antonio, Marlo, and Cash supposed to be the ones providing me with an heir?" Lucas asked.

Alex covered her mouth, feeling sick.

She had been taken for a fool. A big, stupid fool.

Of course, Roman would never fall for her. There was no way any of this was real.

How could it be?

Pain shot through her chest and tears filled her eyes.

They'd had sex. She had given herself to a liar.

"I know all about your little plot to show Alex for the slut you think her to be. Getting Antonio, Marlo, and Cash to bed her. To take her in turns!"

Alex covered her mouth and took a step back, then another. How did she confront him after this?

With the files in her hand, she felt even sicker. This was all a lie. Roman had told a lie. He'd only taken her to bed at the orders of her father.

She had to get away.

The file fell from her hands, and luck wasn't on her side as it landed on the floor on the edge of its bind. The noise seemed to echo, sounding more like a hammer than a simple file.

The birth certificates spilled out, and she stared down at them.

The door opened, and then she was looking at Roman. "Alex."

He took a step toward her, and she moved back.

There was no way he was touching her again.

"Shit, you heard that."

Words failed her. She couldn't think of a single thing to say.

Tears filled her eyes as she looked at him, and she knew it was all true. The lies had been with her. He hadn't believed her or her diary. He was going to hurt her by getting his friends to manipulate their way into her bed.

Only, she had never lied.

"Alex, please, let me explain."

"Don't … come near me."

"Alex, baby, you don't understand."

She tilted her head back and looked at him, then laughed. "I don't understand. Tell me, Roman, what is so complicated about what I just heard. You were ordered to make me fall in love with you. To help you, you used fifteen children. Did you know they were all your capos' … unwanted children?" No matter how much pain she was in, she wasn't going to call them anything cruel or mean.

"What?"

"Of course, you'd probably lie."

"I had no idea," Roman said, turning toward Lucas.

"They're bastards, Roman."

"Don't call them that!" Alex screamed and stepped away. "Oh, my God, I can't believe…" She was going to be sick, but she wasn't going to fall in front of him. She was not going to vomit.

Turning on her heel, she had no idea where her father was, but she ran, going for the front door. She managed to pry it open and took several steps out into the cold air.

"Alex, don't do it," he said, grabbing her arm and trying to stop her.

"Let go of me." She jerked out of his hold. "You don't get to touch me. Not ever. Not fucking ever." She hated to curse, but she had to make him stop. To leave her alone.

Roman held his hands up.

"You were going to make me fall in love with you? And then what? What was going to happen?"

"I wasn't going to do it."

"What about your friends? What about that? I always knew something was going on, but I figured I was just weirded out by your friends."

Roman ran a hand down his face and released a sigh. "We need you to come inside. You can't go out there. It's dangerous."

"Don't come near me and just tell me the truth!"

Silence filled the air.

She was aware of Antonio, Marlo, and Cash. They'd followed them outside.

Tears fell down her face, and she swiped at them, hating how weak they made her feel. Roman didn't deserve her tears.

"You wouldn't take that fucking test, so I thought…" He stopped.

"You thought that I was lying. That I had slept

with other people, and what, they were going to prove your theory correct?" She shook her head as he didn't deny it. "Wow. Really. Wow."

"You can't go, Alex," Antonio said. "The threat is very real."

"Alex will not be leaving," Liam said.

She spun toward her father. "Dad?"

"Alex, go on inside because we don't know the extent of this threat."

She wanted to argue with him. She was so sick and tired of being told what to do. One look at her father's face, and she knew he had nothing to do with this. He was angry, the rage clear to see.

Like so many times before, her father was going to take care of her. She moved toward him, and he wrapped his arms around her.

"I love you, sweetheart. Please, go inside."

"Dad, don't do anything stupid."

"I won't."

Alex moved past Roman, and when he tried to reach for her, she pulled away. There was no way he was going to touch her, hold her, or get into her heart, not ever again.

Stepping into the main house, she looked up to see Lucas. He had paled. He hadn't expected Liam to find out.

Without another look in his direction, she made her way up to the bedroom, but with one look at the room, she felt sick.

In her mind, she saw Roman moving over her, kissing her, and heard the laughter she had shared with him. Then, as she stepped forward, something moved behind her and slammed across her head, sending everything black.

Chapter Sixteen

Roman couldn't believe Alex heard his father! Liam had stepped out for just a minute to take a private phone call, and then Lucas had wanted to know progress, which had turned into him berating him for fucking failing.

Staring at Liam, he knew he was in for a world of pain. The man removed his jacket and started to roll up his sleeves.

"I'm not going to fight you," Roman said.

"That's assuming you will get any hits in."

He didn't want to fight her father. "It was all a mistake," he said.

That didn't stop Liam from advancing toward him. Hitting Alex's father wasn't going to fix anything.

"Mr. Smith, I suggest we go in and talk."

"Do you think I will have anything to talk to you about after what I just heard?" Liam charged at Roman, but he didn't put up his fists or block any of the hits.

He took each blow.

Liam wasn't hitting lightly. He was angry, and Roman understood the rage. The hits sent him to the ground.

"Get the fuck up."

He expected Liam to hit him while he was down, but the man actually had a fucking code.

"I didn't know about the kids," Roman said. "I wanted to adopt them because they are fucking amazing."

"Get up! I already knew they were Greco brats. Alex shouldn't have known."

"And there was a file," Lucas said. "I have no idea how she got this as this was locked up and secured in my office at home."

Roman frowned and looked toward his father. "What?"

"This file, I keep a record of every single child that was placed in foster care or sent to an orphanage. I do keep an eye on them. I'm not heartless. Well, not completely. They could be soldiers one day."

At that moment, he hated his father. There had been moments throughout his life that he hadn't liked the man in front of him, but it had never been downright hatred, not like this. Alex had looked so fucking broken, so sad, and so lost. That had been on him, and he didn't know what to do to bring her back to him.

He'd fucked up big time. He knew that.

Now all he had to do was figure out how to fucking fix this, but how did you fix lies?

"But if you said that it was at home, back in your office, how did it end up here?"

Liam hit him again. He lost his train of thought and glared at Liam. "For fuck's sake, I love your daughter, okay?"

This time, Liam went to kick him, and Roman spun out of the way, getting to his feet, ready to defend himself.

"Do not fucking lie to me."

"I'm not lying. I love your daughter. I love Alex, and I will do whatever it takes to protect her." His nose was bleeding, and from the last blow, he felt like he might have a bit of a concussion. His vision was a little messed up, and he was seeing everything in little spots.

"Phillip. Fucking Phillip!" Roman said.

"What's your brother got to do with this? Antonio asked.

"He's the attacker. The amateur," Roman said.

"Son, I think that is a reach."

"Really? Look where he's reaching from! The second fucking chair. He's the second son. The one no one wants. The one who is constantly overlooked! Fuck. He knows that if he takes out Alex, war will break out between us. Liam would be on a rampage, like he was when he … lost her mother. We'd die—"

"And it would give him the perfect opportunity to rise up the ranks and take over."

A cell phone rang.

Roman patted his chest and pulled out his cell phone, seeing that it was a video call from an unnamed caller. He didn't like this. "Where's Alex?" he asked.

"Who is calling?"

Roman didn't have time to answer as he accepted the call and he saw Alex, lying on a bed, eyes closed, and blood spilling from her forehead.

"Surprise, big brother," Phillip said.

He grabbed the phone tightly, pissed off to see his little brother on the line. The smug smile on his face was enough to make him want to kill him.

"Did you suspect me?"

"Where is Alex?"

"Oh, she is taking a little nap," Phillip said. "You were so busy fighting that I knew now was my perfect opportunity."

"You've been in the house the whole time?" Roman asked.

"Well, of course. I didn't get an actual invite. Seeing as all my other men had failed to put this bitch to ground, I had no choice but to do it myself."

"And because you know where all the secret hiding spots are and tunnels, you were able to get into the bathroom without us seeing you."

"Bingo, so there is more to you than being a pretty boy."

"You leave Alex alone. Your problem is with me."

"Phillip, son, what are you doing?" Lucas asked.

"Ah, dear old daddy, he is there. This is good. I suspect his little buddy Liam is there as well."

Roman gritted his teeth, anger rising up inside him as Phillip sat on the edge of the bed.

"I'm here."

"Good, that is good. I want Roman and Liam to come to me. Don't bring any weapons, or any soldiers. Daddy, I suggest you go back into your office and wait for my call. You are going to want to see this. Oh, and if any of you fail to do as I say, Alex pays the price. You know, I thought she was pretty before, but up close, I can see just how stunning she looks." Phillip traced a finger across her chest.

"Get your fucking hands off her!" Roman couldn't stand to see anyone touching her.

Alex was his. No one else's. No one else should be touching what belonged to him.

Phillip laughed. "Good. I know you'll come, and if you don't, I'm going to take her for a test drive, brother, and see if I can have her screaming my name but for a whole other reason."

The line went dead. Seconds later, a text came through with a location.

Roman didn't even hesitate. He walked toward his car.

"Roman, what are you doing?" Lucas asked.

"I'm going to get my wife."

"This is your brother."

"And Alex is my fucking wife. She had done nothing to deserve being hurt by him." Liam moved toward the car, but Roman didn't care.

"Roman, come on man, we've got to think this

through," Marlo said.

He shrugged. "There is nothing to think through. He's got Alex, and I've got to go and get her."

"He's going to make you kill each other," Antonio said.

"Antonio is right," Liam said. "Whatever is about to go down, we're not going to make it out alive."

"Then you kill me," Roman said. There was no way he was going to be able to take out Liam. He wouldn't hurt Alex in that way.

"You're not thinking straight," Cash said. "This is Phillip. Your brother is a fucking pussy."

"A pussy who has been able to evade us right to this moment, when he wanted to be revealed. We've been his puppets, Cash. I'm not going to let Alex get hurt because I didn't look in the right places." He looked toward his father. "Permission to kill him if I have to."

"He is not going to live," Liam said.

Roman looked toward his father-in-law.

"Son or not, Greco, he dies tonight. He set up men to attack my daughter. He nearly killed her. He attacked her here and tried to kill her himself. Tonight, he dies."

Lucas nodded. "Agreed."

Roman was surprised. His father would never allow anyone to make that call on family.

He climbed into the car, turned over the ignition, and pulled out of the main parking lot, heading down the long drive.

"You know where your brother is?"

"Yes. It's our family safe house. It's not too far from here." Pressing his foot on the gas the moment they cleared the street, Roman kept an eye on the road, also checking for any possible leads of people following them.

He wasn't worried, but he wanted to be prepared for everything.

Glancing behind and in front of him, he was aware of Liam staring at him as he drove.

"What?" he asked.

"You said you love my daughter. Was that a lie?"

"No."

"How can you love my daughter?"

"How can I not?" he asked, glancing over at Liam. "She is not a hard person to love, Sir. It just took me some time to see it."

"And your friends?"

"Look, I thought she was lying. I thought she was … different. The women I've been with before, they loved the attention that my friends gave them, and I always tested them."

"So you treated my little girl like those bitches I've seen sniffing around you."

Roman tightened his grip on the steering wheel. "It wasn't intentional. Alex rebuffed them at every single opportunity."

"Of course she did." Liam tutted. "If she asks for a divorce after this, you are to grant her it, no questions asked."

"We have adopted kids together, Liam. I'm not going to turn my back on them."

"You did it as all part of a plan to seduce her."

"I did it because those kids are amazing," Roman said. "Being around them and Alex, we're a family. I don't expect you to understand that." He shook his head and brought the car to a stop at the side of a curb. "We have to walk from here."

Liam climbed out of the car, and Roman did the same. Side by side, they made their way down the street, coming to a set of gates. They were hidden by overgrowth from years of neglect. His father liked to have safe houses in places where he figured no one would enter. With the iron gates with spikes on top, and walls too high to climb, Roman had to figure right.

First, he opened the box on the side of the house that was hidden by a load of branches. He pried it open and typed in the code. The gate opened slightly with enough room for him to slide on through.

Liam followed close behind him, and the gates closed the moment they were through.

"How did Phillip get Alex here?" Liam asked.

"There are several exits and entrances. He would have had to use the back entrance. He came by car."

"And how the fuck did he get here by car when we were on the driveway?" Liam asked.

Roman sighed and turned to Liam. "Seriously, you've known my father a long time and you haven't figured out he's paranoid and would have multiple exits and entrances?" With his dad, there was always a secret tunnel that led to a single garage, near the back of the property. Roman had once known all the codes, but he'd stopped going to the safe houses years ago.

"Fair enough. Your dad has issues."

"Don't I know it."

Roman made his way to the front door. There was no one to greet them. No soldiers waiting to take him on. What was Phillip's game?

After they stepped into the house, the door closed. It had been a long time since this house was used as the musty smell was a little overpowering.

"About time you showed up."

Roman looked straight ahead and saw a cloth had been wrapped around Alex's face, pressing into her mouth. Phillip stood behind her. He had her long hair wrapped around his fist and was also yielding a knife.

"Alex!" Liam took a step toward her, but Phillip tutted.

"I would be very careful if I was you." Phillip tilted the blade of the knife, and Roman saw blood seep out near the tip.

He was cutting her.

"If you touch her—" Liam said.

"What? Do you think you can stop me?" Phillip asked. "You handed her over to my brother. You signed her death certificate the moment that happened. Alex was never going to be safe."

"And is that what you planned all along?" Roman asked. "To start a war that you hoped would erupt between us?"

Phillip chuckled. "I did my research. I knew Liam wouldn't let Alex's death slide. He'd get to the bottom of it, and I always intended to let it lead back to you, brother. The firstborn son, her husband."

"How?"

His brother tutted. "No, you are not going to distract me from what I have planned. It is simple. For Alex to leave with one of you, you have to kill each other!"

Alex started fighting against him.

Phillip tugged on her hair, making her cry out. "Don't even think of fighting me. Remember what I told you, those little bastards will be dead if you even think to defy me."

Roman turned his cell phone on in his pocket, calling Antonio. He gave it a few seconds, hoping his friend would pick up the call. "Little bastards?"

"You think I didn't know about the whole adoption process?" Phillip laughed. "It's so fucking funny. The heir to the Greco empire being a little step-daddy to all the bastard children."

"And you're going to kill them?" Roman asked.

"I've got men in place. They know if I don't make it out of here, they're to go in and slaughter them all."

"How did you figure it out?" Liam asked. "That they were Greco bastards?"

Roman looked at Alex, and each time one of them called the kids bastards, she got angrier. That was good. His wife was a fighter. She wasn't going to be taken out easily.

He hoped Phillip had underestimated her.

"Do you think it was hard? Lucas didn't even know I existed. He already had his main son. The heir. His pride and joy. I was … nothing to him. He didn't even see me when I stood in a room with him. It wasn't hard to figure out I could learn everything I needed to by just being in the right place and right time. The men would come with their whores, and they would ask him to fix it. So he did. If she didn't have an abortion, or was too far gone to, Lucas made sure the baby was taken, and I found out where. Sometimes the kids were put in foster homes, but like the case of little Stuart, he was hurt, left, and abandoned. It was a coincidence that day that you found him, you know, but I have a feeling that is what led to the Greco Smith alliance."

Phillip glared at Roman. "I should have been picked to marry her. You're the firstborn. You should have been married to a capo's little virgin. Alex was meant to be mine."

"Alex was never going to be yours," Roman said. "Do you really think Dad was ever going to look at you?" He took a step toward his brother and immediately stopped when Phillip pressed the blade a little harder against Alex's neck.

"Go ahead, brother. Tell me how useless I am.

Tell me how Father was never going to pick me. I'll kill her."

"And you know I will kill you," Liam said.

"Which is why you get to kill him," Phillip said. "Kill Roman, and I will let Alex go. You and I, we can form an alliance. A true one. One where I guarantee that I will love and protect your daughter. Roman couldn't keep her safe, but I can. I can give you everything you ever wanted."

"I'm listening," Liam said.

"You cannot be fucking serious," Roman said.

"My daughter's safety and happiness are my only priority. How will you keep her safe?"

"Simple, with Roman out of the way, I will be the only heir to the empire. I will make you my second in command. I will give you more power and money than you could ever dream of. You'll have everything you want, but all you've got to do is kill Roman. Make him suffer. He hurt Alex. He has been plotting to hurt her for months. I heard what he wanted his friends to do. They were all going to share her."

"I was never going to allow that to happen. Not anymore," Roman said. No other man was ever going to touch his woman. Alex belonged to him.

He saw the tears in her eyes, the pain. He didn't know if it was because of the knife at her neck or his words.

"I'm sorry," he said, looking at Alex. "I'm sorry that I fucked up. I'm sorry that I … was willing to have my friends seduce you. I fucked up, Alex."

"Enough. I have said enough!"

"My brother is not going to be good enough for you. I have heard from sources that he has a little dick, and he will never be able to satisfy you. He is a selfish, envious, little shit who wants what he can never have because you are mine and you will never be his." He looked at Phillip. "I took her virginity, and as usual, you will be enjoying my seconds."

"Shut your fucking mouth. You have no idea what you're talking about."

It got Phillip exactly where he wanted him, with the knife pointed away from Alex's neck and losing his temper, so he didn't have time to prepare for the charge.

Roman took him down, easily overpowering Phillip.

His little brother was no match for him, and he twisted his arm, snapping it. As he did, he jerked his hand so Phillip thrust the blade into his own neck. All Roman did was be the force behind the sudden jam.

****

Alex sat on the make-do hospital bed. They were not in any medical center. Her father had grabbed her and pulled her out of the house. He'd removed the tie from her mouth and released her arms. Her neck was sore.

The doctor had already treated her wounds. The tiny nicks on her neck were nothing. The blade hadn't done any lasting damage, but the lamp that Phillip had used to knock her out with, that had cut the back of her head. She had to have some stitches there.

"How are you feeling?" Liam asked, coming into the room.

"Fine."

"Honey, don't lie to me."

"You knew who those kids were?"

"Not in the beginning, but something about the setup confused me. I dug and discovered the truth."

"And you never told me."

"Would it have made you love them all any less?"

She shook her head but then winced as pain exploded inside.

"I suggest you don't do that too much anymore."

"Confirmed. Ouch." She rubbed at her temple.

"Roman killed Phillip. He died at the safe house."

"He was obsessed with power. With taking his brother's place," Alex said.

Thinking about Roman brought tears to her eyes. "I want a divorce, Dad. You're going to have to figure out some way to … bring peace with Lucas, but I can't, not anymore. Not after."

"I know. I have already called my lawyer. I don't mean to be rude, but you did mention an annulment…"

"Dad, that's not possible." She hated saying those words to him.

"Okay." He sat on the bed and wrapped his arm around her shoulders.

"I am still going to be Mommy to those kids," Alex said.

"I figured you were going to say that." Liam sighed. "I have already had the orphanage sign removed and have done the necessary paperwork. That house is now yours, Alex. You can do with it as you please."

"I can?"

"Yes. I've also contacted some contractors. I think it's time it is made into a house. If anyone can take on fifteen kids, then it's you," he said.

"Is that why … you didn't want me to adopt?" Alex asked.

"I knew who they were, and at the time, tensions were still very much in place. If I allowed you to go through with any adoption, I was worried for your safety, and for the safety of the children."

"You should have told me."

"I was doing what your mother wanted."

"You were?"

"She knew what I was capable of. Knew our

lifestyle, and she wanted me to keep it as far away from you as I could. I failed."

"You did great, Dad."

"But growing up, you never had a whole lot of friends."

She shrugged. "Friends can be overrated. I had you and Millie. That was enough." She rested her head against his shoulder.

The doctor suddenly appeared. "Sir, Lucas and Roman Greco are here."

Liam tutted and Alex tensed.

Her father had snuck her away while they'd been distracted.

"I will go deal with them," Liam said.

"Don't leave."

"Honey."

"Can we go?"

The doctor looked at her and then turned to her father. "She needs to be kept awake, and if she does fall asleep, wake her every hour, on the hour, just to be sure." He winked at her.

"Thank you."

Liam helped her up. The pain meds the doctor had given her had made her feel a little lightheaded. She held on to her father, knowing he would protect her.

They left the room and headed out into the hallway. The doctor led the way, and then he looked between them all. "I will leave you people alone," he said.

Alex stared at Roman.

The liar.

"You shouldn't have taken off," Lucas said.

"My daughter was injured. I will do anything for her," Liam said. "And she didn't need to see another dead body."

She winced as they all seemed to be shouting.

"I will take care of her," Roman said. "I've gone through this before. Waking her up, making sure there is no permanent damage."

"I want a divorce," Alex said. Her words rang out in the hallway.

"Not happening," Lucas Greco said.

"I suggest you and I talk before you start telling my daughter what is and is not happening," Liam said.

"I'm not going to stay married to you," Alex said.

"Alex, come on, you know what is at stake."

"Yeah, I do, which is why I've asked my dad to make arrangements so that this can be amicable. I want nothing to do with you or your family."

"Does that mean you will not be adopting those kids?" Roman asked.

"You leave them out of this. Those kids are mine. They may have Greco blood running through their veins, but they will never belong to you."

"They will be soldiers," Lucas said.

"No, they will not," Alex said.

She released her father, clenched her hands into fists, and glared at Lucas Greco. She wasn't afraid of these men.

"You gave up the right to those kids. You can try to take them, but you will be hit with a brick wall. I swear I will make your life and all the lives of your capos fucking hell if you even try to test me." Alex had no idea what she would do, but with him being a mafia capo and the Boss, there were things she could do. She just had to not have a painful head to think about it. "You shouldn't have manipulated me," Alex said, turning to Roman. "I was willing to give us a shot. There didn't have to be love. There didn't even have to be any kind of emotion. I was fine just being your wife, and us just surviving. You lied, and you … you were trying to make me cheat on you to what? Prove what? That I wasn't good enough? Because I'm a Smith and not a Greco?"

"Alex, please."

"It's best if we just end things now." She couldn't add, *before one of us gets hurt.* Alex already felt like she was being torn apart.

Lies. So much of it was lies.

"It's time we left," Liam said. "Alex has been through enough over the last couple of days. It's time for her to heal."

"This isn't over," Roman said.

"It never even begun."

Chapter Seventeen

Two months later

"You haven't signed the papers," Antonio said, lifting the papers on his desk.

Roman went straight to the scotch. Blood stains still covered his hands, but he didn't care. It had dried, and now that his job was done for the day, he needed the numbing silence alcohol granted him.

Two months.

It had been two months since he last saw his wife, and it was all because of Liam. Her fucking meddling father. The evil bastard.

Swigging back the shot of hard whiskey, he then poured himself a second. After downing that, he finally turned to the divorce papers he'd left out on his desk. He'd been served them two weeks after the showdown with Phillip. His father had presented them to him.

From what he'd been told, Liam and Lucas had come to an agreement. An understanding. There would be no bloodshed providing Roman stayed away from Alex. The kids were given to Alex, and she would adopt them herself. In return, Liam would provide the relevant resources to deal with all of Greco's enemies. Help with their drug and gun side business, and offered also an outlet to distribute as well.

It all sounded so nice and neat, and peaceful.

Lucas told him to sign the papers and that he'd have another wife lined up for him soon.

Roman refused. Alex was his wife.

Besides, there was always a risk she could be pregnant. He wasn't being an asshole, but he considered all the times he'd fucked her, and it wasn't a lot, but it only took one time. He hadn't used a condom.

He hadn't used anything. He'd felt her precious virgin pussy wrapped around his dick, and he had spilled his fertile spunk inside her.

Roman didn't know how much time he had to wait, but he was hoping soon. Refusing to give his father the papers was causing some issues. He didn't want a *proper* wife. He wanted Alex back.

"Great detective work." Roman placed his fingers to his forehead and saluted him.

"Don't be a dick," Cash said. "It doesn't suit you."

"Oh, come on, it's because I'm a dick I'm in my home, alone." The same home he'd shared with Alex for a few weeks. They had divided their time between this house and his apartment.

The pillow still smelled like her, and there were times when he was a little lost, when he grabbed it and sniffed. He was turning into a fucking pussy.

"You need to sign these papers," Antonio said. "Your dad is going to get pissed, and I know Liam's not happy about it either."

Roman frowned and looked toward Antonio. He saw him mutter under his breath as he closed his eyes.

"How do you know that?"

"Liam's her father, of course, he's going to be pissed."

"But how do you know that?" Roman advanced toward his friend. "You'd only know that for sure if you've … seen him."

"Roman, come on, we're not the enemy," Marlo said.

"You've seen Liam, haven't you?"

Antonio's jaw clenched, and Roman slammed his fist against his friend's gut.

"Shit."

"Fuck."

Marlo and Cash got out of their chairs, but Antonio held his hand up as if to tell them he was okay. He let out a cough, and Roman was more than happy to punch him again.

"Yes, I've seen him."

"Alex?"

"Shit," Antonio said.

Another fist to the gut. He went to hit him again, but Antonio shoved him hard and quickly put distance between them.

Roman was already up on his feet. He was an expert in dealing with pain, and staring at his friend, his enemy, he was ready to go a hundred rounds with him if he had to.

"Yes, I've seen Liam and I've seen Alex. I've seen all the kids as well."

He'd been banned from seeing the kids, and Roman hated to admit how much he missed the little shits. The cock-blocking, moaning, constantly-eating, and saying-dumb-shit little kids he wanted to protect as well.

"Have you?" he asked, looking to Marlo.

He shook his head.

"What about you?" This time he looked at Cash.

"No, man, I haven't."

"Mr. Greco asked me, okay? He asked me to be the peace offering for us."

"What did you do?" Roman asked.

"I … I helped Alex pick out a car that will help her take the kids to school. They're already going to a school now. She had them enrolled within weeks of her moving to the house. The signs have all been taken down, and it is no longer registered as an orphanage." Antonio dropped his hands.

"You took them to school?"

"No, I took her to go and find a decent van or a bus. She settled on a mini-bus. One that will take fifteen. Alex is training to drive it. Millie already has the right licenses to drive it. Turns out before going to work for Liam, she was a school bus driver."

Roman snorted. He could see that about Millie. He stumbled back, sitting on the arm of one of his chairs. Alex, the kids, driving them to school.

For the past two months, he'd been sniffing out all the traitors Phillip had garnered. Some of them were lowlife crooks. There were a few capos who'd been more than willing to accept Phillip as their boss for a price. It was his job to take care of them all. That was what he'd been doing today. Torturing. Killing.

He nearly had every single person who would have turned their back on his father.

Roman didn't care about the death he caused. They had it coming, but when it came to Alex, she had his attention, always.

"How is she?" Roman asked.

"The bruises are all gone. She's happy. She loves being a mommy to the kids."

"And the kids?"

"Oh, they're doing fine. They are part of a family now. Alex's family."

Roman gritted his teeth. He never cried, not for anyone. Crying only got more beatings, and he'd stopped getting them when he was a young boy.

Tears were for the weak. For the foolish.

"Do they ask about me?"

Antonio sighed. "I only saw them once, Roman. A couple asked after you. They wanted to know where you had gone."

"What does Alex say?" Roman asked.

"She says you're busy. That you've got a lot to deal with right now."

"So she hasn't told them I'm not coming back?"

"No, but you do need to sign the divorce papers."

"I don't need to do jack shit."

"This isn't good for you or for Alex, or for the kids, or for the bigger picture. Guys, are you not going to help?" Antonio asked, looking toward Marlo and Cash.

"I'd rather not get punched in the gut."

"Pussies. Come on, Roman. You have to see sense."

"Why do I?"

"You never wanted to be married to Alex in the first place. Even you said she was beneath you. She's not from our world. An outsider. A loser."

Roman grabbed Antonio's lapels. "Don't fucking call her that."

"For fuck's sake, Roman, make up your damn mind. You don't want her, and now what? Do you not want to be the first man to have a divorce in the Greco line?"

"I don't want to lose her."

"Dude, she's already lost."

Roman glared at Antonio.

"Did you not think asking us to seduce her wouldn't have an impact?" Antonio asked.

"She was never supposed to find out."

"Roman," Marlo said, standing up. "You need to think about why you don't want to sign those divorce papers and why you didn't want her to get an annulment."

"War. I was protecting our families," Roman said.

"Oh, cut the crap, Roman. I'm sick of all your bullshit. We all are," Cash said, standing up as well.

"Yes, there would have been disagreements between both sides, but we all know Lucas and Liam would have figured something out. They had already come together. They would've made it work. You didn't want Alex to call quits because the real reason is you like her. You have always liked her."

"No, I think he's been in love with her," Antonio said. "Even before the wedding, he stopped screwing around. You took your vows seriously, and let's face it, you treated her like crap because you panicked. For the first time in your life, there was a woman you actually liked. Not a woman who was impressed by your money, or who you were, but a woman who cared about being real, and you were afraid."

He glared at his friends.

"And that's why you won't sign the divorce papers," Marlo said. "You're in love with your wife, and if you sign them, you know you will lose her forever, because if you can see how great she is, you know other men will see it as well."

"Don't."

He hadn't been in love with Alex, not in the beginning. Roman wasn't even sure that he liked her. She was different, opinionated, and she wasn't trying to gain his attention. In fact, she never had been.

During their short engagement, Alex never reached out to him. Never sent her father to demand he take her out to lunch. She left him alone.

"I broke her heart and her trust," Roman said.

"Last time I checked, both of them can be healed," Cash said. "With the right words and actions."

"I don't know what to do." He had never admitted that openly to anyone. It was a weakness, and he refused to be weak.

Roman didn't even care if his friends were

sharing a look between them.

"You don't give up," Antonio said.

"And you don't let her forget that you do love her," Marlo said.

"Oh, and I have it on good authority that if you actually tell a woman you love her, you might get a better chance of them listening," Cash said. He held his hands up as if to ward off some evil. "I've said what I needed to. I've got to take a shower, and some of us actually need their dick sucked."

Cash slapped him on the back as he made his way outside.

So did Marlo, and then Antonio.

"Would you have slept with her if you had the chance?" Roman asked.

Antonio was the last one to leave. "Not a chance. I think I had a hunch from the beginning that she was different, and you liked her. Don't fuck it up this time." He closed the door, and Roman rubbed at his temple.

He was tempted to enjoy the scotch some more, but that wouldn't help him to clear his head. Getting to his feet, he stumbled to the desk, and lifted the divorce paperwork. There were tabs on each line needed for his signature, and he hadn't put a damn one there.

Instead, he grabbed the paperwork, opened a drawer, and picked up a lighter. Stepping toward the fireplace, he held the lighter beneath the paperwork and flicked the light.

He watched and waited as it caught light, and he placed it gently, so as not to let it blow out, in the fireplace.

Roman watched the contract go up in flames.

Alex wasn't going to be able to get rid of him quite that easily. Not yet. He knew setting fire to the divorce letter wouldn't stop, but it would give him some time. His dad was going to be so pissed, but that was nothing new.

It was time to win back his wife, but for real this time.

****

Raising fifteen kids was hard.

Alex knew it would always be difficult, but she never realized how demanding it would be. She wouldn't change it for the world. Each morning, she was awake by five thirty to make sure breakfast was on the table. The kids always made it down by six.

Breakfast was a lot of fun, but she had to keep reminding the kids they had school and to rush them along. They were always talking about the dreams they had the night before, which she did love to hear.

Once they were finished with breakfast, it was a mad dash to getting changed. She was pleased they didn't have just the one bathroom, otherwise, she'd only ever get a couple of hours of sleep a night.

After they were dressed and ready, ninety percent of the time, it was car duty, then school drop-off. She often had to drop the oldest off at school first so she could make it in time for the rest of the kids. They were split between three schools, which meant three different drop-offs.

She was lucky, though.

They had all banded together to make this work. She'd overheard the kids talking one night that if they didn't help her out or make this work, there was a chance they'd all be taken away. She wasn't sure if that was accurate, but according to her father when she asked him, there was always a chance that if it didn't look like things were working out, social workers, the police, and just about anyone else, could step in and take them away from her.

Alex couldn't allow that. She loved these kids. They were hers, and she was going to give them the best damn chance she could.

With the kids in school, she often drove home and did a mad dash around the house, cleaning and putting everything neatly. She'd spend a short time studying as she'd taken up her classes again, and with her dad's help, she'd arranged for all her work to be done from home. The lectures were already recorded, so it wasn't so hard to watch them. If she didn't get a chance during the day, when they were all asleep, she did some homework then. In the last two months, she rarely did any sewing.

Her dad had set up a brand-new room in the main house. Also, as an early birthday present, he'd handed over the deeds to the house. This place was now her own, and she loved it.

All she had to figure out was a job that fit into her busy schedule. This was how her day had repeated for the last two months.

Two months since she learned the truth about Roman. Two months without seeing him.

They had been married for that long, before he started to notice her, and now, she wished the few weeks they had together hadn't happened. It would make moments like these, when she was bent over a newspaper looking at all different kinds of job opportunities, and she had time to think about Roman. With the kids home, her mind and feelings were safe. Alone, they were not.

There was so much about him she missed. So damn much.

Tears filled her eyes as she remembered hearing the truth from his dad. How it had all been a lie.

The front door opened, and Alex knew it was either her dad or Millie. She'd gotten around to having the locks changed. Even though Antonio had been by to help her pick out a car or mini-bus, she made sure he didn't take any keys.

Liam entered the room, and she smiled at him, getting to her feet and rushing to his side. "Hey," she said.

"I missed the breakfast run, didn't I?" he asked.

Alex didn't actually get to drive the kids to school, Millie or one of her father's guards often drove, but she was right in the vehicle to see them off to school. She was still taking lessons, and it was a process. She'd get there.

"Yeah, it's fine."

"How were they all?"

Her father, although he wouldn't admit it, had fallen a little in love with the kids. They called him Grandpa, and she saw how happy that made him.

"Amazing. Tyler is kind of freaking out though. He wants to try out for the football squad. He was going to ask you about it when you stopped by."

"Well, I'll be picking them up this afternoon. What's this?" Liam asked, glancing down at the table. "You're looking for a job?"

"Yeah, I've got to learn to pay my way, you know. A job does that. It helps to bring in money." She didn't feel comfortable taking from her dad all the time.

"Sweetheart, you do know that with all of these being … Greco bloodline, that is where a great deal of money is coming from?"

"What?"

"Lucas didn't set this all up for his men to get off easy. All of them have to provide, even those men where their kids have already been fostered. It creates an income all in itself."

"Lucas has been paying for them?"

"Yes. I've also been providing, but when I went over the books, I realized Lucas made a donation into a bank account every month. It's linked to this house." Liam pulled a card out of his back pocket. "And I can honestly say, you deserve this."

Alex took the bank card from him.

"There's more than enough in there for you to change the place if you want, raise those kids, and to start some college funds."

"I still need to get a job." The money would be put to good use. She would make sure all of the kids had a college fund set up, which could either send them to college or at least assist them, or give them some money if they decided to leave. She had already started to make plans.

"I will support you, Alex. Always."

"Dad, I've got to do this."

"Sweetheart, you're taking care of fifteen kids. It's a full-time job by itself. You don't need to worry about having some money. We can help take care of that." Liam pointed down at the paper.

"Did he sign them?" she asked.

Roman kept refusing to sign the divorce papers, even though it was the best thing for both of them.

"No," Liam asked.

She sighed.

"I've got to ask though, sweetheart, do you really want him to sign them?"

"Yes, of course, I do. It's time that we cut each other out of our lives for good. I would have done it sooner, but, well, I didn't think I was able to."

"And not for any other reason?" he asked.

"What other reason could there be?"

"Oh, I don't know, how about … you're in love with him?"

Alex stared at her dad for several seconds, not even able to move. “Don’t be ridiculous.” She picked up her empty coffee cup and headed toward the kitchen, which was spotless.

She had to get started on dinner.

With so many mouths to feed, it was a lot of vegetables to plan ahead for.

Liam followed her into the kitchen. “I know you’re hurting.”

“Dad, I’m not in love with Roman.” The lie spilled easily from her lips.

“I don’t believe you.”

“Does it matter? He lied, and I want a divorce. I can’t trust him. Why are you even questioning this?”

“Because I want what is best for you.”

“And you think Roman Greco, liar and manipulator, is the best thing for me?” she asked.

“I think Roman Greco, the man who has fallen in love with my daughter, who arranged the adoption of fifteen children, and who refuses to sign divorce papers, has a right to be given a second chance. We all fuck up in this life, Alex.”

“I can’t believe I’m hearing this, from you of all people. You’re the one who says there is no chance for making mistakes or fucking up. You always say that.”

“And I could be wrong half the time, Alex.”

She shook her head. “I don’t want to hear this.” Staring in the kitchen, she needed to get out and have some fresh air.

“He does love you, you know,” Liam said.

This made her turn around to look at him. “No, he doesn’t.”

“Roman Greco is a selfish little bastard. He did every single thing his father ordered him to, but he always made sure he was the one who came out on top.

Always. He played hard, Alex, but the moment he got engaged to you, those women he was with before, they didn't get a chance with him. They were gone."

"Dad, we, he was, we were not good together. He needs a wife who is this sweet innocent virgin who won't cause him trouble and certainly doesn't stand out at all these events. I never fit in."

"I know you didn't, and that is on me. Your mother, she was exactly like you, but she didn't care to fit in. At some of the parties we were at, she'd be surrounded by people in designer gowns. Talking about how expensive their clothing was. Your mother always made her own gown, her own clothes, and when asked where she got hers, she'd give a fabric store, the yardage, and how long it took her to make. Sometimes she'd give a pattern, but she didn't give a fuck."

"Don't bring Mom into this."

"I loved her, Alex. Even when she said she wouldn't marry me because she didn't believe in it, and also, it would make me work harder, because at any moment, she could still leave."

"You know, there are times I thought that was a little cruel," Alex said.

"I didn't because your mother was right. I worked my ass off to keep her. She never allowed me to take her for granted. She was all fire. Roman, in the early days, he might have wanted this doormat you talk about, but I've seen the way he looks at you, and believe me, that is a man in love."

"Dad, stop it."

"You need to think about why that makes you upset."

"I'm not upset." Tears sprang to her eyes, and she felt like her heart was breaking. The truth was, she had missed Roman, so much. More than she cared to admit.

They'd lived together in this house for such a short time, but it had been long enough to leave a lasting impression.

She missed him so much, all the fucking time, and it was … unfair.

"Sweetheart," he said, moving toward her.

Alex covered her face, trying to control her feelings, but it was too much. She couldn't handle this. "Dad, please, it hurts."

Liam wrapped his arms around her and pulled her against him. "I've got you, sweetheart."

"I … I think I was falling in love with him, but it was all a lie. What do I have to believe? How can I believe anything he has ever said to me?" She began to sob, and Liam held her, but she didn't want her father. No, she wanted her husband, the man who refused to divorce her. The man who'd finally made a dream of hers come true and wasn't here to share it with her. "Don't … kill him for this."

"Honey, please, you know I won't kill him. You love him."

"Don't, maim him, or hurt him, or injure him," Alex said.

"Now, unfortunately, you do know me, and I'm a little disappointed I'm not going to get the chance to have a whole lot of fun." He started to pout, and Alex couldn't help but laugh at how … silly he looked.

"I love you, Dad."

"I love you too."

Chapter Eighteen

The locks on the door had been changed, so his key didn't work. Alex had forgotten to change the passcode on the front gate, so he was able to get inside the grounds, just not in the house. If he knocked or rang the bell, there was a chance he'd wake the kids. He'd already gotten the details on the kids, and how well they were doing at school, and they were all doing great.

It helped to have Greco as a last name. The doors and avenues it opened were priceless. Alex wasn't going to raise those kids alone.

He'd already come to the conclusion that she wasn't pregnant.

Roman was done waiting for a meeting, and instead, was sneaking into his wife's house. No, *their* house.

He knew where her bedroom was, and it was a hazard with how high it was, one that he was more than willing to make.

"Who's there?" a voice said, calling out.

Roman gritted his teeth, looked up onto the porch, and saw Kyle, one of the oldest kids sitting on the front porch.

"Roman?" Kyle asked.

"What are you doing out late at night?"

"Why are you sneaking around?"

"I'm the adult here. You better not be … fucking around."

Kyle smirked. "I'm not. I've got a chem test to study for, and Stuart, just lately, he doesn't sleep light. My bedroom is next to his and the walls feel like they're vibrating. I've got to think, and I like being outside."

Roman nodded.

"Are you sneaking in to Alex?" Kyle asked. "That's kind of illegal and a little stalkery?"

"Is Alex in her bedroom?"

Kyle folded his arms, and Roman gritted his teeth again. "Are we about to have a standoff? Is that it?"

"You and Alex broke up. She said you're getting a divorce."

"Not accurate. We didn't break up. A little misunderstanding, that's all. I can't divorce her," Roman said.

"Why not?"

"I burned the divorce papers."

"You know they can print and sign some more. The process can begin again."

"And they'll all meet a fire, Kyle. I'm not divorcing my wife."

"Why not?" Kyle tilted his head to the side.

Roman debated lying, or making up some bullshit, but that had gotten him into trouble with Alex, and he wasn't going to make the same mistake again.

"I love her, Kyle. I'm in love with her and have been for a very some time now, but I fucked up. I made mistakes, and Alex believes the worst of me, but I want to spend the rest of my life with her. I want to help raise you guys. I want to be a … father to you all, or a friend, or whatever you guys need."

Kyle nodded. "I knew it. I knew you weren't a bad guy, that shit just got out of hand."

"Language. I will tell Liam that you need grounding if you continue."

He chuckled. "How about, you don't tell Grandpa about my language, and I don't tell him that you were thinking of sneaking into his daughter's bedroom."

"That is a deal, but don't forget, Alex is my wife."

"Who is attempting to divorce you."

"Tit for tat," Roman said.

Kyle laughed and pulled a key out of his front pocket. "This will help you inside. If Alex attacks you, beats the crap out of you, then I'm telling her you stole it."

Roman forced a smile to his lips and nodded at the kid. "Good work on that studying."

Kyle continued to laugh, but Roman tuned him out as he made his way to the front door.

After letting himself inside, he locked the door and posted the key outside the mailbox. He heard Kyle pick it up, and then Roman looked inside the house. There was a light on for the main landing, so all the kids would have something to see if they woke up needing a bathroom break in the middle of the night.

Roman climbed the stairs, keeping his footsteps light and hoping not to disturb the rest of the house.

He couldn't recall ever having to sneak into a woman's house before, at least one that ended well.

After making his way down the hall, he stopped at Alex's bedroom, and then he placed his palm flat on the surface. He didn't know if she'd be awake, asleep, or waiting on the opposite side with a baseball bat.

He grabbed the handle, gave it a twist, and let himself inside.

Alex was nowhere to be seen.

He listened and heard her in the bathroom, at first, he thought she was singing, but then, he heard the faint sounds of sobs.

Alex was crying.

Now, he was fucking pissed off. Whoever had made her cry was going to pay for it. Anger rushed through his body, and he was ready to fucking kill them all.

He was about to enter the bathroom, when Alex opened the door. Her eyes were red and bloodshot, and tears spilled down her face. Her hair was wet, and she held a towel wrapped around her body.

"Roman?"

"Who made you cry?" he asked. "Tell me and I will go and deal with them, now."

Alex shook her head. "What the hell are you doing here? You shouldn't be here."

"But I am here, Alex. Tell me." He grabbed her shoulders, forcing her to spin around to face him, and she pushed him away.

"Stop it. You don't get to pretend with me."

"I'm not pretending, Alex. I'm being serious. I want to know who made you feel this way?"

"You really want to know?" she asked.

"Yes. I want to take care of it."

"Then look in a mirror and take care of yourself," she said.

"I made you cry?"

"Yes. You made me cry. *Us* made me cry. How useless it was, that is what made me cry." She glared at him with a death grip on the towel at the apex of her tits.

Roman was a little distracted. For two months, all he had was memories, and they were not enough.

"Alex..." He moved toward her, but she pulled away.

"What are you doing here?" she asked.

"I'm going to win you back."

She shook her head. "That is impossible."

"No, it's not."

"Roman, sign the divorce papers."

"Not a chance. Not now. Not knowing that you're crying because of me."

"Does that make you feel good or something?"

she asked.

"It makes me feel like shit, Alex. I don't like to see you cry or to know that I'm the cause. I love you too damn much."

"You're lying."

"I'm not. I won't lie to you."

"I can't believe you." She shook her head, and he moved toward her, cupping her face.

"You don't have to believe me, because it is the truth, and I'm not leaving this house, not ever again. I'm not leaving your side, not until you give me a chance."

"Is this another order your father gave you?" Alex asked.

"No. He ordered me to sign the paperwork, and I burned it."

"You burned it."

"You got that right, baby. I burned that sucker because I refuse to sign it. You're worth a lot more to me than that paperwork!" He tutted. "I'm not going to let you go."

"Roman, don't you see? You and I, we don't mesh, we don't make any kind of sense. You need to be with someone who understands you, who wants the same kind of things you do."

"Funny you should say that because all I can think about was how good we were together."

"That's sex."

"I'm not talking about the sex, Alex. I'm talking about hanging out together. Being with each other. We had some good memories, and I know if given the chance, we can have a lot more. All you've got to do is give me a chance. That is all I'm asking for."

Tears came to her eyes. "Stop it."

"No, I'm not going to stop it." He stepped toward her once again, cupping her face. She didn't push him away, she couldn't. Alex had a death grip on the towel.

Her cheeks were flush, and he stroked his thumb across her plump bottom lip.

"I'm going to prove to you just how good we are together." He dropped a quick kiss on her lips, but that wasn't enough. He needed more.

Sliding his fingers back into her hair, he cupped the back of her head and pulled her in close, slamming his lips down on hers and taking the kiss he actually wanted. There was no holding back.

It was demanding, passionate, and everything he wanted.

Alex was his.

She gasped, putting her hands on his chest, but she didn't push him away. The towel she wore fell to the floor, and as she tried to reach down to pick it up, he captured her wrists, stopping her.

"Don't."

"Roman?"

"You look so beautiful." He didn't let her bend down to pick up the towel, he did it for her and wrapped it around her body. "I'm not going anywhere. You heard my dad that night. You didn't hear everything that I had to say."

"You didn't deny it."

"How could I? My dad did order me to seduce you, to make you fall in love with me. I never used the kids as a way of making that happen, Alex. I wanted to adopt these kids. To give them a chance, to have a family of my own. One that I could … enjoy with you. I never got this growing up. I never had a dad who wanted to play in the backyard. His idea of playing was sending me to one of his guards who would teach me to take pain. That was what I got to do."

"What about kids of your own?"

"One day, we'll have them, Alex. They're not going to be any different than those boys and girls out there. *Our* sons and our daughters, and I hope one day they will … call me Dad, but I know that is a long shot. I know they hate me because I hurt you."

"They don't know anything, Roman. I couldn't bring myself to say anything bad about you."

"Kyle seems to know something went down."

"He's the oldest and just because I haven't said anything doesn't mean my dad hasn't. They all call him Grandpa. I think he likes it."

Alex disappeared into the closet and came out a few minutes later, dressed. She held the towel within her grip and was patting at her hair, drying it. "You can stay," she said.

"I'm staying here."

Alex sighed. "I'm not going to have sex with you."

"I'm not asking for sex. I'm asking for a second chance, and when we do have sex, you'd have forgiven me, and we can both move forward."

"Doesn't your dad have another bride lined up who is more suitable for you?" she asked.

"I don't care because the only woman I want is you."

"Roman, do you really think this is going to work?"

She hadn't kicked him out, and he found her crying, and he was going to assume it was about him. "Yes, I do."

It wasn't a brag either. He was going to make this work because he wanted to.

He loved Alex. Truly loved her.

Now it was time for him to show her. Roman didn't have a plan. He had no idea how he was going to prove it to her, but he wasn't going to stop until he got what he wanted.

****

The kids adored having Roman back, and if she was honest with herself, she did as well. Not that she'd admit it to him. No way would she be that honest with him.

Roman already had a big ego, although she wasn't really seeing it of late.

They had been living with each other for a week. She'd expected him to be gone within three days. Roman took over from the guard and Millie, driving the kids to the three different schools.

He was always awake at five thirty, and they had been ready for breakfast on time. Each morning, he rounded up the kids, helping with buttons, hair, and collecting all their homework. After a braid disaster, he did stop helping the girls with their hair. Alex had to unknot their hair. Alex couldn't even understand how he'd been able to make it so bad, but this was Roman, and well, he clearly knew what he was not good at. The dishes were always done before they left for the school trip. Each morning, he fist-bumped the boys, telling them to have an amazing day. The girls kissed his cheek, and he told them the same, but added to kick all guys in the balls.

Alex tried to talk to him about that, but he wouldn't have any of it.

When they got home, he insisted she did her studies and he cleaned the house. This was another new adventure.

Roman had never cleaned a day in his life. The first day of his attempts to help, he smashed multiple pictures and had somehow burned out the motor on the vacuum cleaner. Again, she had no idea how he did it.

She had a feeling he tried to vacuum up some spillage of water, but he denied it.

In the end, Alex ended up showing him how to clean. They did a little bit each day, and when he felt she was doing too much, he forced her to study. When she was in the study, Roman was there, complete with a laptop and doing his own work. From what she figured out, he was working from home. His dad called him all the time.

Liam stopped by, but he also made sure to give his son-in-law a warning.

Alex knew her father was pleased he had turned up though.

One week, turned into two.

Then three.

Before she even realized what was happening, they'd been living together for over three months. The weeks just blended together.

Roman was there, always. There were a few occasions he left to go and take care of business. Whenever he came back, she knew when the work had been dangerous as he was dressed differently. He never brought it home.

The kids were demanding, but Roman was always there, helping. They had gone out together as a family to theme parks, and the beach.

The first couple of weekends of doing nothing, Roman had made it his mission to bring experiences.

They were a little stressful as Alex liked to keep a constant eye on them. Going to the beach, allowing some of the older kids to go off and do their own thing, was hard. She got through it, keeping the youngest entertained.

Little by little, Roman was fixing and changing the house, with Antonio, Marlo, and Cash's help, along with a few skilled workers Roman vetted.

Alex stared across the lawn, watching Roman as he was going over the details for a tree house. He didn't want one built out of his sight and insisted it be near the house. He had also brought in an architect to draft one.

Roman had gotten all the kids around the dining room table with a notepad, and he made them all, in an orderly fashion, talk about what they wanted their tree house to be like.

He'd listed every single item.

She smiled just thinking about it.

"Can you believe the lengths he's willing to go to?" Antonio asked.

Over the past several months, Alex had learned to forgive his friends, and it had taken time, but she did believe they weren't trying to seduce her anymore in some illicit plot to out her to his family.

Roman had already taken her virginity.

"He loves to make them happy," Alex said.

"And you," Antonio said. "All of this is for them and for you. You're his family. I'm not saying that because he put me up to it or anything. I'm speaking the truth."

"You don't have to," she said, holding her hand up.

"Yeah, I do. You think I don't see this between the two of you? Months ago when he made up his mind not to give up and to find a way of winning you over, I thought he was wrong. I figured a clean break was what you both needed, but I was wrong. What you both need is each other. You love him, Alex. You know you do."

Antonio left, and Alex turned to watch Roman. He was pointing at the design.

They slept in the same bed with each other. Every morning, she woke up in his arms, feeling the evidence of his … arousal against her hip. She was the one who always pulled away first.

Damn it.

This wasn't supposed to happen.

Not to her.

Not to them.

Roman clapped the man on the back and then headed down toward her. He kissed her lips, which he always did, regardless of who was around them. "It's a done deal. He can have it done in about four weeks."

"Wow, okay."

"He is going to source all the tools, and then we can move this baby on the road. Those kids are getting a tree house. Hate to brag, but it is going to be a little bigger than your one back home with your dad."

Alex cupped his face and stepped toward him. She had no idea what she was doing as she pulled his face down and kissed his lips.

Roman's hands didn't touch her at first, but then he wrapped his arms around her and pulled her in close. She released a moan, then a whimper. His hands went to her ass, then sank into her hair, before gliding back down to grab her ass.

They needed to be alone.

Alex pulled away. "I've got to … er…"

"Yeah, me too."

She took a step toward the house, then another. The kids were at school, and they had a couple of hours before picking them up.

Once inside the house, she didn't stop until she got to her bedroom, stepping inside. If he followed and closed the door, they were doing this, if he didn't, then that was that. He wasn't ready.

The door closed. Alex spun around.

Roman advanced into the room. They stopped

and stared at each other for the longest time.

Her lips felt a little dry. He stopped a foot away from her, and she watched him.

Alex reached for her shirt first, pulling it off over her head and then wriggling out of her shorts.

He groaned. "Alex."

Within seconds, she stood before him naked.

"Do you not want me?" she asked.

Roman closed the distance. "Of course, I want you." He took her hand and pressed it against his rock-hard dick. "I will always want you. I can't stop thinking about you. Do you have any idea what it's like to sleep next to you? To feel you in my arms and not be able to touch you? To sink inside you? To fuck you?"

She knew. Each night was as much a torture for her as it was for him.

"Fuck me, Roman," she said, sinking to her knees before him and reaching for the button of his pants.

He tugged his shirt off as she pulled his pants down.

Roman helped her ease them down the length of his cock, and the moment he was clear, his dick sprang forward.

Feeling bold, she wrapped her fingers around the length and started to pump it, working up and down his shaft. Glancing up his body, she stared into his eyes and saw them close.

Alex licked her lips, and then she slid her tongue across the tip of his cock.

Roman growled, opening his eyes and staring down at her. "Oh, fuck," he said.

His hands stroked through her hair, and he wrapped it around his wrist. He tightened his grip, and Alex took the tip of his cock in her mouth and started to work over him. Taking him to the back of her throat, lifting up.

"Don't use your teeth."

Pulling back, she sucked on his cock and bobbed her head. Then Roman pulled her off and lifted her to her feet.

She let out a gasp as he pressed her to the bed, spread her thighs open, and then his mouth was on her pussy, licking and sucking at her clit.

Alex cried out his name, not wanting him to stop as he sucked her clit into his mouth. He used his teeth. Not enough to cause pain, but enough to make her ache and yearn for more.

His name was a mantra spilling from her lips, making her beg for more. Hoping for more.

Roman plundered two fingers deep inside her pussy as he lapped at her clit. Pleasure rushed through every single pore of her body. Her orgasm took her completely by surprise as with only a few licks and sucks, he had her coming, screaming his name, begging for more, and not wanting him to stop.

He didn't. Roman kept licking her pussy, sending her into a second orgasm before he moved up the bed.

She stared at him in a pleasured haze, a little taken aback as he pressed the tip to her entrance, and then, inch by inch, slowly began to sink inside her.

Her teeth sank into her bottom lip as she felt him.

"Fuck, I've missed you, Alex. So fucking much." He seated himself to the hilt within her.

"Roman?"

"Yeah, baby."

"Don't hurt me again. Not ever."

"No, I'll never hurt you again. That I promise." He lowered down so they were flush against each other, their bodies melding together. "I love you, Alex, so fucking much, and I will never hurt you again. I promise.

You are mine, and there is a lot of shit I can give up in this world, but I can't give you up. I refuse to give you up."

"I love you too, and I don't, I don't want to be afraid to love you."

"Don't be. I am here. I am with you, every step of the fucking way. I promise you. I will earn your forgiveness. I will never give you another moment to doubt me."

She stared into his eyes, and she knew he spoke the truth. Roman hadn't run away. He'd stayed by her side. He had proven time and time again that he was here to stay. To help raise the kids, to bring them into this world, and to build a life and family with her.

Alex … loved him.

"I already forgive you."

Her father had told her that no man would stick around this long if he didn't love her, and Alex knew. She felt it.

He started to move inside her.

Roman began slowly, but as he pressed inside her, his strokes sped up, driving into her, pistoning deep and fucking her hard, and she gave him back, rocking her hips to meet his, feeling his cock pulse. When he couldn't hold back anymore, she held on to him as he pushed in deep and came, spilling his seed within her.

They hadn't used a condom, but Alex didn't care.

"No more divorce papers?" he asked.

"Roman, I already stopped sending them. You only burned that one. I don't make a habit of wasting paper."

He chuckled. "I'm so fucking lucky to have gotten you."

Tears filled her eyes, and she cupped his cheek, knowing that she had also gotten lucky in getting him as well.

Epilogue

Nine months later

Roman took his wife's hand and locked their fingers together. She was a little uncomfortable going to a formal event his father had invited him to. It was a family event where all the capos and their families were going to be. At first, Lucas Greco had only invited him, Alex, and Liam. Roman refused. He had a big extended family. Fifteen children who needed an extension added.

He took his role as father seriously.

Alex wasn't just nervous about their children going to a Greco gathering where all their original fathers were going to be, but also the fact she was eight months pregnant.

Her stomach was … huge, but Roman couldn't get enough of it. He loved spending hours late at night, rubbing creams into her stomach. Millie had told him it would help to soothe Alex and the baby. He didn't care if it worked. Any excuse to touch his wife was a blessing as far as he was concerned.

The whole family was excited.

At first, Little Stuart was worried. They had been sitting around the table, and Stuart had refused to eat. When Roman asked why, Stuart then blurted out the question, "Are you going to get rid of us now that you have a real baby on the way?"

It had broken his heart and he knew it had shattered Alex's.

Roman had dealt with it. "Is that what you all think? That with a new baby on the way, you're all going to be removed, or kicked out, or ignored?" All their heads had bowed at the table, including Kyle's.

"Well, then I guess I have sucked as a dad,

because as far as I am concerned, you are getting a brother and sister. I know you don't call me Dad, and you see me as Roman, and Mr. Greco, or Alex's husband, but I see you as my sons and my daughters. Nothing is going to change. I love you all, and a baby is not going to change that."

That night, as he helped to put the kids to bed, they all said the same thing. "Night, Dad."

He'd nearly fallen to his knees, he'd been so fucking happy. A grown-ass man, and he finally had what he didn't realize he wanted, a family.

Arriving at his father's house, their minibus looked out of place. He and Alex argued about what to call it. She said it was a family car. He called it a minibus. Either way, it was a car that got them all from A to B.

After climbing out of the car, he rounded to Alex's side and helped her out. Then, one by one, he helped the kids out of the car. There were a lot of them.

The sun was high in the sky, and he heard the soft melody of music. This was a ruse. His father wanted to deal with a couple of the capos and had used a family gathering to achieve that. Antonio, Marlo, and Cash all approached.

The kids called them all uncles, and he knew his friends liked that.

"Dude, this is a picture," Antonio said, pulling out his cell phone.

Roman didn't care. His kids and his wife all gathered around to have their photo taken. He wasn't ashamed of his family. He loved them all.

"Time to go and see Grandpa," Roman said.

Alex grabbed his hand, and he knew she was nervous. The kids didn't know who their real dads were, and this was a risk, but it was one he was willing to take.

There was no way he'd go to a family gathering and not take their kids. They were a family, and his dad had to realize that.

They didn't need to go through the main house. Guards were near a gate, and one by one, the kids entered. Roman and Alex, stepped into the backyard together.

As to be expected, he and Alex hadn't been seen together in over a year, and it drew attention to them.

His father was talking with a couple of capos, but at their entrance, he had no chance to ignore them. Liam was already making his way over here, and the kids rushed toward him, calling him Grandpa.

Liam lapped it up.

Out of their two dads, Liam was the one who accepted their decision. His dad often tried to get him to foster the kids out, to move them on.

Not happening. He loved them all.

Lucas approached. as did his mother, who looked nervous.

The kids were laughing and happy.

"Dad, Mom, I'd like you to meet my family," Roman said.

Now it was up to his dad. He could either send them off to play as some of the other kids were not doing because they were afraid of being told off, or he could tell them all that he was their grandfather.

He stared at Lucas, waiting. "I'm your grandfather, kids," Lucas said.

Again, his children were … wonderful, and within seconds the Boss of the Greco mafia was swarmed by fifteen kids, all wanting a hug, or to shake hands. Kyle had taken up shaking hands.

Alex wrapped her arms around his waist. "They're all staring."

"Let them stare. Evil bastards that they are. They don't get to share in this moment. This is ours, and will always be ours."

"Roman Greco, I don't think I have ever seen you quite so sexy as I do right now," she said.

"Oh, you haven't, huh?"

"I guess a man taking care of his family is … well … quite something."

He stared down into her eyes, feeling her swollen stomach against him. "Stick around, Alex, because I will rock your world when it comes to our family."

And he did. Rather than stand around, talking shop and work, he ran after his kids and completely destroyed his reputation as being a hard-ass bastard with no heart. He'd make them all pay, but for now, he had his family, and that was all that mattered to him.

The End

Sam Crescent

BESTSELLING BBW ROMANCE

SPICY ROMANCE FOR REAL WOMEN

EVERNIGHT PUBLISHING ®

www.evernightpublishing.com